BABY,
BABY

Books by Kylie Adams

FLY ME TO THE MOON

BABY, BABY

Published by Zebra Books

BABY, BABY

Kylie Adams

ZEBRA BOOKS
KENSINGTON PUBLISHING CORP.

ZEBRA BOOKS are published by

Kensington Publishing Corp.
850 Third Avenue
New York, NY 10022

First Printing: August 2002

Printed in the United States of America

Acknowledgments

This romp is dedicated to the BABY, BABY crew in my own life—a super-sized lot of nieces and nephews . . .

Roman—Was having serious conversations before he could walk. Knew bigger words than most rock stars, too. Beautiful, brilliant, and a razor sharp sense of humor. Born for the Ivy Leagues.

Paul—Is there a more photogenic boy in the world? Sorry, even Brad Pitt is a swamp monster compared to Paul. Add natural athlete and super smart to the list. And blond, too. Basically Robert Redford.

Noah—This one is 100 percent boy, a real romper-stomper with an infectious laugh that makes up for any chaos caused. Plus, he's gorgeous. Watch out, world. He's on his way.

Sophia—A true beauty in the making. Really. She's a pint-sized Liz Taylor from way back when. Will drive the boys nuts and have her poor father popping Paxil like breath mints.

Ryan—We call him Yidda Yidda. Don't ask why. It's an inside thing. His smile is worth five million—and that's selling him cheap. Was reading his own little books at six months. He's practically Bill Gates.

Berkley—Yidda Yidda's twin sister. People do back hand-springs to earn her approval. Sometimes it works, sometimes she walks away unimpressed. Already wise to the power of exclusivity. Will likely marry a future president and be the real one running the country.

Brent—A baby Federal Expressed straight from heaven. Is there a more peaceful, docile child? Okay, maybe you know one. But does that baby love Mozart? Probably not. Brent wins. A total angel.

Carson Grace—Seven pounds of breathtaking beauty. I'm not biased. Ask anyone at the hospital where she was born. Even that stranger in a coma. He woke up just to ooh and ah over her. Carson has already been forced to call block all the fashion magazines. She can't be bothered right now.

It's better to be looked over than overlooked.
—Mae West

Prologue

Ziegfeld Theatre, New York

It was an all-or-nothing roll of the dice. This movie would either do for her what *Basic Instinct* had done for Sharon Stone (make her a Hollywood goddess) or send her the way of Elizabeth Berkley in *Showgirls* (kill off any hope of a big-screen career). In about two hours, Tatiana Fox would know the outcome.

The opening credits were rolling. She sat there, glittering in a chevron sequined strapless Carolina Herrera gown, holding court at her first star-studded premiere. But all she wanted to do was throw up. Of course, she couldn't bend over in this dress. So that was that.

A sudden wave of dizziness sent her reeling. *Sin by Sin* could mean triumph, a life of hard knocks, and lousy movies finally paying off. Then again, it could mean humiliation, a

failure so high-profile that late-night comics would make
her part of their five-minute monologues.

Greg Tapper picked up on Tatiana's anxiety, threaded his
fingers through hers, and squeezed tight. "It's Wednesday.
The picture opens Friday. You're going to be a star by
Monday."

Her heart took a jump. "I won't know what to do."

Greg released her hand and patted her knee. "No one
ever does."

She watched him in the dark. He was the name above the
title in *Sin by Sin*. Even without a finished screenplay, studios
lined up to pay him twenty million dollars a film, just to
have him attached to a project. That's how huge a star he
was.

What if she got that big? Tatiana let her imagination
take flight. Coffee at Meryl Streep's house. In walks Julia
Roberts. A few minutes later, Susan Sarandon. Then Julianne
Moore. Everybody's clustered around the kitchen table, sipping Starbucks, discussing the biz. This script sucks; that
project is Oscar-worthy; so-and-so is a brilliant director.
They could form an exclusive sorority. Goldie Hawn would
want in, but the girls would vote no because she giggled
too much. Aspiring actresses would daydream about her
meteoric rise, telling anyone who would listen, "I want to
be the next Tatiana Fox."

But things could easily go the other way. She felt a dull
ache in the pit of her stomach and didn't know what to
blame it on—that she hadn't eaten in two days, or that she
was scared to death. In theory, Hollywood had a twelve-
foot wall built around it, and only a chosen few managed
to climb over and join the party. The industry loved to put
people in their place. Like the TV actor who quits a popular
series to do movies. *Sorry, buster, you are strictly small-
screen material.* Or in her case, the straight-to-video

B-movie starlet who takes a stab at the big time. Her last credit was *Lady Cop Undercover IV: Red Light District.* There was a *Playboy* pictorial in her past, too. She could actually hear the proverbial knives sharpening.

Tatiana's character in *Sin by Sin* was a sexually carnivorous, cold-blooded murderer hell-bent on revenge. She did everything from stab an enemy during the act to give the hero a blow job in a convertible during a high-speed chase. There was no middle ground with a role like this. You either hit a home run or got tossed out of the game.

Each year the Golden Raspberry Award Foundation held a press conference to give out "Razzies" as a way to honor what really sucked at the multiplexes the year before. Sylvester Stallone had been nominated, like, over twenty times. She could easily be a shoo-in for worst actress next year.

Tatiana felt a hand on her bare shoulder and knew right away that it belonged to Kip Quick, because his palm was clammy and his nails needed clipping. "You steal every scene that you're in. The other actors might as well be props."

Kip had cut his teeth on music videos. *Sin by Sin* marked his debut in features. What did he know? It wasn't as if he were Martin Scorsese. Tatiana just smiled nervously and tried to watch the rest of the movie without breaking into hives.

Everybody had come out for the big night. This included Monica Lewinsky, who was invited to almost everything in New York, according to Kitty Bishop, Tatiana's publicist. "There are no real stars anymore," Kitty had complained as they found their seats. "The cast from the first *Survivor* are still on priority mailing lists. It's sick."

They were three quarters into the movie now. So far, nobody had laughed or stomped out in disgust. This was a good sign. But then again, the audience could be speechless in their horror. Tatiana's big scene was coming up, her most dramatic one in the film. She took in a deep breath in an effort to calm her wild heart.

"After tonight, you can tell everyone to kiss your ass," Kitty said.

Or be thought of as one. Tatiana stared blankly at the screen until suddenly she couldn't watch anymore. It made more sense just to close her eyes until it was over. . . .

Chapter One

Hotel du Cap, Cannes, the French Riviera
Six Months Earlier

Tatiana was popping Klonopin like Tic-Tacs and still felt on edge.

Mental note for Dr. G to up the dosage or prescribe something else. Maybe Vicodin? No, too many people ended up in rehab for that. And the last thing she needed was to sit in a group therapy circle and listen to Matthew Perry, Melanie Griffith, and Robert Downey Jr. blather on.

She thought a nap might help quell her nerves, but just as she began to lose herself to sleep, the banging on the door and the ringing of the phone kicked in simultaneously.

Tatiana stretched out to deal with the nearest interruption first. "Hello?"

"Good evening, Mrs. Fox." Alonzo from the front desk. A tall, dreamy blond guy with beautiful hands. "It is my pleasure to inform you that a Federal Express letter has arrived.''

She felt a tickle of curiosity. "Can someone bring it up to my room?''

"It would be my pleasure, Mrs. Fox.''

"Would it also be your pleasure to get me the part in *Sin by Sin*? That way I won't have to beg for it later tonight.''

Alonzo said nothing.

"Honey, I'm kidding. About you getting me the part. I fully intend to beg.''

Stilted laughter. "Of course, Mrs. Fox.''

She hung up, wondering what the package could be. Probably an official letter from Jeremy Johnson, the agent who just days ago had dismissed her for refusing to sign on for *Lady Cop Undercover V: Sex Crimes.*

"Wake up, Tatiana,'' he'd spat into his headset phone. Apparently, all the busy Hollywood types spent their days looking like Judy the *Time-Life* operator. "This is as good as it gets. Who do you think you are? Gwyneth?''

"I could be . . . one day . . . she did make *Hush*, you know! It's not like everything on her resume is sprinkled with Oscar fairy dust.''

"That was a rhetorical question.''

Jeremy's voice had taken on such a severe tone that it conjured up all of Tatiana's rationality. There were no other offers on the table, and facts were facts. She had a husband, Kerr, who wrote poetry full-time (translation: a very sensitive man but always dead broke), twin babies to provide for, a mortgage to cover, and a nanny and personal assistant to employ. But no matter the people counting on her, she had to stop and think. How long could she continue to star in these crappy movies and expect to keep her sanity?

"I need some time to—''

Jeremy had cut in with an exasperated sigh. "If the Dob-

sons don't have an answer by the end of the day, they're
going to cast another actress.''

Don and Glee Dobson were the husband-and-wife production team behind more than forty low-budget features.

Typical Don Dobson: ''There's nothing wrong with ex-
ploitation.''

Typical Glee Dobson: ''Breasts are the cheapest special
effect in the business.''

A few years ago, still as desperate for work as she was
today—hmm, so much for progress—Tatiana had sought
them out in Santa Monica at the American Film Market, a
place where ugly men smoking big, fat cigars and wearing
thick gold chains hustle lousy movies—the kind that avoid
the multiplexes and head straight for video stores. How
much sex and nudity? How much action? How much violence? That's all anyone wants to know because that's all
the age sixteen-to-forty male demographic cares about. *This*
was her public. No wonder her weekly therapy session with
Dr. G was like a lifeline.

Anyway, one thing led to another with the Dobsons, and
they signed her up to star in *Lady Cop Undercover*. Standard
erotic thriller formula—killer runs amok; heroine takes lots
of showers, beds two men (one good, one bad); and gets
stalked, attacked, almost murdered at least half a dozen
times. But the fans loved it. Then Tatiana needed a new car,
so she agreed to make *Lady Cop Undercover II: Massage
Parlor*. The same boneheads went ape for that one. Meanwhile, Kerr wanted to put in a pool, so she said yes to *Lady
Cop Undercover III: Escort Service*. Next, Tatiana saw Meg
Ryan's house in *In Style,* got redecorating fever, and agreed
to headline *Lady Cop Undercover IV: Red Light District* to
foot the bill for the shabby-chic-meets-casual-Zen-with-a-
little-feng-shui thing she had in mind.

But one day a dream smacked her between the eyes. It

happened at Starbucks. Tatiana had just finished detoxing in a strenuous, hour-long yoga class and dashed in for a half-caffeine, double-short, nonfat, no-whip mocha. The new issue of *Daily Variety* had been left at a two-top, so she thumbed through it as she sipped. That's when she read about *Sin by Sin*. The new Greg Tapper picture had hit a snag because Nicole Kidman bailed out of the lead female role.

She'd considered it nothing less than a sign from God and immediately fished out her cellular to call Jeremy. When he finally came on the line, she brought him up to speed on her brilliant plan, finishing up with a ferociously upbeat "Get me a script! Get me this part!"

"Get a life!" One thing was certain: the asshole was no Tony Robbins. "An offer's out to Ashley Judd already. The studio wants a big female star. You'd be lucky to get on as an extra. But here's some good news—I'm playing phone tag with the Dobsons. There's another *Lady Cop* movie in the works. I'll call you." Click.

Luckily, she'd had a session with Dr. G scheduled for later that day. The first thirty minutes or so had been run-of-the-mill self-esteem meltdown: my career's over, I'll never rise above the ranks, my agent doesn't believe in me, why does Catherine Zeta-Jones get everything, etc. And then Dr. G had started in with her psychological tricks. *How does that make you feel?* Ugh! Tatiana hated that one. And it was, like, Dr. G's greatest hit.

But after a little soul-digging, she'd come to the realization that the lousy feeling she carried around inside was often fertilized by other people. Like Jeremy. What a bastard. He'd never really worked on her behalf, not the way a real agent who truly believed in a client would. And then there were the Dobsons. What frauds. They made their movies cheap and fast, hired loser directors who yelled things like,

"I've got a headache, so let's finish this fucking scene in one take," and regularly dispatched her to scream queen conventions where she sat in a booth for seven hours and signed eight-by-ten glossies to college dorks. Yeah, right, she was their *special* leading lady.

"The ability to say no is a powerful thing," Dr. G had pointed out.

So she did. Say no, that is.

But Jeremy had wanted none of it. "I'm advising you to take this offer."

"Well, this time I'm not going to follow your advice."

"Is this some kind of joke?"

"No, the real joke is the idea to make a fourth sequel to *Lady Cop Undercover.*"

"You know what? You're not marketable enough to be a high-maintenance client. Find another agent." Click.

At first Tatiana couldn't believe it. But soon a dull dial tone was buzzing in her ear. Like any other struggling actress with no prospects, she'd started to cry.

Kerr had come running. "What's wrong?"

She'd given him the truth but made Jeremy sound even meaner to ratchet up the sympathy.

But Kerr had just urged her to call him back and say she'd take the part. "We really need the money, Tat."

"Then why don't *you* get off your ass and make some?"

That had shut him up for the rest of the day.

Someone was still pounding on the hotel room door. This snapped Tatiana back to the present. She forced herself out of bed and shuffled over to answer.

Into the room burst September Moore, looking pretty ridiculous in an off-the-shoulder cheetah print dress and matching handbag.

"Isn't Cannes enough of a zoo?"

September sailed past her and flopped down on the chaise.
"Yes, but don't we all love the animals?"

"Where have you been?"

"The Miramax party."

Tatiana shrugged. "I wasn't invited."

"Neither was I. But I crashed. Great champagne. So-so
food. Ben Affleck was there. I want to have his baby. Actually, I just want him to get me pregnant. He can have the
child."

September Moore had been a victim of too much too
soon. She peaked at twenty with a Best Supporting Actress
Academy Award for her role in *Postcards from Paris*. Now,
almost fifteen years later, she was doing guest turns on *Law
and Order* and starring in bad cable television movies. Her
latest was *Just A Few Bites, Jenny!* in which she played the
distraught mother of a teenage girl with an eating disorder.

"I saw David Walsh in the bar," September said silkily.
"He looked lonely."

Tatiana wondered if she could actually go through with
the plan. Here she was, at the Cannes International Film
Festival, with no movie to promote and no agent to represent
her, just an out-of-work actress looking to seduce a producer
in hopes of landing a lead role. Definitely a career low. If
only Hugh Grant would drive up and tell her to get in the
car, then it would be official.

Miserable, Tatiana flung herself onto the bed. "I don't
know if I can do it. I don't mind playing a whore in a bad
movie, but in real life a girl needs to have some standards."

This show of morality failed to impress September. "Do
you have any idea what I've done to get where I am today?"

"You mean the bottom-left corner of *Hollywood
Squares*?"

"Hey, don't knock it. The pay's decent, and they give
you a nice gift basket after the show."

Three knocks on the door.

Tatiana groaned and got up to answer.

A bellboy stood there with the Federal Express letter.

The return address puzzled her. It was from Kerr. She tore open the package and began to read.

Dear Tat,

   This is the hardest thing I've ever had to do. You know how much I love you, but our marriage hasn't worked for a long time, and I'm going to be the practical one and suggest that we end it.

Tatiana halted. One paragraph and already she felt as if as many variants of emotion that happen in the typical Shakespeare play were passing through her. *Hasn't worked for a long time.* If that wasn't the merest tip of the iceberg! And *practical*? The man was a poet! And not even a published one. He lived in a dream world, believing someone would just tap him on the shoulder one day and magically pronounce him the next William Blake. She took a deep breath and continued.

   If nothing else, though, I owe you the truth, don't I?

Stop. God! She hated it when people asked questions in letters. Her mother did it all the time (well, twice a year, actually, in her amazingly inappropriate birthday and Christmas missives). Steaming now, Tatiana soldiered on.

   There's a part of me that I've kept buried for years.

Yes, that would be the part of you that earns a paycheck.

Now I have the courage to bring it out into the sunshine, and I have to thank Jaron for that.

Wait a minute. Who the hell is Jaron?

He's the man I love, the man I plan on spending the rest of my life with.

A home-wrecking bitch, that's who! Hurt and anger battled back and forth inside her like blood corpuscles in full-scale war.

I suppose I've always been gay.

You think? It's not like a head cold, you moron!

Until I met Jaron, though, those feelings never came to the surface.

Well, excuse me while I go find the perfect Hallmark card and volunteer to help with your float for the gay pride parade!

There's no denying who I am now. My name is Kerr Fox, and I'm homosexual.

Tatiana stopped again, silently cursed him for plagiarizing the Alcoholics Anonymous mantra, and locked eyes with September. "Kerr left me for another man."

"Bless him! A scandal like this could give your career a real boost. First things first. You need a great publicist."

Tatiana went back to the letter.

I don't want this to change our relationship or the dedication we share for Ethan and Everson. Of course, I'll be moving out and asking that you assume full custody while I begin this new adventure in my life. I need to take the time to find out who Kerr is.

Tatiana stomped over to the minibar, grabbed a Scotch, and downed it straight from the tiny bottle, feeling it burn a path down her throat and into her stomach. Immediate guilt. Her first minute as a full-time mother and already she had a drinking problem. Hopeless!

"This is perfect," September said. "A stint in rehab will milk this even longer. The press loves stuff like that."

"Right now I couldn't give a shit about the media."

September gasped. "You don't mean that! It must be the booze talking."

Tatiana considered another Scotch.

"You just have to pull yourself together and go find David Walsh. A role like the one in *Sin by Sin* happens once in a lifetime. You can always find another gay husband."

Tatiana sucked in a breath. Her lips quivered. A crying jag was on the way.

September stood up, crossed the room, and shook her violently. "Hold back the tears! Your eye makeup is perfect. Don't ruin it."

"He's leaving me," Tatiana whispered faintly. "And he's giving me full custody of the twins."

"Oh, this is horrible!" Now September raided Scotch from the minibar. "One of my ex-husbands tried to do that, but I wouldn't let him."

"You have a child?"

September nodded. "A daughter. I never liked her, though. Too clingy."

Tatiana just stared back, as if this bizarre woman with

warped values had all the answers. "How could this happen?"

"Have you seen the guy he dumped you for?"

"I don't think so."

"Well, he must be gorgeous. You know, it's really exhausting. These days you have to compete with women *and* men to keep a guy."

Tatiana sank down onto the bed. September's words were like white noise. In a crisis, she needed her friend Candace, a woman who actually made sense. "This is *so* unbelievable. How am I going to take care of two kids all by myself? I *knew* we weren't ready for children. I told Kerr that over and over again, but he insisted on adopting." She flailed her hands in the air like ravens. "And now he's running off!"

"Can't you send the kids away to boarding school?" September asked, inspecting a nail, looking bored.

"They're *fifteen* months old!"

September shrugged. "Oh." A moment of deep thought. "You could call the birth mother and tell her you've changed your mind."

"Do you have *any* maternal instincts?"

"I felt very protective toward a personal assistant once. But then I had to fire her."

"Stop, please, I'm getting a lump in my throat."

September huffed a little.

"I can't believe you suggested that. I told you the story, didn't I? Kerr met the birth mother in a poetry workshop. The teacher always ripped her pieces apart for not communicating enough emotional despair. Later on this woman decides to give up her twins so she'll have something painful to write about."

September looked impressed. "She sounds very dedicated."

"No, she sounds *insane*. And her kids are better off with me. Now isn't that a scary thought."

Tatiana pictured them, Ethan and Everson, boy and girl, blond and blond, two beautiful, innocent darlings who needed her to provide unconditional love and slavish attention. But even with the nanny and an occasional hand from Enrique, her personal assistant, could she really pull it off? Just trying to factor the odds, a feeling of instant exhaustion set in.

A scene flashed in her mind: two chubby children with squat noses, faces dark red from crying, cheeks and upper lips a mess of tears and mucus. The only thing Tatiana knew how to do was plug bottles into their mouths. Certainly you needed to know more, though. Perhaps she could pick up a brochure at a baby store.

Suddenly, Tatiana felt dizzy. The room dipped and swayed. Obviously, the Klonopin was kicking in. And the Scotch. And the nervous breakdown. *Damn you, Kerr!* It seemed reasonable to blame him for all of the above.

"You have to put this out of your mind," September said. "Focus all your concentration on David Walsh."

Tatiana shook her head. There was no way she could go through with her vamp act now. Not in this state. She could barely think beyond the next few minutes.

September walked over to the closet, sifted through Tatiana's hanging clothes, and flung a hot Betsey Johnson number onto the bed. "Wear this. With a thong. No bra. Chances are you'll get the part *and* top billing."

"I can't." Tatiana stood there, frozen.

"Somebody is going to star in *Sin by Sin*. Why shouldn't it be you?"

"You don't understand. I don't care about that stupid movie!"

September reared back, apoplectic, her mouth agape.

"I've never heard such deranged talk. I'm calling a doctor."
She started for the phone.

"I don't need a *doctor!* My agent fired me! My husband
left me! I'm a single mother of twins!"

"All good points. Forget the doctor. You need a sani-
tarium."

It was strange, Tatiana realized, that her impulses were
to mourn the less emotional losses. Her spirit had been hurt
more than her heart. This brought to mind the words of
playwright Jean Giraudoux. Dr. G had handed them to her
a few sessions ago, neatly typed onto an index card: "If
two people who love each other let a single instant wedge
itself between them, it grows—it becomes a month, a year,
a century; it becomes too late."

For Tatiana and Kerr, it had become too late a long time
ago. Husband and wife had metamorphosed into awkward
roommates. Sexually they were at an impasse. Of course,
the fact that he was gay made her feel better about this. But
perhaps the biggest divide had been the debate over children.
Her ambivalence had lit the fuse for many fights, some
dragging on for days. So how ironic that, after she gave in
on the issue, he'd helicopter out and leave her to raise those
kids all alone. Hello? Did she look like Rosie O'Donnell?

"I know a clinic in Switzerland that puts you to sleep for
thirty days. I went there after my first face lift. Maybe that's
what you need."

"A face lift?" Tatiana ran to the bathroom mirror, horrified.

"No . . . well . . . How old are you?"

She paused a moment to remember. The Dobsons thought
she was still in her twenties. Ditto Jeremy. The lie passed
her lips so often that she'd started to believe it, too. "I'm
thirty-four."

September gasped. "And you haven't had work done yet?" Her eyes narrowed. "Liar."

"I'm telling the truth."

"Bitch."

Tatiana turned back to the mirror. Staying out of the sun was the best thing she ever did. It gave her skin a porcelain quality. She smiled at her reflection, at the absence of lines around her mouth and eyes. "Don't be jealous. I'll probably age ten years by the end of the week."

"Just don't go out there and get new tits. Too many women do that when their husbands start acting like idiots. All it leads to is back trouble and limited fashion choices. The designer's muse is not the big-breasted woman, you know."

Tatiana was barely listening. A quiet panic began to consume her. Was seeking out David Walsh the right thing to do? Or should she call up Jeremy, beg his forgiveness, and say yes to *Lady Cop Undercover V*? Granted, it wasn't *Norma Rae*, but it was a paycheck, and she had to keep the household going. The nanny came bustling in with bags of diapers, formula, and baby food about every ten minutes. And not a dime was in the bank for college.

September glanced at her watch and grimaced. "I hate Cannes. There's never enough time in the day. I have to decide between a dinner and a cocktail party, and it's like choosing which leg to amputate."

"Don't let me keep you. I'm fine."

"Are you sure?" September already had her hand on the door as she said this.

"Honey, go, do your thing."

September reached into her bag and pulled out a small bottle of September Rain, the perfume she hawked on QVC every couple of months. "For good luck. Men go wild for it."

"Thanks," Tatiana said, offering up a half smile. She didn't have the heart to tell her the truth: the stuff smelled like furniture polish. In fact, people in Hollywood jokingly referred to it as September *Pain*, this after a rumor circulated that a young model had actually fended off an attacker by spraying him with it.

Alone with her insecurities now, Tatiana snatched her cellular and punched in Jeremy's number.

His bitchy assistant answered.

"This is Tatiana Fox. I need Jeremy right away. It's an emergency."

Annoyed sigh. "What kind of emergency? He doesn't represent you anymore."

Tatiana knew what she had to do. Acting rude got you nowhere in Hollywood. Acting crazy got you all the attention in the world. "I'm sitting here with a bottle of pills in my hand."

Within moments Jeremy came on the line. "Tatiana, where are you?"

"In Cannes."

"Why?"

"September Moore convinced me to go. David Walsh is here."

"You won't take *my* career advice, but you'll listen to *September Moore?* Maybe you should swallow the pills."

"Jeremy! I don't have any pills. Well, I've got Klonopin for anxiety, Prozac for depression, and Ambien to help me sleep at night, but those are in my beauty case, not in my hand. I just said that because I knew you wouldn't take my call otherwise."

"This better be good."

"I've decided to take the part in *Lady Cop Undercover V.* I need the work. My hus—"

"Too late. Tori Valentine has already signed."

Tatiana experienced a flush of red heat. Tori was a *real* twenty-something, a former Dallas Cowboys cheerleader, and, coincidentally, also represented by Jeremy. The worst part: she was a terrible actress, so bad that they didn't invite her back for the sequel to *Sorority House Slaughter,* and she was the only sister who survived in the original!

"*Tori Valentine?*"

"That's what I said."

"Are you sleeping with her? I bet you were just waiting for the chance to steal my franchise away from me! Listen, there's only one *Lady Cop Undercover,* and that's me god-damn it!"

"Sorry. They've already rewritten the script. Your character turns up murdered in the opening scene."

"*What?*"

"Tori plays your younger sister who's just out of the police academy. She finds you dead in a dumpster."

Dead in a dumpster. Was this art imitating life?

"And don't be so dramatic," Jeremy scolded. "I'm not banging Tori. Didn't you know I was gay?"

"I should introduce you to my husband. That's why he left me."

"Really? Is he hot?"

Tatiana almost hung up. Going from September to Jeremy was enough to drive anyone to pills. "My life's upside down, Jeremy. I need to work. I'll even do a monster movie. But nothing where a creature drags me under the water. I know an actress who almost drowned making *Return to Swamp Thing.*"

Jeremy's pause was a pregnant one. "When are you going to pack it in? Let's face it, you're getting a little long in the tooth for the sex bomb roles, and you don't have the acting chops for character work."

Tatiana just sat there, letting the words sink in, more than a decade of struggles playing like home movies in her mind. She'd left college early to model in Europe, where she made decent money but grew tired of being hit on by Italian playboys. Then it was off to Los Angeles. More modeling. Ridiculous acting classes. One teacher had told her to lie down on the floor and pretend to be a piece of bacon frying. There were occasional walk-ons in movies and episodic television. Her big break had been a speaking part in a Toyota commercial. Then, finally, a chance to star in a movie, even if it was *Lady Cop Undercover*. Next came an offer from *Playboy*. It was supposed to do great things for her career. It didn't. But it earned her the down payment for a house. Not bad for a day of topless sunbathing and gymnastics on a skyscraper.

Jeremy had been with her for the whole ride, treating her with casual regard from day one. Never taking her calls. Rescheduling appointments at the last minute. Making her wait interminably when she did have one. Year after year, humiliation by humiliation, this sank in, eroding her confidence until almost none remained.

But Tatiana had a little bit left, and she dug deep to access it right now. She felt a surge of energy, megavolts of angry determination, if not outright defiance.

"Listen to me very carefully, Jeremy. You're going to rue the day that you dropped me."

He started to laugh. "Give me one good reason."

"Because I'm going to make it, you son of a bitch. And I mean *big*."

Chapter Two

"All over me like a rash, he was . . . rooted me silly . . . dead set!"

Jack's eyes fluttered open.

"How's my rotten form? Pig's arse! I'm a top sort."

Jack propped himself up on his elbows.

"He got his end in all night! Now I could eat a horse and chase the jockey."

Jack attempted to piece together the past several hours. Limousine from airport to hotel. Walk around the wharf area known as Woolloomooloo. Drinks with a sports-writer friend. Party stop at the Pier One Parkroyal. Lots of flirting with a hot barmaid named Danni. Lusty ride up in the W's glass-walled cargo elevator. Call to room service to send up champagne. And now the morning after.

"I dunno . . . hoo-roo!" She hung up the phone and

twisted her body around, surprised to find him awake. ''Want some brekkie?''

Jack had no idea what this girl was saying. But he knew one language that they both spoke fluently, so he just smiled and leaned in to kiss her.

Danni drew back, covering her mouth with her hand. ''I got breath like an abo's armpit!''

He took that to mean *not* Pepsodent fresh.

She broke into a wide grin. ''Can't believe I had it off with Jack Thorpe. You're top of the wozzer.''

''Ah,'' Jack said, running a hand down her smooth, slender arm. ''That's what all the girls say.''

''We were both on the slops and out to it. Think I'm *still* half-cut.'' She got up, modesty not an issue, and ambled her way into the bathroom.

Jack noticed her tattoo for the first time. It was Buttercup, the feistiest of the Powerpuff Girls, needled in just above the crack of Danni's ass. Pretty sexy.

''Feel like I'm away with the pixies!''

''I feel like I woke up in Ouagadougou,'' Jack murmured, stretching, sighing, hungry as hell.

''Can barely see! My eyes are pissholes in the snow!''

Jack groaned. *Somebody flash me subtitles!* He considered calling the concierge to see about having an interpreter sent up. It amazed him how he'd been born in nearby Darlinghurst but was an Australian on paper only. The country's raucous, down-to-earth, colorful idioms separated the sunburnt diehards from all the rest. He was definitely the latter, having moved to Leytonstone, East London, before his fifth birthday.

Mum, a hairdresser, and Dad, a gas fitter, had no idea what lay ahead, because it all started innocently enough, as most paths do. It began the year they moved to Chingford in Essex. Like every other seven-year-old, Jack had been soccer crazy, a footballer from the jump. That meant hours and hours at Chase Lane Park, learning the fundamentals of touch and control, practicing dead ball and corner kicks until well after dark. Then he would run home and play keepy-uppy with the ball before bed.

By the time his days at Chingford High came around, Jack was done for. You could always find a football under his arm, but rarely a stack of books. At fourteen he signed schoolboy terms to play for Manchester United, planning to turn professional two years later once he was able to leave school. In the beginning, his parents were reluctant, though when the club manager paid a visit, they came around. Jack could still remember Terry Harrison's sales pitch.

''Little Jack's got it all: total belief in his own ability, technical focus, and inner calm. That's the holy trinity all the best athletes share. He's going to be an icon, so let him go, but hang on tight for the ride.''

Football was about discipline and team spirit, and from sixteen on, Terry kept a tight reign on Jack, allowing him no opportunity to rebel or stand out from the crowd. Put under the charge of Mrs. Conran, a humorless landlady who was built like an ox and drill-sergeant tough, Jack knew only endless training sessions and lights-out at ten o'clock sharp.

Terry didn't have all the young United players on eagle watch. Jack had seen other guys his age frequent pubs and discos, smoke fags, and use their pro footballer status to score girls and gain access to VIP parties. But it never bothered him. He preferred taking a bag of balls onto the field and honing his free kicks to perfection. His eye was on the prize. And years later, the prize was in his hands, slippery, but there.

It seemed to happen almost overnight. A picture hit all the sports pages in Britain: Jack at the Euro 2000 competition

in Belgium, up against Portugal, going after a ball with the
ferocity of a lion, finely sculpted athletic body pulsing with
aggression, blond locks wind-strewn, face a mask of determination for team and country. The headline read simply,
"JACK ATTACK," and from that morning on, everything
changed.

Victories and honors began to tumble all over themselves.
Premier League title, Champions League most valuable
player, a Football Association Young Player of the Year
award, the coveted World Cup. Jack's boots sold at auction at
Christie's for megabucks, his signed shirts were like precious
stones, and fans and collectors rumbled through dustbins
outside his hairdresser's salon for locks of hair to tape in
scrapbooks or to sell on e-bay. It was insane.

And it got worse, or better, depending on the day. The
entertainment and fashion press started clocking his every
move, snapping shots of him out on the town. His penchant
for wearing juvenile T-shirts—GI Joe, Sailor Moon, Superman, even Hello Kitty—was hailed as a stroke of ironic
brilliance. Designers called him a "visionary" and regularly
sent him clothes at no charge. *GQ* voted him most stylish
man of the year. Photographers trailed him everywhere.

Next came the money. At contract renewal time, his
agent pounced, brokering a merciless deal that made him
the highest-earning player in the league. Sponsorship
offers poured in. Ditto the commercial opportunities. A
line of Jack Attack apparel hit retail and flew off the racks.
The official Jack Thorpe poster papered the public transit
system and the walls of awe-struck boys and swooning
girls.

On the field, Jack let all the madness seep into his game.
To whip up the crowd, he played Hollywood passes, show-
boated, and hit flash. When the fans would roar, you could
actually feel the stands begin to shake. "Jack attack; no

turning back!'' Their shouts had a rolling sound, like thunder. The high was like a drug.

Off the field, he got buck-wild, too, dating a series of high-profile pretty young things: the model who left him for a rock star, the daughter of the construction millionaire, who wanted marriage right away, the soap opera actress who liked to tie him up.

All this brought on a brutal verbal blast from Terry. ''Do you know how many careers I've seen cut short by this kind of shit? Booze, girls, pretty boy posing—that's the quickest route to the transfer market. Stop being a lad and start being a man!''

The lecture didn't take. As if it stood a chance in bloody hell anyway. A guy had to hit rock bottom, right? At the next match against Argentina, he did. One of the midfield players crashed into him. Jack's knee twisted on the way down. He heard a sickening crack, then experienced pain so intense that he just lay there, poleaxed, everything a red mist. Unaware that Jack was hurt, the player bent down to give his hair a tug. Jack didn't care if it was innocent fun or not. The gesture fueled him with rage, and he tripped the jerk with his leg that could still move. The hooligans in the stands turned on him, booing and snorting. Drunk with agony, Jack gave them all his middle finger. Manchester United ended up losing the match on penalties, paving the way for a premature exit from what could have been back-to-back World Cup titles.

Jack's knee required surgery. This meant months of rehab . . . and never playing football again, at least professionally. At twenty-six, his career was over. It felt so strange. For eleven years Jack had lived in this claustrophobic world, with few chances to meet people outside the environs of football. And when he did, they were just girls who didn't last or phony friends who glommed on for the sake of proximity to fame.

Trying to build a life without football had been rough going. But silver linings were slowly turning up. There was the comfort and freedom of being set for life financially, and the ego salvation that a BBC sports magazine show wanted to sign him on as a coanchor.

Suddenly, Jack noticed the message light blinking on the bedside table phone. Maybe Hugh had good news about the BBC offer. Before he could reach the receiver, it started to ring. Must be *very* good news. Ha! The anxious bastard couldn't even wait for a buzz back.

"I hope you held out for all the perks, mate," Jack said right away.

"Mr. Thorpe?" It wasn't Hugh.

Jack pulled the covers over his naked body and laughed. "Sorry. Thought you were someone else."

"I'm calling from the front desk. The credit card you presented to secure your stay with us was declined. We left several messages for you."

Jack pushed off the covers. "I was out most of the day." A terrible sense of foreboding came over him. "I'll ring my manager straight away and try to figure out what the trouble is."

"Thank you, sir. We appreciate your prompt attention."

Jack hung up, genuinely stunned. A declined credit card? He never knew what was coming in or going out. Everything business or personal went directly to Hugh Haliwell, who, since the day Jack turned pro at sixteen, had managed anything to do with money, from investments to speeding tickets.

He punched in Hugh's number. It rang. And rang. Eleven times and still no answering machine. Jack got a bad feeling. Finally, someone picked up with a faint, slurred greeting.

"Hugh?"

"Jack!" Too sunny, too soon. Definitely something wrong.

"Where are you?"

"In Australia with a worthless credit card. What's going on?"

A long silence. Followed by a muffled cry. Then a drawn-out sob.

Jack couldn't believe it. "Hugh?"

"Who's on the blower?" Danni asked. She was back, fresh from the shower, gloriously naked, towel drying her wet hair.

Jack gestured for her to be quiet. "Talk to me, mate. Come on, it can't be that bad. Is it Victoria? One of the kids?"

"I messed up, Jack. I messed up bad," Hugh whimpered.

"My friend Desiree's throwing a barbie," Danni said. "They're probably cracking tinnies right now. I'm not clapped out. You?"

Jack slapped his hand over the receiver. "Shut up! Can't you see I'm on the phone? And Christ, go learn some English!"

"Don't go crook at me! I'll piss off quick!" Danni glared. "I will!"

"This is serious," Jack said, lowering his voice. But he knew the annoyance was all over his face and flashing from his eyes.

"Ain't *you* up yourself. That sticks out like a dog's balls. Well, fine. I'll nick off then." Danni huffed and began to seek out her scattered clothes.

Jack ignored her. "Hugh, I'm back. Tell me what happened."

"It's all gone," Hugh said, voice cracking, tone devoid of hope.

"What's gone?"

"Your money. My business. Everything. It's gone."

Jack's stomach did a flip. His heart took off. "Wait a minute. *My* money?"

"I messed up, Jack."

"We've established that, mate. Give me some detail."

"I invested in the first phase of something called the Cassandra Project, and the return was twenty-five percent in just a few months time. The sec—"

"Hold on," Jack cut in. Something about the Cassandra Project rang a bell. He scanned his brain for the answer. Then it hit him. Those stories that ruled the London papers. An investment scheme went straight into the toilet. One man had lost everything and jumped to his death from the Lloyd's building. But that had been days ago. "Did you risk *my*—"

"The second phase came available," Hugh explained desperately. "They promised a thirty-percent return. I—"

Jack shut his eyes. "How much did I lose?"

There was silence.

"How much, Hugh?" Jack's voice went down an octave.

"Everything."

Jack cursed himself for surrendering control of his future to Hugh, for being too lazy to look after it himself. And wait until Mum hears about this. "You put too much trust in that bloody manager of yours," she always nagged. "He's not family. Remember that." But year after year, Jack had ignored her wisdom.

"You can't mean everything," Jack said.

Hugh's sigh came from somewhere deep within. "I mean everything."

"My pension?"

"Gone."

"My retirement accounts?"

"Gone."

Jack started to sweat. At least he had a home. His warehouse apartment in Shad Thames, a fashionable quarter on the south side of the river by Tower Bridge, was like a sanctuary. Then a worst-case scenario moment washed over him. No . . . bloody hell . . . he couldn't mean the apartment, too. "My place?" Jack's voice croaked a little.

"Gone. The car, too." Hugh started to cry again.

Jack felt sick. Any minute now he could throw up. Just hurl. Literally. The BMW Z8, a swank, superfast ultimate driving machine. He broke up with a girl once because she spilled coffee on the front seat. That's how much he loved his baby.

Hugh blubbered on.

"Stop crying!" Jack hissed. "*I* should be crying right now. I'd *like* to cry. But I'm too *pissed* to cry. Shit! How could you risk everything I own on one deal? Who gave you the authority to do that?"

"You did."

"Oh." Jack stewed in the moment. "Well, what the fuck do I know? I'm just a dumb jock."

"I'm sorry, Jack. This is killing me. If it's any consolation, *I* lost everything, too. Victoria left me. My kids won't talk to me."

"That helps a little," Jack said. "But what the hell am I going to do? Football is the only thing I know."

Danni squeezed into the last of her clothes. "Sounds like you're on the bones of your arse. Too bad." She curled up her top lip and started for the door.

"Don't go," Jack pleaded. "I like to have sex after I hear bad news. It helps curb the misery. I just lost everything I own."

"Owd ya be?"

No clue what that meant. But judging from the scowl on her face, it didn't appear to be supportive.

"What kind of drongo would put all his eggs in one basket?" Danni asked.

"My manager."

Danni shook her head. "Dillbrain." And then she left, slamming the door behind her.

Jack felt seized by desperation. "I'm stuck in this hotel, Hugh. I need some money. Christ, I need a job." A quivering arrow of hope shot into his heart. "What about this BBC thing?"

"It fell through. Management couldn't get past you flipping the bird at the World Cup."

"I wasn't in my right mind!" Jack argued. "I'd just busted up my knee. I was in horrible pain!"

"The image overshadows the circumstances."

"I shoot one bird and suddenly I'm O. J. Simpson?"

"I don't know, Jack."

"What about my stuff?"

"Everything's been seized. There are some tax problems with the earnings from phase one."

Jack lay there speechless, half expecting Hugh to come charging in on his cell phone, accompanied by a camera crew from some bad reality TV show. Everyone would get a good laugh, right? This couldn't be happening. But it was.

Homeless.

Carless.

Careerless.

"I have a friend in Los Angeles," Hugh said. "David Walsh. He's a film producer. I talked him into seeing you for a bit part in the new Greg Tapper movie. It'll pay something and get you a Screen Actors Guild card."

"It probably isn't necessary to tell you this officially, Hugh, but . . . you're fired."

Chapter Three

Los Angeles, California

"I've got bad news and worse news." Enrique chose to announce this at baggage claim.

Tatiana merely stared—at the conveyor belt. Her Vuitton case was sandwiched between a battered Samsonite and a set of golf clubs, making its way toward her—slowly.

"Did you hear what I said?"

"Shut up unless you have good news."

"Okay . . . Tori Valentine was run over by an SUV."

"Really?" Was this a sign that *nobody* could succeed her in the *Lady Cop Undercover* franchise? For a fleeting moment, Tatiana danced upon the air. Just as suddenly, she halted, putting herself in check, experiencing a moment of self-hatred. How could she celebrate this kind of news? Tori was only an innocent girl. She didn't know the state capital, and after seeing *Pearl Harbor*, she actually believed that

Ben Affleck had fought in World War II. *Shame on me.*
Now, if *Jeremy* were to get run over by an SUV . . . Hell,
make it a Hummer and put the Dobsons in the path of
destruction, too.

"I'm kidding," Enrique said. "You know that, right?"
He checked out a girl passing by who was a dead ringer for
Penelope Cruz. "Tori did break up with Mookie, though.
They had a huge falling out at Deep. I was there."

Mookie played drums for the popular rock band Suicide
Hotline. He was covered neck to feet in tattoos, pierced like
a pin cushion, and always in a scrape with the police. But
he had an enormous tallywacker (ten inches according to
some), so women stuck to him like Krazy Glue.

Finally, Tatiana's Vuitton came around. She pointed at
it.

Enrique struggled with the luggage. For a hot guy who
worked out all the time, he really wasn't that strong. "What
do you have in here?" He huffed and puffed.

Tatiana rolled her eyes. "Not a set of encyclopedias,
Hercules." She reached down to take the bag from him and
managed the transfer with little effort. Honestly. Maybe it
was this instant-mommy business that had turned her into
Supergirl. Lately she'd been observing women with children,
and these ladies could lift! Kids, car seats, diaper bags,
fifteen Wal-Mart sacks—all at the same time. As if Arnold
Schwarzenegger could do that. Well, maybe with a stunt
double.

Enrique's Jeep was illegally parked. To no surprise, a
ticket had been slipped under the windshield wipers. "Shit."

Tatiana gave him a scolding glance. Enrique got parking
fines as often as porn stars got hepatitis. She even had to
bail him out of jail once. The whole affair had taken hours
and caused her to miss an audition for a breath mint commercial. Her personal assistant sometimes *cluttered* her life as

opposed to clearing a path for efficiency. How dumb was that? But he was a sweetheart and great scenery to have around (imagine Ricky Martin, only *hotter*), so she kept him on.

"You're going to get arrested again."

"This sucks." He glanced around pugnaciously, as if he were going to pull a Zsa Zsa and slap the cop who wrote the citation.

Tatiana heaved her luggage into the back and climbed inside. "And that makes how many unpaid tickets this week?"

"Just one. I swear." Enrique lurched into a busy lane without looking, triggering a cacophony of horns, profanity, and obscene hand gestures.

Tatiana opened the glove compartment and a pile of unpaid tickets came spilling out. "Enrique!"

"Okay, I got three this week. All the rest are ancient."

"I'm *not* going to bail you out again. Next time you stay in jail. I'm serious. You do realize that you'll be somebody's bitch before the cell door closes, don't you?"

He didn't answer.

"This is so irresponsible. What if you had the twins and got pulled over? They would take you in and turn Ethan and Everson over to some female officer in a uniform two sizes too small. You know how sensitive Ethan's skin is. He might get a rash from the polyester. I would be your one call, but say I'm on the phone with September. You know she hates it when I do the call-waiting thing. Usually, I ignore it, and most of the time I forget to check the messages after I hang up. It could be *hours* before I find out where you are. *Hours*! The twins could pick up a terrible habit in that time. Like bad grammar. Or a Krispy Kreme addiction. I don't want them eating too much sugar. I read the Marilu Henner book about healthy kids, you know."

Enrique shook his head. "All this from a parking ticket?"

Tatiana gave him a haughty look. "It's called chain reaction."

"Not paranoid schizophrenia?"

"Oh, you're a stand-up comic now? Forgive me. I thought you were a struggling personal assistant."

Enrique cut in front of a Range Rover. "You're just avoiding the inevitable." He gestured to the floor board. A tattered copy of the *Star* lay near her feet. "Deal with the worst news first. Page sixteen, I think."

Tatiana picked up the scandal rag and turned right to it, zeroing in on a thumbnail image of herself in the left-hand corner, boxed under this hideous headline: "OBSCURE SEX-POT LOSES HUBBY TO GAY AFFAIR."

"Obscure?" She stared lasers at Enrique.

For once in his life, he watched the road.

Reading on, Tatiana didn't know whether to laugh, cry, or just bulldoze through the *Star* editorial offices. The short article was chockablock full of inaccuracies. Okay, she was *not* a nude model. She *never* said, "Now I wonder if I'm enough woman for any man." And she *didn't* race into the arms of Stephen Baldwin. Pause to let wave of nausea pass. *Stephen Baldwin?* He was, like, the worst Baldwin brother. Well, maybe next to worst. For a second there she forgot about Daniel. But at least give her Alec or Billy! It was a total lie anyway. Why not be creative in a positive direction? Disgusted, she threw down the tabloid.

"Don't worry. You didn't make the cover, so hardly anybody will see that," Enrique said.

"That's because I'm *obscure*. I'm not worthy of the cover." Tatiana snatched up the fish paper again to survey the front. "But the Bush twins sneaking a wine cooler are. I *hate* this town!" She turned to Enrique with great seriousness. "Do you think I need a publicist?"

"I think you need a nanny."

"I already have one. Melina's wonderful."

"That's the worst news."

"*What?*" Tatiana experienced instant panic. Ethan and Everson adored Melina. Plus, she wasn't exactly legal citizenship-wise, and therefore was very affordable. Tatiana never felt guilty about this, because she had no intention of ever running for congress or being appointed secretary of labor.

"She's quitting to go work for someone else."

An avalanche of hurt. "Why?"

"More money, a guesthouse, and the chance to drive a Mercedes—a station wagon, but still. I'm jealous."

"She's at least giving me two weeks notice, right?"

Enrique said nothing.

"*She's not?*"

"They want her to start right away. She's even getting a signing bonus. But I convinced her to stay on until you got home."

"Bitch! I should call Immigration!" Tatiana stopped herself. "No, I don't mean that. Well, I kind of do. But I don't *want* to. I'm a mother now. I need to set a good example." She took a deep breath. "*You* call Immigration."

Enrique laughed. "How about I call the nanny service instead?"

Tatiana steamed in the passenger seat. "Make that your *second* call." She let out a frustrated sigh.

Enrique fiddled with the CD player and soon Blink 182 came thrashing out of the speakers, loud, angry, and aggressive—precisely how Tatiana was feeling. In just a few days she'd lost her agent, her role as the original *Lady Cop Undercover*, her husband, and her nanny. The sum of it all triggered a crying jag.

"Are you really upset or just being emotional?" Enrique asked.

Tatiana glared at him through red, tear-filled eyes. "What do *you* think?"

He shrugged. "I don't know. You burst into tears when we were watching a repeat of that very special episode of *Blossom*. Remember?"

"This time I'm *upset*," Tatiana wailed. "Which reminds me—call Dr. G and get me in as soon as possible. I don't care what time. And make sure *all* my prescriptions get refilled." She pulled a thatch of hair around and inspected it. "Oh, yuck. I need to see my colorist, too. Call Brenda. Beg if you have to."

"Uh . . . it might be better if *you* called Brenda."

"Why?"

"We hooked up after a Matchbox Twenty concert a few weeks ago, and I never called."

"Enrique!"

"I know, I know, a serious violation of my personal assistant covenants. But she looked so hot in those low-riding jeans. I couldn't resist."

"Do you know how long it takes to build a healthy relationship with a colorist? Brenda and I have something special. I'm going to tell her that I let you go. I'll say you stole from me or something. And if you even *think* about sleeping with Dr. G, you are so fired! You know, I still miss Gem from Fred Segal. You totally ruined that connection. She used to save me all the new arrivals before they got picked over."

Enrique bobbed his head up and down to the turgid rock beat. "Gem was hot. She had this thing about smelling my armpits, though. It was a little weird."

After long seconds of silence and internal reflection, Tatiana finally called up the courage to ask the million-dollar question. "Have you seen him?"

"Who?" Enrique asked blankly, playing drums on the steering wheel.

She twisted down the volume and stomped on the *Star* with her left foot. "Kerr!"

"They came by yesterday to pack up the rest of his things."

"They?"

"Kerr and Jaron."

"Kerr *and* Jaron? They're a *they* now?"

Enrique nodded. "He's an executive at Cartoon Planet. You know, the cable channel."

"How am I ever going to live this down?"

"Live what down? Kerr did you a favor. I'm glad he accepted who he is, because you didn't have a clue."

She turned on him sharply. "So you knew Kerr was gay?"

"From the jump."

"This is ridiculous. The woman who's the last to know. I'm a walking cliché."

"You constantly complained about his lack of interest in sex, and he stared right through me whenever I swam in the pool. One plus one equals two."

"Thanks for sharing. So what does this Jaron person look like?"

"He's older, a major twirler but a really sweet guy."

"What's a twirler?"

"A man who's *really* in touch with his feminine side."

"Oh, God!"

"I know this hurts," Enrique began with surprising philosophical directness. "But at the end of the day, it's for the best. Hadn't Kerr become more like a brother than a lover?"

"I suppose there's some truth to that."

"You're too young not to have that knots-in-the-stomach feeling over a guy. Especially when you're not even thirty yet."

Tatiana smiled. Enrique actually believed her Hollywood age. What an angel. Maybe she should give him a raise.

"And I know how straight men think," Enrique went on. "A woman who's been in a dead-end thing with a gay guy is a great catch. It gives us the chance to swoop in and show her what she's been missing. That makes us feel all macho and shit."

They pulled up to her pied-à-terre in the Hollywood Hills, a one-story nineteen-hundred-square-foot stucco with two bedrooms, three baths, a pool, and great views of the city.

At $839,000, it was more home than she could really afford, but the *Playboy* pictorial money had come in just as she fell in love with the property, so the mortgage company allowed her to take on the debt. Now she was like most of America—not poor but definitely broke, and one paycheck away from disaster.

Melina was standing next to a Jaguar as they pulled up the drive, watching an older man in a black suit pack her belongings into the trunk. The moment Melina saw Tatiana, the nanny began to sob.

Before Enrique came to a complete stop, Tatiana tumbled out of the Jeep and ran to embrace her.

"Oh, Miss Tatiana," Melina cried. "Please don't hate me. I love my babies. I don't want to leave. But I need more money. I have my own children to think of, and this new family gives me a nice car, too."

Tatiana drew back and stared at Melina's swollen face. "What am I going to do without you?"

"Everything will be OK," Melina said gently, grasping Tatiana's hands and squeezing tight.

"But you're so good with Ethan and Everson. I can't imagine trusting anyone else. What if I hire a nanny who takes long naps? They could be playing with matches and sewing kits and cleaning supplies while she sleeps. And what do I know about raising children? There's a reason I buy silk plants!''

"Stop talking this nonsense," Melina scolded. "You have what it takes to be a good mother. I trust your instincts.''

Tatiana was taken aback. "Do you mean that?'' The words barely made it out of her throat.

"If I didn't, I wouldn't leave. I love those babies. But I know you'll do the right thing for them."

Tatiana beamed. This vote of confidence took a little bit of the edge off.

"They'll be waking up from their nap soon. Kiss them for me.'' And then Melina slipped into the purring motor car and was whisked away, down the drive, out of their lives.

"I vote for a hot au pair from France," Enrique said.

Tatiana gave him a disapproving look, decided against his raise, and stepped inside. The moment she darkened the door, the house felt different. Kerr's absence was palpable. It was just her now. And two innocent babies who needed her to have racehorse stamina, an amazing immune system, and nerves of steel just to keep up with them.

She pressed an ear against their bedroom door and heard nothing, not even a stir, so she headed straight for her master bath to wash her hands and splash cold water on her face. All the crying had ruined her eye makeup. What she saw when she looked down at the double basin pierced her heart. Kerr's razor, Zirh facial scrub, toothbrush, and Blistex were gone.

Suddenly, the magnitude of her situation hit home. It was all up to her now: the twins, the mortgage, finding the right nanny . . . everything. Granted, Kerr had never been much help. He just wrote poetry, smoked pot, and played with the kids, always managing to disappear at feeding and changing times. But no matter his uselessness, there was still the psychological comfort of being in it with someone else. Tatiana had been lonely but not alone. Now she was lonely *and* alone.

"You're going to love this!" Enrique shouted, making his way through the house.

Tatiana dashed into the hall and fiercely hushed him. "The twins are sleeping!" she hissed, then halted, reflecting on what had just happened. "Oh, honey," she whispered, laughing a little. "That was such a mommy moment. I'm so proud of myself."

Enrique stood there, cell phone in hand, perplexed. "Dr. G can see you tomorrow at one. Not a moment too soon, apparently."

"I'll need you here in the morning to watch the kids."

"What time?"

"No later than nine."

"There's a big party in Malibu tonight, but I'll try."

Tatiana felt the quick flash of anger. "You'll *try?*" At times like these, the twelve dollars an hour he earned seemed like overpayment.

"Depends on how drunk I get."

She punched his right arm, smack dab on his Superman symbol tattoo.

"Ow! That hurt."

"I have no nanny, no husband, no agent, and no job. If you don't show up on time tomorrow, I'll have no personal assistant."

"How does eight-thirty sound? I'll bring doughnuts." Enrique grinned.

"Better." Tatiana softened. This Latino stud was adorable. Ten years ago she would've been hooked by any line he threw at her.

* * *

I'll bring doughnuts. What a load of bullshit! Nine-fifteen and no sign of the asshole. Tatiana could just picture him, sacked out with a wannabe actress in the upstairs bedroom of some Malibu beach house.

Ethan had been the first to wake up. Six on the dot. The strategy had been to put him in the playpen, and shower before Everson opened her eyes. But a mother's plans were always subject to change. By five minutes after six, the little girl was wailing something wild.

For the past three hours it had merely been a matter of keeping them out of the emergency room. Stop Ethan from playing with the electrical wires behind the leather sofa. Grab Everson before she climbs on the Noguchi table and starts dancing.

She watched helplessly as Ethan ate his waffle but smeared Gerber plums all over his face and wherever he could reach on the high chair. Meanwhile, Everson held her waffle but refused to bring it to her lips, defiantly refusing all morsels of food and only taking in a few sips of apple juice.

As the clock flirted with nine-thirty, Tatiana popped a Xanax. It seemed the logical thing to do. Then she scooped up the twins and trotted them upstairs to plop them inside the playpen. All manner of toys were at their disposal— little Fisher Price people, Barney, Baby Bop, and BJ, even Tinky Winky and Po from the Teletubbies—yet all they cried out for were the makeup items visible on the vanity. Desperate for peace, Tatiana tossed them a few Chanel products.

"Don't eat these," she ordered firmly, then dashed to the sink, shaking with anxiety. In thirty minutes she had to be on the Univision lot, in one of the bungalows, reading for the lead in *Sin by Sin* with producer David Walsh and director Kip Quick. Impossible! At this rate, anything before noon was iffy. But somehow she had to get there.

The positive aspect about being pulled in ten thousand different directions was that Tatiana didn't have time to realize the enormity of the situation. Or how terrible she looked. Auditioning for David Walsh. This was huge! Yet all she could do was wash her face, apply some mascara, swipe on some lip gloss, and gel her hair into a ponytail.

The telephone jangled.

Instinctively she knew it was Enrique and picked up on the second ring.

"It's not my fault!" he screamed before she could even say hello. "A chemical truck overturned on the Pacific Coast Highway. My mobile's dead. I'm borrowing this phone from a woman in an Aston Martin convertible. You know, she's pushing forty, but she's still pretty hot. I wonder . . ."

"Save it for your sex addict group therapy circle! There's nobody to watch the twins!"

"Call Kerr."

"I'd rather take a swim in those chemicals that spilled."

"What about September?"

"The twins would be safer fending for themselves." She took a deep breath. "Screw it. I'll take them with me. Meet me at Univision. Ask for David Walsh at the gate."

"It could be hours, Tatiana. I'm in the middle of a total traffic fuck."

"Take a helicopter if you have to!" And then she slammed down the receiver, slipped on her favorite pair of Earl jeans, threw a white tank over her head, and grabbed the twins.

Everson became instantly fascinated with the diamond studs in her ears. Already a smart girl!

Ethan proceeded to gnaw her shoulder.

"No biting, honey," she said, wincing in agony. "We're

going on a very important trip, and I need you to be perfect little angels. That's right. A sweetboy and a sweet—''

Ethan spit up without warning—all over the front of her shirt. Some of it ran down into her cleavage.

There wasn't so much as a second to stop and change. She simply blotted the mess with a wiping cloth and secured the twins in their car seats, which seemed to take forever since it was only her second or third time doing it. How had Melina always managed to buckle them in quick as lightning?

She started out driving like a maniac. Then she suddenly realized that there was more at stake than a movie role. Two little lives had to be considered. In her rearview mirror she watched the twins, and the realization of how much they needed her scared her silly. It triggered a real fear. By comparison, approaching David Walsh at the Hotel du Cap in Cannes had been kid stuff. . . .

Tatiana had hung up with Jeremy and left the room like a hurricane, furious, full of bravado, determined to do *anything* to get the part in *Sin by Sin*. She'd found David at the bar, nursing what looked to be a fourth round.

''Celebrating?'' she'd asked, slipping into the banquette right beside him.

''Trying to forget.'' David hadn't appeared surprised by her audacious familiarity. Cannes was a crazy place, and a man as successful as him had likely seen it all.

''I bet my life is more screwed up than yours.''

He'd studied her with amusement. ''The movie I produced opened the festival, and everybody hated it.''

At that point, Tatiana had recalled September mentioning a wretched film called *Hard Times for Lovers*. ''How much did it cost to make?''

"Thirty million."

Tatiana had waved a dismissive hand and shrugged. "Honey, it's not like anybody's going to be comparing it to *Ishtar*. Besides, Hollywood memories are short, and *Sin by Sin* will gross at least that much on opening weekend."

"Who are you?"

"I'm the star of your next picture."

"Is that so?" David had laughed heartily. He had a kind voice and a comforting smile. It all added up to an avuncular quality that had put her instantly at ease.

"Show me a man who's bet against me, and I'll show you his tombstone." She'd quoted a line from the *Sin by Sin* script and nailed the delivery.

The smile had faded from David's lips.

"Introducing Tatiana Fox as Nikki Alexander," she'd said grandly. "Is it too soon to inquire about special billing?"

He grinned, this time more impressed than amused. "Just a bit."

"Greg Tapper and I were in the same acting class years ago. I was one of the few girls he never slept with. How's that for sexual tension?"

"Who's your agent?"

Tatiana had hesitated. "Actually, I'm in between agents now. I was with Jeremy Johnson—"

"He's no good."

"The son of a bitch dumped me because I said no to a shit project going straight to video to take a chance on *your* movie."

"Well, at least he's practical. You could do worse."

Tatiana had leaned back a little. "Don't give me the 'we're looking for a big name' speech. I might have to pour that drink over your head."

David had laughed, holding up his hands in surrender. "Don't shoot the messenger. That's a studio mandate."

"Sharon Stone," Tatiana had said matter-of-factly. "Remember a little movie called *Basic Instinct*? Can you imagine Geena Davis in that part?"

David had tilted his head in agreement.

"I rest my case." Boldly, she had reached over to take a shot off his drink. "There's enough marquee power with Greg Tapper attached. A big-name actress is what we call diminishing returns. I learned that concept in a college economics class. Besides, no actress who's really made it is going to submit herself to the sex, nudity, and violence involved. You're fooling yourself if you think otherwise."

"I see," David had said contemplatively, pausing to nurse his poison for a spell. "You know who should star in *Sin by Sin* and how much it will gross on opening weekend. Maybe you should produce the film, too."

At first Tatiana had worried that she'd gone too far . . . until she noticed the mischief in David's eyes. "I thought about it, but then I figured, you do a pretty decent job. Why should I stress myself out?"

David had laughed again, harder this time. "What do you say to an invitation to come read for the director?"

Tatiana had sucked in a breath and waited for the second invitation—the one up to his room that would secure the original invitation to read for the part. But it never came.

"You've got a certain quality," he'd continued. "It's worth a formal look. Kip Quick's helming the picture. Heard of him?"

Tatiana had been unable to concentrate, because she was still waiting for the inevitable come-on to drop. Vaguely she shook her head.

"He's a video director. A few commercials, too. But the kid's a phenomenal talent. I think—"

"Are there strings attached to this reading?" Tatiana had cut in. "I mean, if you expect a blow job, then just say so."

David regarded her curiously. "You would give me a blow job?"

"For just a reading? No. But if you were offering me the part . . . I would try to negotiate down to a hand job and maintain my dignity."

"You're such a prude."

Tatiana had merely stared back at him, confused.

"Unlike most producers in Hollywood, I'm happily married—and staunchly faithful." David had paused to finish his drink. "Not that your proposal isn't enticing."

Quite suddenly, she'd leaned over to kiss him on the cheek, her lips brushing against his short beard. "You are an absolute doll! I can't wait to meet your wife and tell her this story. It's so rare to meet a man who wouldn't have to unzip his pants for brain surgery."

"I don't—"

"Oh, but she *must* know! Give me your address. I'll write her a letter. I love personal correspondence. And I just got some beautiful stationery from Smythson of Bond Street that will make it even more special."

David had laughed and fished a business card from his front pocket. "When are you heading back to L.A.?"

"Tomorrow morning."

He'd nodded enthusiastically, scribbled something on the card, and slid it directly in front of her as he stood up. "I'll see you in Hollywood, Tatiana." And then he'd winked and ambled away, stopping to chat with Kevin Spacey.

Tatiana had glanced down. The reading was set for the day after tomorrow. She'd made a mental note to sleep with cucumbers over her eyes to offset the look of jet lag. . . .

* * *

But so much for beauty rituals. She'd been exhausted after getting Ethan and Everson down last night and had fallen asleep going over the *Sin by Sin* screenplay, only to wake up with a terrible indention on her cheek from one of the script's brass butterfly clips. Though only hours ago, it seemed like days.

"Car!" Ethan screamed.

"Bus!" Everson screamed louder.

"That's right," Tatiana said patiently, employing the tone of a Stepford nursery-school teacher. "There are lots of cars and buses on the road." She glanced at the stereo clock and grimaced. "And they're all in our way."

"Milk!" Ethan whined.

Had she thrown an extra bottle into the travel bag? She remembered tossing in diapers, baby wipes, an extra outfit, animal crackers, a few books and small toys, a tube of Cortaid, their favorite blankets, and Xanax (for her). Hey, she was entitled! But no milk. Oh, God, how could she have forgotten?

The fact that she didn't replenish his milk as fast as David Copperfield could make an elephant appear made Ethan sob.

And, of course, Everson started to cry, too.

Desperate, Tatiana negotiated a semidangerous merge to the right and turned into the lot of a convenience store. If she locked them inside the running car and dashed inside, the whole errand would take only a minute or two.

As she slipped out, the twins cried louder. It nearly broke her heart. She felt like the worst mother in the world. But better than her own, at least. No need to beat herself up entirely.

Tatiana grabbed a quart of whole milk and sprinted toward the register.

Behind the counter, a dense-looking girl struggled with the credit card machine. "Your card messed up."

Tatiana recognized the man in question. He costarred on a popular NBC sitcom. She guessed his personal finances could absorb a purchase of gas, cigarettes, and beer.

"You swiped the wrong side," he snapped.

The others ahead of her began to sigh and shift impatiently, staring lasers at the dumb clerk.

An unthinkable scenario flashed in Tatiana's mind. What if a carjacker broke the window and took off with the twins? Her heart picked up speed. She rummaged through her purse. The only bill she had was a fifty. *Whatever.* In a fit of panic she threw it on the counter and ran out of the store.

"We don't take nothing larger than a twenty!"

Tatiana marveled at the stupidity. The cashier didn't recognize a forty-nine-dollar tip. Once back in the car, she refilled Ethan's bottle and peace was instantly restored. He rode quietly the rest of the way to Univision. Everson sat there engrossed in a flip book about Rainbow Fish. By the time they reached the bungalow, it was a few minutes after ten.

She didn't bother with the stroller. It took too long to get the damn thing out of the trunk.

"Poo poo!" Ethan said.

Tatiana leaned in to unbuckle him. "Poo poo is right." The smell nearly knocked her over. She tried to stop breathing through her nose.

"Poo poo," Everson said, giggling.

"Yes, we have official confirmation of a poo poo," Tatiana murmured.

With a heavy bag over her left shoulder and a baby in each arm, she closed the rear door with her foot and stormed inside. There was a sleek outer office, decorated with framed posters of David Walsh's most celebrated films: *Divided Hearts, Crime After Crime, Second Sight,* and *Just One Lifetime*.

Tatiana stood there in awe, not quite believing her luck. She was here to read for the starring role in David Walsh's next picture. Gooseflesh sprang up on her arms. But then the smell of Ethan's poop brought the moment to a crashing halt.

She fumbled for her cell phone and pressed speed dial to reach Enrique.

"I've moved maybe half a mile since we last talked," he said.

"Damn you!"

"Damn *me*? Damn the truck that spilled chemical shit all over the highway."

"Damn *you* for going to that goddamn party! What can I do?"

"Get the secretary to watch them."

Tatiana glanced around for signs of life—a coffee mug, a half-eaten muffin, school pictures of homely children, anything. "I'm in the waiting area and nobody's here."

Enrique paused a beat. "Stick them in the car and turn on the radio."

Tatiana hung up.

Just then a tall, athletic dream of a guy stepped out of the inner office, closed the door behind him, and right away winced at the smell of Ethan.

Without even thinking about it, she rushed him, transferring the twins into his arms.

The man looked stunned but accepted the precious cargo anyway.

"You're my only hope," Tatiana said. "I have to audition for a really sexy part, and walking in with these kids could send out the wrong vibes.'' She let out a deep breath. ''I don't know what I can offer you. I just spent fifty bucks for a quart of milk, and that's all the cash I had. How about gum? Somewhere in this bag there's a fresh pack. And it's sugarless. Always a plus. Oh, this is the boy.'' She patted Ethan on the head. ''He needs changing. Don't forget to rub some ointment on his bottom. I think he's getting a rash.''

And then she took a moment to compose herself, licked her lips, and marched into David Walsh's inner sanctum, determined to make her dreams come true.

Chapter Four

"I want a man who can make love all night long, and if you're not that man, then just do me a favor and drop dead." Tatiana delivered the line with such deadly insouciance that she stunned the room.

David Walsh stared back as if she were Charlton Heston in *The Ten Commandments* and had just parted the Red Sea.

Kip Quick looked equally mystified. He flipped his Dave Matthews Band cap to the back and regarded her strangely.

She gestured to the battered script on Kip's lap. "It's your line, unless I'm auditioning for the male lead, too."

"Oh, right," Kip blurted. "My line." He searched for his place on the page. "Is it true about your last two husbands granting you that favor?"

Tatiana stretched and spoke in a breathy voice enriched with dirty promise. "It's true that they were lousy in bed. It's true that I buried them. The rest is just gossip."

Kip lost his train of thought again, gazing at her in awe-struck wonder.

She couldn't believe that he would actually be the movie's director. After all, he looked as if he needed a note from his mother to be here. In fact, he still lived with his parents. Probably had a *Penthouse* stashed under his mattress, too. Yet here he sat, after only a few videos on MTV and one Pepsi commercial, playing with the grown-ups on a big-budget film for a major studio. Only in Hollywood.

Tatiana cleared her throat.

"Does nudity make you uncomfortable?" Kip asked.

She glanced down at her pages. *Not* part of the *Sin by Sin* screenplay. This man/child had obviously missed her series of *Lady Cop Undercover* movies. Chances were he hadn't peeked at her pictorial in the April 1999 *Playboy*, either. If he had, it would have been while under the covers with a flashlight.

"My comfort level depends on the situation," she announced matter-of-factly. "A relatively closed set is no problem. Shooting on Sunset Boulevard at high noon is another matter entirely. I mean, I'm not Madonna."

David smiled at Kip as if to say, "See? I told you so."

And then a horrifying thought struck Tatiana. It hit like a clap of thunder. She went from confident actress audi-tioning for the big part to manic mother wanting to put child safety locks on, well, *everything*. Shame rained down, soaking her. She was officially the *worst* parent in the world. By comparison, Joan Crawford was Carol Brady. "I can't do this right now." She started to shake. She needed a cigarette. She didn't even smoke.

David's smile faded faster than Cindy Crawford's hope of a movie career after the release of *Fair Game*.

"I just realized that I left my children with a complete stranger," Tatiana said breathlessly. "I mean, he could be

a serial killer, or one of the Kennedy boys that Jackie O
didn't raise, or Paula Poundstone in disguise." She placed
hand over heart and shut her eyes for a moment. "Promise
you won't tell Social Services. This is all new to me."

"I didn't realize you had kids," David said.

"Don't you read the tabloids? My ex-husband insisted
on adopting twins and then decided he was gay and left me
for another man. Anyway, yesterday my nanny quit without
notice, my personal assistant is AWOL, and the only other
person available was September Moore. She's a good friend,
but I wouldn't let her watch my purse. Would you? Let her
watch your wallet, I mean. Or your man purse. I hear those
are big in Europe. Okay, so I packed up the kids and here
I am. By the way, if you smell something sour, it's because
Ethan threw up all over me on the way to the car." Tatiana
took a deep breath. "Is this too much information?"

David and Kip stared back in slack-jawed amazement.

"This is *my* part. I *am* Nikki Alexander. Plus, I need a
job. But now I have to go. Don't worry. I'll work out child
care issues before shooting starts. You know what would
be great? On-set day care." She paused a beat. "I'm kidding.
I don't want the kids to see me running around with a knife
or shooting people or having simulated sex with different
men. That could be traumatic for them. And that's instinct.
I didn't have to read Dr. Spock to come up with that. Pretty
good, huh? I think I'm getting the hang of this mommy
business. Okay, are we done here? Do you need to see my
boobs or anything before I leave?"

There was a long second of telepathy between David and
Kip, after which they traded a discreet nod.

"We'll set up a reading with Greg Tapper," David said.

This meant she was on the short list. Under normal circumstances she would be so excited that cartwheels in rush-hour
traffic might be in order. But she was worried sick about

Ethan and Everson. "That sounds great," she said, somewhat absently. "I'll wait for your call."

Unable to stand it one more second, Tatiana dashed back to the reception area. The twins were perched on either side of the man's hips like Anne Geddes bookends, listening in peaceful rapture as he read a story from the sports section of the *Los Angeles Times*.

"Sammy Sosa hit three homers in the first round to barely squeak into the semifinals but made the finals by outhomering Luis Gonzalez," he was saying softly in his heavily accented voice. Could be English, could be Australian. Tough to call. But she wanted him to read the Yellow Pages. He sounded *that* scrumptious.

Ethan and Everson peered up at him, little mouths agape, as if he were Barney or something.

Tatiana was instantly suspicious. They *never* sat still like this for her. "Did you give them drugs?"

He stopped reading and just stared at her.

"I've never seen them stay in one place unless they're sleeping. Or eating. Well, Ethan does hold his position behind the sofa when he's pooping. But the rest of the time it's an insane level of activity. I can't keep up."

"These kids are perfect."

No, honey, you're perfect. The words were almost on her lips. She zeroed in on his firm forearms, mesmerized by the muscles flexing under his skin as he folded up the newspaper and tossed it aside. He looked sharp and mod—three-day beard, dirty blond bed-head hair, lean body coiled into well-worn jeans and a 1999 World Cup T-shirt ripped at the left sleeve, skin basted a honey bronze.

Los Angeles was loaded with great-looking guys. They worked on it just as hard as the women, if not harder, slaving at the gym, sticking to the Zone diet, checking the mirror twenty times a day to ask, "Am I handsome enough?" Hot men were in such supply that Tatiana could fill a tour bus with just the ones she'd seen this week. So it said something about the one front and center that he could not only make her take a second look, but hold it—steady. Simultaneously, he gave off grit and luminosity. An unbeatable combination.

"How did your audition go?" he asked.

"They want me to come in for a reading with the star."

"Congratulations. You should ring your mum. I always ring my mum when there's good news."

She was instantly put off by this and decided to openly mock him. "Well, I'm not speaking to my *mum* at the moment. What about your audition?"

"Christ, it was horrible."

Now she felt bad. There was a slow, vague sweetness about him. "Which part were you reading for?"

"Greg Tapper's partner."

"But he dies in the opening scene after just one line."

"I tried 'See you tomorrow, Josh' several different ways, but they just weren't feeling it."

Tatiana giggled and moved in to scoop up Everson, who started to cry immediately.

He stood up, hoisting bulky Ethan onto his hip with Mr. Strong ease, then smoothing Everson's unruly hair with his free hand, a gesture that instantly mollified her. If fifteen-month-old girls could fall in love, then Everson Janey Fox, positively swooning now, was head over heels.

"Who are you? I should know your name since my kids think you're better than Big Bird."

"Jack Thorpe, god-awful actor, smashingly good baby-sitter."

She smiled in a way that she hadn't smiled since running into George Clooney in an elevator at the Beverly Center. "I'm Tatiana Fox."

"I know. I subscribe to *Playboy*. You're the girl who posed naked climbing on the side of a building."

"*Half* naked. I *was* wearing a thong. So how long have you been a bad actor?"

He checked his Patek Phillippe watch. "About fifteen minutes. I don't think I'll stick with it. I'm actually a footballer." He pointed to his knee. "Or was. An injury put an end to my career."

"Which team?"

"Manchester United."

Tatiana's memory registered nothing. *Manchester United?* It sounded like a bank, not a football team. "Is that one of the new leagues?"

He smiled at her, revealing immaculate porcelain teeth. "I forget that you call it soccer here in the States." A sudden look of inscrutable sadness came over him, weighing down his features like old age. "I miss my mates."

Tatiana wanted to know where he came from, why he was here. This unnerved her. She usually only cared about her own problems. Meanwhile, Ethan clung to him like a koala bear. It was really adorable. Now she felt melancholy, too, thinking of Kerr and the way he'd run off to be with Jaron, leaving the kids without a full-time father around.

Everson started to squirm and stretch out her arms. She wanted Jack Thorpe again. The deafening cry that came next could have been picked up as far as Venice Beach.

Reluctantly he stepped forward to take her.

The very second Everson's tiny hands touched him was the very second she stopped fussing.

Tatiana's humiliation was only ameliorated by the sight of him standing there, shrugging with pride, the twins climbing all over his hard body. It *defined* sexy. Any woman who melted whenever Tom Selleck showed up on cable in *Three*

Men and a Baby needed to take a memo. That was then, Jack Thorpe was now.

She gestured to Everson. "This one's madly in love. I should just let you take her until it's time for the first visit to the gynecologist."

Jack laughed. "If she's like all the other women in my life, then the honeymoon won't last long."

Hmm. Definitely code for single, available, and unlikely to propose marriage. "Thanks for being such a good sport. You must think I'm crazy."

"Why?" He feigned innocence. "Leaving your kids with the first person you see isn't an American custom?"

Playfully she glared at him. "You *are* a bad actor."

"Don't say that too loud. I still need a job."

Tatiana gestured to the twins, who were positively blissful. "You know, my nanny quit yesterday. . . ." She trailed off, as if she were just kidding, but, strangely, she found herself to be half serious. Why couldn't he be Ethan and Everson's nanny? With Kerr gone, they needed a male figure around.

Jack smiled. "One of these days I might be desperate enough to consider that."

She attempted to laugh off her comment as mere silliness. But it really wasn't so ridiculous. The only big deal was the gender role issue, and that was his problem. Certainly a support group existed somewhere for men with girly jobs. Enrique could go, too! Tatiana routinely dispatched him for tampons and makeup, so he already knew what it felt like to have a sissy career.

"That was a joke," Jack clarified. "I changed this chap's diaper to be nice, not to impress."

She stopped short of rolling her eyes. The Mr. Man act bored her, except when firefighters and carpenters did it. Then it was sexy. But a professional athlete who got hurt and became an out-of-work actor? Save it, buster. You're not in Paul Bunyan country anymore.

"Luckily, none of my old mates had to see me do that."

"Yeah, luckily." She couldn't tear her gaze away. First, he was gorgeous. Second, she liked this idea of his taking over for Melina.

Jack stood there, shifting uncomfortably, a child in each arm. "I probably should get going."

No! Stay until I figure this out. That's what she wanted to tell him. But instead she just grinned like a dork and kicked her mind into hyperdrive. Whatever she came up with had to appeal to his masculine ego, no doubt bruised from the sports injury and current state of unemployment. Light bulb! Oh, God, this was good. He would eat it up and ask for seconds.

"It's amazing to me that you're not still in training with a professional team. You've got an incredible body," Tatiana said.

Jack's chest jutted out a bit, and eyes that once gleamed suddenly gleamed more. "Thanks. I try to stay in shape."

Tatiana reached out to test the firmness of his biceps. "I bet you know everything about fitness and sculpting the perfect body."

He shrugged. "I know enough."

"If I get this part, it means a lot of nudity. The camera adds ten pounds, you know. I'll have to be in flawless shape."

He gave her a once-over. "You look pretty flawless from where I'm standing."

Tatiana put on a show of humility. "Well, honey, you are obviously too far away."

His gaze narrowed. "Now that you mention it, I suppose your arms could stand some toning."

Tatiana blanched.

"Your lower abs need a little concentration, too. And maybe—"

"Okay," she cut in sharply. "Let's just say I'm not Jennifer Aniston and leave it at that." Pause to stifle urge to push him in front of a bus. Had she asked for a complete body review à la Roger Ebert? That would be a definite no. "As you so tactfully pointed out, there are some key areas I need to work on, bodywise. So how would like to be my personal trainer?"

Jack's lips curled into a sneaky smile. "I'm one tough bastard. Sure you can handle me?"

"Hey, I got these two dressed, fed, and out the door before ten. Anything you throw at me will be kid stuff."

The baby bag started to ring.

Could it be David Walsh already? Tatiana dashed to fish out the cellular. Shit. It was Enrique. "Hello?"

"I'm on the Univision lot. All these bungalows look the same. It's like a housing project."

"What—"

"Oh, I see your car now. There's a Taurus parked next to it. Nobody in Hollywood drives one of those. Must be a rental."

She let out an annoyed sigh. "The reading is over."

"You sound tense."

"Yeah, well, it hasn't been the easiest couple of days."

"Hey, I've set up two nanny interviews for later today. Gretchen Guy and Lexi Epstein. One used to work for Rosie O'Donnell, and one just got fired for doing the man of the house. But you don't have a husband anymore, so I figure no worries on that score."

"How thoughtful. Listen, meet me back at the house. I need you to watch the twins while I go to my session with Dr. G."

"This isn't fair. It's not like I've had any experience with kids. Growing up, I never even had a puppy."

"But you've had lots of dumb girlfriends. Ethan and Everson are smarter and don't need half as much attention." Click. She gave Jack a look of apology. "My personal assistant."

"An assistant, a trainer, a nanny—I assume Dr. G is a shrink."

"I prefer *therapist*."

"Noted." There was laughter in his eyes. "Any other helpers I should know about?"

"There's a pool boy who comes once a week. Does that count?" She stole a pen from the reception desk and scribbled her number on Jack's arm as Everson looked on with interest. "Call me to set up my first torture session. *Soon*. I'm free from four o'clock on. You should know that I hate to exercise, and I'm famous for sending my assistant out on late-night runs to Taco Bell."

"That'll have to stop. Once you're under my training, nothing but water after seven o'clock."

"Honey, you are tough. Very Louis Gossett Jr. I feel just like Richard Gere in *An Officer and a Gentleman*."

A puzzled look skated across Jack's face. "What's the going rate here? I don't know how much to charge you."

"Not a problem," Tatiana said, reaching for the phone again to speed dial September Moore. "I have a friend who's more high-maintenance than I am."

It rang and rang.

Tatiana huffed.

Finally, a groggy September picked up.

That's when Tatiana realized how early it was. September rarely did anything but scan the columns before noon. "I know it's early . . ."

"It's okay. I should get up and take a shower. My acupuncturist is coming. Besides, I can't just sit here and read about all the stars going in and out of rehab. I need to save some fun for later.''

"Quick question: How much do you pay your personal trainer?''

"Which one? I've got one guy who really knows what he's doing. He's got a best-selling book and everything. There's another guy who's in really great shape but doesn't have any formal training. He just puts me through a few calisthenics, and then we usually end up having sex on the weight bench.''

"The first guy.''

"Three hundred an hour. I think he has an opening. Angelina Jolie was driving him crazy, so he dropped her. Do you want his number?''

"No, thanks. Just doing some market research.'' Another call beeped in. "I'll ring you later.'' She hung up and clicked over. "Hello?''

"Same time, same place. Tomorrow. It's all set up with Greg Tapper.'' It was David Walsh.

Tatiana closed her eyes. If God let her get this close to her dream and then yanked it away . . .

"Tatiana?''

"I'm here.''

"Now would be a good time to find a new agent. I put in a call to Cleo Mars. She can see you at three o'clock if you're interested.''

"*Cleo Mars?*'' Tatiana gripped Jack's arm for support. Hmm. Nice and strong. It felt good.

"Do you know her?''

"*Know* her? She's, like, the best!'' At the peak of September's Oscar glory, before the slide to Lifetime movies and guest stints on *ER,* she'd been represented by Cleo Mars. Building stars was the famed agent's specialty. It almost didn't seem possible that Tatiana had a real chance of landing her.

"We go way back," David went on. "You're not obligated to go with her, of course, but it's worth a meeting to hear what she has to say."

Relax. Play it cool. Don't sound like an out-of-work actress desperate for the first thing that comes along. "I'd give up a kidney to sign with Cleo Mars!" *Damn it! Not the attitude I was going for.*

David laughed. "I don't think it'll come to that. Get some good sleep. We'll see you tomorrow." And then he hung up.

A jealous Everson was alternately slapping Tatiana's hand and trying to pry her fingers off Jack's arm.

"Good news?" Jack asked.

Tatiana could hear her own heartbeat. "Extremely." She took a deep breath. "Will you help me get them into their car seats?"

Jack smiled. "I think I can manage that." He leaned back to address his new friends. "Let's buckle in, gang. It's the only way to travel."

Ethan and Everson beamed and watched in peaceful wonder as he strapped them in and gifted each with a kiss on the top of the head.

Jack winked and turned to Tatiana. "Suppose I should strap you in, too."

She found herself smiling. After all, it wasn't a bad line. "I got it covered, Pele. But thanks."

"Sure?"

"Absolutely."

"I'll be calling to set up our first personal training session."

She shut the door, turned on the engine, and zipped down the window. "You better."

"How much does your friend pay her trainer?"

"Three hundred an hour."

He propped his hands on the hood of her car. "My fee's four hundred."

The man didn't kick balls for a living anymore, but he sure as hell had some. "Why?"

"I'm better. Ask those two in the backseat. They'll vouch for me."

"Do you have any references who can actually *talk?* Nothing against any models you might have dated, of course."

Jack shook a finger at her. "You're bad."

"I can say those things. I used to be a model."

BEEP!

Tatiana spun to see Enrique sitting in his Jeep, the engine idle as he watched the pre-seduction unfold.

"Get a room!" Enrique shouted, laughing at his own remark.

Jack appeared unfazed. "Who's that?"

"My personal assistant."

"What does he get per hour?"

"Too much."

Jack fingered the ink scrawl she'd made on his arm. "I better call you before I shower."

Tatiana moistened her lips. "Good thinking. Guess you're not just a pretty face after all." And then she slowly backed out of her parking space.

Jack watched her for a moment, then slipped inside a taupe-colored Taurus.

Tatiana turned to Enrique.

The young stud's gaze was aimed dead at her, his grin teasing. "Flashy car. Friend of yours?"

"Hey, at least this one's straight." Tatiana pursed her lips in a serious display, but there was laughter in her eyes.

"In that ride? There's no doubt." Enrique laughed and zipped away.

"How does that make you feel?"

Tatiana leveled a hard glare at Dr. G. *"How does that make me feel?"*

Dr. G merely nodded. "Yes, that was the question."

"My agent dumped me, my gay husband asked me for a divorce, and my nanny quit to drive a bigger star's station wagon. Chances are, I'm not quite ready to head out on the next Up With People tour. *That's* how I feel."

Dr. G, a plump woman in her early forties with naturally auburn hair parted down the middle, began taking notes on the yellow legal pad that always adorned her lap.

This drove Tatiana crazy. Unless a doctor was scribbling out a prescription, she hated to see any jotting of *notes*.

"You're experiencing a kind of chaos that can trigger all sorts of emotions," Dr G said softly.

Tatiana rolled her eyes. "Is pissed-off an emotion?"

Dr. G paused. "Anger . . . is a very natural reaction."

Tatiana breathed in deeply, then exhaled. "I can't be angry at Kerr. I mean, he's *gay*. That's fundamental. What's to be mad at? And at last it explains our nonexistent sex life in a way that exonerates me, so I guess I should be grateful. Really, though, I'm just confused. Why me? I'm a sexy girl. You know, a pin-up type. I was in *Playboy*. Have I mentioned that?"

"Yes," Dr. G said patiently. "You also gave me an autographed copy of that issue. My husband uses it periodically as visual stimulation to pleasure himself."

"That is so sweet." Tatiana halted. "Where was I? Oh, yes, Kerr. I just don't understand why he chose to marry

me. Gay men are supposed to go after women like Liza
Minnelli. You know, someone they actually want to *be*.''

"Homosexual men want to be Liza Minnelli?''

"Well, they've always loved Judy Garland, and Liza's
the next-best thing. Granted, there's the other daughter,
Lorna Luft, but she made *Grease 2*.''

"I'm not following.''

"Did you see *Grease 2*?''

"No.''

"Rent it. We'll revisit this topic after you've seen it.''

Dr G appeared mildly frustrated. "Let's get back to your
anger.''

"Well, I can't be angry at Melina either. She took another
job for more money and a better standard of living. You
know, for an illegal alien, she's very American. A true
capitalist mindset. How can I be angry at that?''

Dr. G shrugged.

"But I *can* be angry at Jeremy.''

"Your agent.''

"*Ex*-agent. The son of a bitch dropped me.''

"And this angered you.''

"Not exactly. I finally realized that I've *always* hated
Jeremy. The guy is a total asshole. He never treated me with
respect. Not even once. But that's good. It makes me want to
get even. You know, the whole success-is-the-best-revenge
thing, like Vanessa Williams, the former Miss America. All
those people dumped on her, but she showed them—movies,
Broadway, hit records. She even sang the theme song to
Pocahontas. And that was a Disney film! When you take
the time to think about it, her journey is really incredible.''

"What about *your* journey, Tatiana?''

Sometimes she just couldn't stand Dr. G.

Chapter Five

"I reviewed some of your work over the lunch hour,"
Cleo Mars said.

Tatiana stiffened. This was just moments into the meeting.
There'd barely been time for a hello-how-are-you, and
already the subject of her crappy *Lady Cop Undercover*
movies was on the table. Not a good sign.

"Don't worry. I've had clients overcome worse."

At first, Tatiana couldn't believe it. "Really?" Then she
stopped herself. *Don't doubt your own potential—at least
out loud. A future star must radiate confidence.* "Well, of
course. I mean, Sandra Bullock in *Speed 2*. Come on."

Cleo returned a shrewd grin. "A major bomb, I agree.
But Sandra was able to console herself with, if memory
serves, an eleven-million-dollar salary. How much did you
earn for *Lady Cop Undercover 4: Red Light District*?"

"About the same . . . if you subtract ten million nine
hundred thousand bucks."

Cleo delivered a brief, triumphant nod. "Here's an important rule to live by: Don't be smug on your way up the food chain. It doesn't wear well."

Tatiana sat frozen, part of her three inches tall, another part of her ravenous to hear more lessons from this legendary industry mover.

"David Walsh is very high on you," Cleo went on. "He says you have a quality. I see it, too. And when we both agree, we're never wrong. At least, we haven't been yet."

"He's the sweetest man," Tatiana gushed. "I think he's the only producer in Hollywood who doesn't cheat on his wife."

Cleo's phone buzzed. She pressed a button. "Hold my calls, Maxine."

"But it's—"

"Hold my calls," Cleo said firmly. She looked at Tatiana and smiled savagely. "New assistant. But if she doesn't develop an ear for listening, she'll be looking for another job next week." Cleo exhaled and gulped from the big Evian bottle on top of her desk. "A million years ago David gave me my first job in the business. Story analyst for his production company. I'll never forget it. The day of my interview he was casting strippers for some Burt Reynolds movie. Picture this: In the waiting room there's me . . . and a platoon of centerfold types." Cleo laughed at the memory. "I'm finally called in, and David says to me, 'I don't sleep around, so if you're looking to get ahead that way, this isn't going to work out.' I said, 'I'm a dyke,' and he goes, 'You're hired.' "

Tatiana giggled. "Were you serious? Are you . . ."

"A lesbian? Always and forever."

"Wow. You were ahead of your time. To be so open about it, I mean."

"It's always been my philosophy that whether or not you

are out is more of an issue than whether or not you are gay.''

Tatiana tilted her eyebrows. ''I wish my husband had shared your philosophy.''

Cleo winced. ''So it's true?''

''Do the tabloids ever lie?''

''Usually not.''

''Well, the stuff about me and Stephen Baldwin is total bullshit, but the rest of it's fairly accurate.''

''I have a new colleague who can help you with the press. I'll introduce you to her later.''

This comment put Tatiana partially at ease. It sounded as if Cleo taking her on as a client was inevitable.

''Closeted people are weak,'' Cleo continued, ''and hiding something prevents true success. Think about it. Have you ever known a powerful person to wear a toupee? A bald Master of the Universe shows his dome.''

Tatiana mulled this over. One of the actors who played a detective in *Lady Cop Undercover II: Massage Parlor* had worn a rug. But she could hardly classify him as powerful. Though he did land the lead in that Tums commercial that was still running. Hmm. Powerful or just a lucky guy?

''I could go on all day about this, but we're here to talk about you.''

Tatiana lengthened her spine.

''If the reading tomorrow with Greg Tapper goes well, this part in *Sin by Sin* is yours.''

Tatiana's heart picked up speed.

''That little speech you gave David in Cannes was pretty effective. Besides, Greg is committed to other projects, and if they don't use this window to shoot *Sin* now, it could be delayed by two or three years.''

''Greg and I were in the same acting class.''

Cleo gave her a wry smile. ''Don't be hurt if he pretends

not to remember that. Greg's memory doesn't go back any further than his first big movie.''

Tatiana's mind traveled back to the New York listening party for Ben Estes's new CD. She'd attended with her friend Candace Rowley. Greg had been there but walked right past her without so much as a nod. Dickhead.

"My main negotiating point would be a script rewrite.''

Tatiana did a double take. She thought the screenplay was great. Well, she thought the same thing about every *Lady Cop Undercover* movie. This one will hit big! What did she know?

"Your character dies in the end. If this movie is huge, the studio will be on their knees panting for a sequel. And if the public expects Tatiana Fox to return as Nikki Alexander, then you can demand megabucks. Suddenly, your asking price for all other projects skyrockets.''

Tatiana liked the sound of it. After all, at present, there wasn't a nickel in Ethan and Everson's college fund.

"I can do my best to get a good offer for *Sin*, but don't expect much. This movie will make you famous. Your next one will make you rich. Can you live with that?''

"I've been living with much less for the last ten years.''

From behind her massive desk, Cleo stood up, revealing a very pregnant form.

Tatiana gasped.

"I'm due in eight weeks.''

"Congratulations. Is this your first?''

"Our second.'' Cleo reached for her water bottle again. "My partner carried the first. Now it's my turn. Same sperm donor, though. He's a medical student at UCLA. Great-looking and smart as a whip.''

Tatiana smiled. You had to admire the woman. Cleo was a tiny thing, barely five feet tall, but she lived life like a seven-foot giant. With her short crop of trendily cut black hair, alpine white skin, dramatically shadowed eyes, and darkly painted lips, she commanded attention and instant respect.

"Are you seeing any other agents?" Cleo asked.

Tatiana shook her head.

"Good. You're better off with me. With my female clients whose sexuality is a major part of the package, I prefer an all-girl management situation. Don't get me wrong. There are lots of men in this town who can get the job done. But at some point a certain amount of sexual anxiety enters the relationship. This way we're free from engaging on that level."

"My last agent was gay."

"Jeremy Johnson?"

"That's him."

"He wishes it were that simple. Since I've known him, he's been gay, straight, bi, a cross-dresser, and for a spell he got into that stuffed-animal fetish cult."

Tatiana made a face. "Yuck."

"Men like him are notorious in this town. They're offered so much sex so often that they get bored and are willing to try anything for a thrill."

"What's wrong with a quiet dinner and a leisurely night of lovemaking?"

"Romance? Oh, they'll never try that," Cleo said, laughing. She led Tatiana into the reception area, past an original Roy Lichtenstein mural, and down a corridor lined with framed film posters and entertainment magazine covers featuring Cleo's impressive roster of first-name famous clients. "I want you to meet Kitty Bishop. I've started a boutique approach to client relations. If you sign with the Cleo Mars Agency, you have priority access to a publicist, a business manager, and a stylist. There are fees, of course, but better deals than you would pay elsewhere. Kitty just moved here from New York. She's a PR whiz and helped put Ben Estes on the map.''

''I went to a party for his new CD several months ago.''

''He's a natural for films. Kitty and I are trying to convince him.'' Cleo stopped at an open doorway.

A no-nonsense blonde sat at a desk that looked as if it had been ground zero to an avalanche. Her hands were free to file her nails as she sprayed venom into a headset telephone. ''Honey, do I need to hire a skywriter? No fucking questions about the divorce! That subject is off limits. Period.'' She hit a button and shook her head. ''Jesus Christ.''

Cleo tapped on the door.

Kitty glanced up, still fuming. ''Connie Chung only hears what she wants to hear.''

Cleo ventured inside. ''I want you to meet—''

''Tatiana Fox,'' Kitty cut in, standing up to offer a firm handshake. ''The next Sharon Stone.''

Tatiana merely grinned, embarrassed. All this positive attention was like a whole new world. She came from a place where agents insulted you and directors cussed you out for flubbing a line.

''Cleo filled me in.''

Tatiana felt as if her chances were being jinxed. ''Nothing's happened yet.''

''But it will,'' Kitty said. ''No big-name actress is going to be that slutty and that unsympathetic on screen. Unless it's Oscar-worthy. And everybody knows *Sin by Sin* is a popcorn flick. This movie cries out for a new face. I already put in a call to Kip Quick. I hired him to direct Ben Estes's first music video, and that mama's boy owes me.''

''You're hired,'' Tatiana said.

''Good. First order of business: Dump Stephen Baldwin. He can't do anything for you.''

"Believe me, I know. That story's not true. I've never even met the guy."

"Well, we need to get a better story out there. You know, do some damage control. I'll plant an item that you're seeing Mark Wahlberg."

Tatiana looked at Cleo.

"I'll give the two of you some time," Cleo said. "Tatiana, expect a call from me tomorrow." And then the superagent quietly slipped out.

Kitty thundered on. "Once shooting starts, you'll need to have a hot fling with Greg Tapper. There's nothing better than an on-set affair."

Tatiana hesitated. "I have twin toddlers to think about. I just can't be linked to men indiscriminately. It's not right."

"I've got two words for you: Pamela Anderson. She plays the mommy-whore thing like a harp. And it works. Trust me. *Sin by Sin* is a very sexy movie. You can't play a role like that and then want to be thought of as June Cleaver. The public won't let you. We should think about setting you up with a rock star, too. Lenny Kravitz is hot. Do you dig him?"

Tatiana's cell phone jingled. She was eternally thankful for the interruption.

It was Enrique.

Instantly, she began to panic. She assumed this was the normal reaction. After all, she'd left her young children under the care of an oversexed twenty-something errand boy with the attention span of an ADD case before the daily dose of Ritalin. "What's wrong?"

"Nothing. Did you forget about the nanny interviews?"

"Oh, shit!" Maybe *she* needed the Ritalin.

"The first one's here. Kerr and Jaron approve and are ready to make her an offer."

Something snapped in Tatiana. "What the hell is Kerr doing there?"

"He called earlier, and I told him what was happening. He said this is a very important decision, and he wanted to be part of it. I didn't think you'd mind. He *is* still their father."

"Well, what is Jaron? Their stepmother?"

"They could do worse. Have I told you about my stepmom?"

"Enrique! Don't let them decide anything until I get there. This is insane! I'm leaving right now." She snapped the phone closed and stewed a moment.

"Sounds like this meeting's over," Kitty said.

"I'm sorry. I have to go home and murder my soon-to-be ex-husband. How's that for publicity?"

Kitty shrugged. "Okay. But the queer angle's better. We can get more mileage out of that. Besides, the lighting on *Court TV* sucks. You would look all washed out."

On the way home, Tatiana practiced breathing exercises she'd learned in yoga class. She was so mad that it felt like her blood was boiling. Kerr had a lot of nerve to dump the twins on her and then show up with his boyfriend to weigh in on who would help raise them.

A Mercedes SLK convertible and a Dodge Neon were parked in the drive. Either the nanny candidate had done very well for herself or Kerr had found a sugar daddy.

She stormed inside only to discover them out by the pool, beached on the lounges, sipping margaritas (Enrique's specialty), and laughing like old college pals.

Enrique saw signs of instant termination and rushed to intercept her. "Don't freak out," he whispered. "I made drinks so she'd relax. That way we'll get to know the real Lexi Epstein."

Tatiana looked past him to see that Lexi could find work

as a lingerie model in a snap. "She's the one who got fired for sleeping with the father of her charges, right?"

Enrique nodded. "But there's no chance of that here," he murmured under his breath. "Kerr hasn't checked out her ass. Not even once. I've been paying attention."

"To Kerr or to Lexi's ass?"

Enrique gave her a dumb look. "I have two eyes, you know."

She pushed past him, deliberately made no eye contact with Kerr, regarded Jaron like a mess on the side of the road, and approached Lexi.

"Hi!" Lexi yelped, with way too much familiarity. "We were just talking about you. I'm dying to see *Lady Cop Undercover*. It sounds like a really good bad movie. You know, like *Attack of the Killer Tomatoes* or whatever."

Tatiana wanted to push this twit into the pool and hold her under for, say, the running time of this good bad movie she wanted to see, which would mean just under ninety minutes. "What are my twins' names?"

Lexi looked confused. "Huh?"

"The names of the children you would be taking care of if you were lucky enough to get this job. What are they?"

Lexi threw glances at Enrique, Kerr, and Jaron, as if seeking emergency aid. "I don't know. They've been napping since I got here."

Tatiana gave her a hard look of disapproval. "I don't think this will work out, but thank you for stopping by."

A stunned Lexi turned helplessly to the others.

Kerr gestured for Lexi to stay put and pulled Tatiana off to the side.

She yanked her arm out of his grasp. "Let go of me! By the way, that's the first time you've touched me in months."

"This isn't about us," Kerr said. "We have a situation here. Melina is gone, and the twins need proper care."

Tatiana scowled back. "I couldn't agree more. But she is not my idea of proper care."

"How do you know? You haven't spent five minutes with her. Jaron and I have been visiting for the last hour."

"My point exactly. Has she asked you anything about the twins? Their names, their likes, their dislikes, their daily routine?"

Kerr shook his head.

"Proper care, my ass. She doesn't even have proper curiosity."

Kerr's brow furrowed. The obvious set in. "Maybe you're right."

Tatiana glared triumphantly, then turned to Enrique. "Show Lexi to the door. By that I mean the front one, not the bedroom."

Kerr stayed put, giving Lexi a weak smile and a weaker wave as Enrique walked her out. He sighed heavily. "I know this is weird, Tat, but I hope we can be friends."

She stared at him. He was a good-looking man—dark hair, trim goatee, lean runner's body. And despite being a lousy husband, he'd always been a pretty nice guy. "Why?"

"Because of the kids. It's better—"

"No," she cut in. "Why did you marry me in the first place? You don't just wake up gay." She halted. "Unless you're Anne Heche."

"Marrying you was the most selfish thing I've ever done. I actually thought those feelings would go away."

"Like what? Menstrual cramps? We're talking about sexual orientation, Kerr. God, haven't you ever seen *Dawson's Creek*?"

He beamed. "Jaron's been bringing me up to speed. We watch it every Wednesday. Don't you love Jen's grandmother?"

Tatiana slapped his head. "You left me with two kids that I never thought we could handle in the first place."

"But you're doing so well. You spotted that bad nanny faster than I can blink." Kerr reached for her hand. "Come on, I want you to meet Jaron."

The other man/home wrecker/whatever was fortyish, handsome in a Donald Sutherland-meets-James Woods kind of way, and very swishy. By comparison, Frasier and Niles were closer to teamsters than to fussy opera boys. Jaron opened his arms. "Give me a hug, girl!"

Suddenly Tatiana was wrapped up in a warm embrace that reeked of Thierry Mugler's Angel Men fragrance.

"I didn't steal him from you, girl. Even as much as I love Elizabeth Taylor, that isn't my style. I hate what she did to Debbie Reynolds. And I never understood why those two fabulous women were fighting over Eddie Fisher."

Tatiana drew back.

Jaron clasped her hands. "Those movies don't do you justice. The lighting director should be hung up by his toenails. You are gorgeous."

Tatiana almost started to laugh. Kerr left her for *this*?

"I know this is strange," Jaron went on. "You're probably thinking, what is my husband doing with this old queen?"

Hmm. At least he's perceptive.

"The answer is simple. We're soul mates. When I read Kerr's poetry, I knew. It's like he was inside my heart making it go pitter-pat. I can't explain it."

"You don't have to," Tatiana said. "I've always hated Kerr's poems. The two of you definitely deserve each other."

Jaron teared up. "You're so sweet. Sort of bitchy, but sweet. I don't want this to be awkward. I want us all to be friends. Really. In fact, I made Kerr get a job so that he could provide for the kids. Who knows when Oprah will select his poetry collection for her book club?''

I do: never.

"In the meantime, he needs to make his own money. That's why he started selling Mary Kay this week.''

Tatiana glanced over at Kerr.

Her husband (at least legally) wore a sheepish grin. "Do you mind if I host a party here?''

She managed a tight smile. "How soon can we get this divorce finalized?''

Jack couldn't stop thinking about her. Tatiana Fox. The crazy woman with the red hair and the wild eyes and the incredible body. Meeting her and entertaining her kids had been the highlight of an otherwise bloody-awful day.

If he could find Hugh Haliwell right now, he'd practice dead-ball kicks with the bastard's head. So much for his former manager's claim to a *friendship* with David Walsh. The audition had been humiliating, what with David looking fuzzy at the first mention of Hugh's name, and Kip Quick demanding a Boston accent for the one-line character who gets killed inside of the movie's first two minutes.

Everything had gone bust. The bit part in *Sin by Sin* was supposed to mean an instant paycheck, plus a Screen Actors Guild card to pave the way for more work. Now what? Jack tried to focus on his next step.

He glanced around his hotel room—one of those extended-stay properties that rents by the week. It stank of mildew, and coming back from the audition, he'd been greeted by a huge roach. Something had to give. And fast. He smoothed his fingers over the number Tatiana had scrawled on his arm. Impulsively, he reached for the phone and dialed.

She answered, sounding put-out right away. "Hello?"

"What did you have for lunch?" Jack asked. "And don't lie."

"Gum, a few animal crackers, and a margarita."

Even through the receiver, Jack sensed a smile from her. "Once you're under my strict training regime, you'll have to do better."

"Well," Tatiana replied. "I'm not under you yet, am I?"

He grinned at the double entendre. This woman could flirt with the best.

"By the way," she went on, "I'm not paying you four hundred dollars an hour. That's outrageous. My friend pays her trainer three hundred, but he has a fitness book on the bestseller list."

"Last year an unauthorized biography of me was a big seller in England," Jack fired back.

"Not the same thing." She paused. "But still impressive."

"What do you think is fair?"

"Let's see . . . my therapist charges one hundred fifty an hour, but she has lots of degrees hanging in her office. How about I pay you fifty bucks but offer a twenty-five dollar bonus for your accent, which means you have to talk—*a lot*. Say, 'Go for the burn.' "

Jack shook his head, feeling silly, but chanted the workout cliché regardless. "Go for the burn."

Tatiana giggled. "Sounds cute. You're my new trainer."

"I'll need to work with you at least six days a week."

Tatiana gasped. "Am I that out of shape?"

"Not really. I need the money."

"Oh, well, that reason goes down a little easier. Deal."

"Good. We start tomorrow at seven. Make sure you have a sensible breakfast at least an hour before."

"That means getting up at six."

"So?"

"I don't open my eyes before nine. Then I read the columns, watch *Regis and Kelly*, gossip with my friend September, and go back to sleep until noon."

Jack couldn't believe it. He knew senior citizens who were more active in the morning. "Do Ethan and Everson just fend for themselves?"

"Oh!" she remarked, as if shocked. "I forgot about them. And I still don't have a nanny. Shit. I'll probably be up at five washing nipples. For their bottles. Not my own. I'll be lucky to get a quick shower."

Jack hesitated. "What about their father?"

Tatiana sighed. "Don't get me started. He suddenly realized he was gay and took off to play house with his new lover. I'd call him, but I already know that he's in a Mary Kay seminar all day tomorrow."

"Mary Kay?"

"Door-to-door cosmetics. You know, the pink-Cadillac thing."

Jack's brow furrowed. "Yeah, I've heard of it. Your ex-husband is selling that stuff?"

"Honey, I *wish* he were my ex. That'll take some time. Anyway, he's got to make a living. His boyfriend is rich but insists that Kerr pull his own weight. I wish I'd been such a taskmaster. I let that freeloader sit around and write bad poetry for years."

For a minute, Jack thought Tatiana was just playing around. But a certain earnest tone in her voice made him believe otherwise. "This sounds like an episode of *Jerry Springer*."

"No, honey," she remarked easily. "It's just L.A."

Chapter Six

Tatiana fell asleep standing up, one hand resting on Ethan's back, the other on Everson's. It was the only way the twins would go down for the night.

Now in her own bed and prying her eyes open to go over the *Sin by Sin* script, she second-guessed herself on the nanny issue for the millionth time. Yes, Lexi was a tramp. And yes, Gretchen was deliberately misleading. Turns out the Rosie O'Donnell she worked for happened to be the nonfamous Kansas City, Kansas, Rosie and not the famous comic/talk show host/magazine publisher Rosie. Still, could Tatiana honestly weigh in on child care matters? At least Lexi and Gretchen had experience.

All the stress worked against her tonight, zonking her out instead of keying her up. She woke with a start a few hours later, having dreamed about losing the twins in a pumpkin patch owned and operated by Tori Valentine and her creepy rock star boyfriend, Mookie. On a tablet she kept on the nightstand, Tatiana scribbled down everything she could remember about the dream, hoping Dr. G could analyze it for the deeper meaning at her next session.

Unable to get back to sleep, she reached for the phone and called September Moore.

"Speak." It was a man's voice.

Tatiana assumed that she'd dialed wrong and started to hang up. But something held her back. "Hello . . . I was calling for . . ."

In the background she heard September laughing, then a playful tussle. Suddenly her friend came on the line. "Who's this?"

"I've got a better question. Who's *that?*"

"Oh, hi, Tatiana." September's voice went up an octave with each word, in that conspicuous way that lets you know you're being talked about.

Tatiana hesitated. "Sounds like you have company."

"I do," September cooed, with more than a hint of vulgarity. "A gentleman caller."

Another wave of laughter. Then she heard the man ask, "Will you miss me if I take a shower?" His voice rang familiar, but Tatiana couldn't quite place it.

September moaned. "I'll join you in a minute." A long, spent sigh. "Tatiana? Are you still there? I'm sorry."

She was officially annoyed now. But was it because she didn't have September's attention or because she wouldn't mind a man needing a shower in *her* house? "Honey, you've never been sorry about anything."

"True," September admitted. "But I am polite on occasion. That's what lying is for."

"So who's the guy?"

"Promise you won't get mad."

Tatiana's defenses went up. Only three forbidden names came to mind. The first, and most obvious, was Kerr. But even Hugh Hefner's harem couldn't lure him back to the straight team. The other name, and the most surprising to her, was ... Jack Thorpe. Of course, there was always George Clooney. That would really piss her off. "I can only think of three men that I never want you—"

"Greg Tapper."

Tatiana felt a flush spread up her neck. "Well, make that four." She gripped the phone tighter. September never did anything by accident, and tumbling with Greg Tapper the same week he was casting *Sin by Sin* was *not* a coincidence.

"He thinks I should read for the role of Nikki," September said. "We might be up for the same part. Is that weird?"

No, it's backstabbing, you bitch. "Have you met with David Walsh?" Tatiana tried to keep her voice light.

September groaned. "Not yet. He's been blowing off my agent, so when I ran into Greg at Spago, I decided to make my own move."

"You'll love David," Tatiana began in an unfettered tone that was certain to drive September crazy. "He's a sweetheart. Today he set up a meeting for me with Cleo Mars. I signed with her this afternoon."

Deafening silence.

Tatiana relished the direct hit. September had been Cleo's success story way back when. Now she was saddled with some junior guy at Creative Artists who had zero clout. Granted, a little mean to rub that in, but tonight her friend deserved it.

"Congratulations," September managed. Badly. No sign of a former Oscar winner in that response.

Deep down, Tatiana knew she meant no harm. September was famous for going after roles that didn't suit her. First, she gave off major ice queen vibrations, what with her patrician features, aloof attitude, and size-two figure. So lobbying for the part of the farm woman who fights to save her property from foreclosure in *This Land Is My Land* was just plain dumb. Ditto the lead in *Sin by Sin*. The script called for a woman with curves. September was a stick. Several boyfriends (without meeting up to compare notes, mind you) had even nicknamed her Bones. "I don't want this to come between us," Tatiana said. "This is a good opportunity. We should both go for it."

"I didn't know you had a thing for Greg Tapper."

Tatiana pulled back the receiver to stare at it for a second. "I don't. I'm talking about the part."

September sighed miserably. "Oh, I'll never get that."

Tatiana wanted to scream. Typical September. It was the night before the biggest reading of Tatiana's life, and she had to spend it boosting September's cables. "Don't say that. Positive-speak only." But really, the chances were greater that Mariah Carey would show up fully clothed for an event. Boffing Greg Tapper wouldn't cut it. She should have at least considered a three-way and brought in the director, Kip Quick.

"Who am I kidding?" September sniffled. "Do you know how long it's been since I've been cast in a feature?"

Tatiana hoped this was a rhetorical question, because she knew and didn't want to answer.

"*Do* you?" September demanded.

"Uh . . . *Shallow Water*?"

September started to cry.

Shallow Water was a shark movie so bad that, by comparison, *Jaws 3-D* could be regarded as cinematic brilliance. At least the latter had several scenes featuring Dennis Quaid without a shirt. The former had offered up Ed Begley Jr. Yuck.

"I'm a joke," September wailed.

"Stop that. Jesus, you've won an Oscar! And look at all

the great television you've done. How many times have you
guest starred on *Touched by an Angel*?''

''I've lost count.''

''See!''

''Maybe you're right.'' A little stronger now.

''Of course I am.''

''I shouldn't even have to audition for this part!'' From
self-doubt to beyond cocky. The girl was back. ''If Greg
Tapper thinks he's getting a second round in the kip, he's
crazy. That son of a bitch can shower and hit the door!''

''You go, girl!'' Tatiana sang. A grossly overused phrase,
yes, but appropriate for the situation.

''You know, I've always wanted to direct.''

''No, sweetie.'' Someone had to stop her before things
got too ridiculous.

Everson woke up first. Five o'clock. Ethan woke up second. Four minutes after five. Tatiana carried them back to
her bed, begging for ten more minutes of sleep. Okay, she
actually pleaded for two hours, but she would have easily
settled out of court for ten minutes.

After they bunched in, though, it became quite pleasant,
comforting in a way she'd never experienced before. The
twins were curled on either side, their faces just a few inches
from hers. Greedily she breathed in their sweet, sleepy scent,
took in their mercurial, beatific grins, and satined her cheek
against their warm foreheads, touched by the music of their
heaving, happy sighs.

''Ma . . . Ma,'' Everson murmured, kissing her full on
the lips.

Tatiana froze, momentarily overcome with emotion.

Ethan stirred and muttered something, but she couldn't
make out what. Probably just babble.

Everything about them was guileless, unguarded, yet so intent. The degree of innocence astonished her. Suddenly, she had an inkling of what a mother tiger must feel like. The realization stayed with her as they drifted off into an indulgent slumber.

At the sound of the doorbell, she woke with a start, craning her neck to squint at the clock. Just a few minutes before seven. Who the hell would show up at . . . ? Jack! Gingerly she extricated herself from the twins' body knot, scooted them to the middle of the bed, built a prison of pillows around them, and dashed to answer the door, stopping first to gargle Listerine for a few seconds.

Jack stood there looking divine—fit (that's why she hired him), well rested (bastard), and hot (not a bad first sight of the day) in a Jack Attack T-shirt and Nike running shorts that stopped midthigh. "Good morning," he chirped, giving her Winnie the Pooh pajamas a double take.

"I just woke up," Tatiana confessed.

Jack shifted slightly to leave. "I can come back . . ."

"No." She grabbed his wrist and pulled him inside. "You're going to train me. By the way, what's a Jack Attack?"

He glanced down at the phrase emblazoned across his chest. "It *was* me doing all manner of heroic things on the football field. Now it's just anxiety, I'm afraid."

Tatiana laughed. She enjoyed a man who could make fun of himself.

Ethan started to cry. Already she could distinguish his wail. It was louder, more dramatic, and sounded as if the sky were falling—or worse, that Barney and Baby Bop's plane had gone missing over the Bermuda Triangle.

"It's just going to be a little complicated this morning," Tatiana said.

Now Everson kicked in.

"I take it you didn't find a new nanny," Jack said.

Tatiana perked up her brow. "Muscles *and* brains. I like it."

There was a light pattering on the floor, then the sight of Ethan peering around the corner. Everson crept up behind him. They watched Jack for a moment, feigning shyness at first, but soon breaking into little smiles as their tiny memories placed him.

Jack squatted down and stretched out his arms.

Ethan and Everson made a few tentative steps before suddenly bolting toward him, delighted as he swooped them up and spun them around.

"Somebody's stinky, and it's not me!" Jack bellowed.

The twins performed a giggle duet in response.

Tatiana still marveled at how quickly and passionately they took to Jack. They merely allowed Enrique to tend to their needs, usually stoic with consternation as he clumsily helped with this and that. Even Kerr had never merited this much enthusiasm. It was uncanny.

"Do you mind changing them while I get breakfast ready?" Tatiana asked.

"I thought the twenty-five dollar bonus was for my accent."

"Don't be so mercenary," Tatiana scolded. "Look. They adore you."

Jack leaned back to regard Ethan and Everson, who were positively beaming.

"Besides, since *you're* here, they won't let me have anything to do with them."

"Lucky me."

You *are* lucky, Tatiana thought. The devotion of a child was such a beautiful thing. Part of her felt downright envious. "Their room is right down the hall. You'll find everything you need."

He proceeded to hop there like a giant bunny, which sent the twins into a fit of laughter and screams that rattled the whole house.

Tatiana busied herself in the kitchen, alarmed to discover that Ethan's favorite Gerber mixture, apple and pears, was nowhere to be found. Not thinking of the hour, she rang Enrique right away.

A groggy girl answered. *Imagine that.*

"Enrique, please."

"It's that bitch you work for," she heard the girl say as she passed the phone.

Enrique came on the line.

"Who was that?" Tatiana demanded. "She just called me a bitch!"

"Lexi," Enrique whispered, sounding embarrassed. "We made another batch of margaritas at my place, and one thing led to another."

Tatiana heard him stretch.

"Man, it's not even eight yet. Is something wrong?"

"Ethan's out of his favorite food. Get some more yogurt, too. And milk. Oh, and Secret deodorant. Kerr took mine."

Enrique laughed. "Well, it is strong enough for a man."

"Can you hurry?"

There was a groan. "Let me get some coffee down first."

"No time for that. Stop at Starbucks on the way, and since you'll already be there, get me my regular, too."

"Do you mind if I get dressed first?"

"That's up to you." She hung up and set about getting the highchairs in place and preparing the first meal of the day. Once finished, Tatiana surveyed the scene, quite pleased with herself. Being a single mom wasn't so hard. Why did people make such a big deal about it?

Jack sauntered in with a baby in each arm. "I had to

change their clothes, too. Not much to choose from. I recommend a shopping trip ASAP.''

Ethan and Everson wore matching pink Tommy Girl T-shirts and frilly shorts.

Tatiana laughed. ''Oh, buddy boy,'' she managed, leaning in to kiss Ethan's cheek. She glanced at Jack. ''You know, it really is kind of cute.''

''Yeah, that's probably what RuPaul's mother said at this age.''

''Good point.'' Tatiana dialed Enrique again.

Thankfully, he answered, saving her a death match with Lexi.

''One more thing: Take the twins shopping today. They need new clothes. And be sensible this time. Leather is not practical attire for toddlers. Are you dressed yet?''

''I just zipped up my pants.''

''Good. Get out of there before you-know-who zips them back down.''

''I told the agency what happened,'' Enrique said, munching in her ear.

''Stop eating on the phone. It sounds gross.''

''It's just pizza from last night.'' He took another bite. ''Anyway, they're going to send us a grandmother-type from the Valley. Her name's Agnes. I hear she's shaped like an ox.''

Tatiana focused in on Jack, who was enticing Ethan and Everson to eat waffles and chopped fruit with no argument. ''Hold off on that.''

Enrique tapped the phone. ''There must be something wrong with this line. It sounds like you said 'hold off.' ''

''I did.''

''Hold off for what? I know this might sting a little, but Kerr looked very happy with Jaron yesterday.''

''For your information, that doesn't sting. I couldn't be

happier for those girls. I might have another plan, that's all. Keep Edna on standby for now."

"Agnes."

"Whatever." Tatiana huffed impatiently. "Are you in the car yet?"

"I just stepped outside." One beat. "Shit."

"What's wrong?"

"One of my roommates' dates is blocking me in." A brief pause. "But the door's open and the keys are in the ignition. Man, she must've really been wasted. Oh, well, I'll just take her ride."

Tatiana heard the car turn over.

"It's a Porsche. Big fun."

Tatiana listened as he revved the motor NASCAR-style. "Be careful!"

"This engine rocks! Did you say something?"

Annoyed, she hung up, turning to Jack with a smile.

"Have you eaten?" he asked.

She mulled the question, finger on her lips. "I found one of Ethan's graham crackers under my pillow. It was stale, but I ate it anyway. How's that for body fuel?"

Jack shook his head and gestured for her to take over with the twins. "I'll make you a smoothie. You can't work out with nothing in your stomach. I don't want you to get sick and then blame me for not getting the part."

At first, she thought Ethan and Everson might stage a revolt, but with Jack active in the kitchen and still within view, they cautiously allowed her to fill in.

Jack clapped his hands. "Blender?"

"Bottom-left cabinet."

He bent over and came up with only the base. "Is this a scavenger hunt?"

"Oh, look in the dishwasher. I forgot that Enrique made margaritas yesterday."

Jack fished it out and rummaged through the refrigerator and freezer, putting in a little of this, a little of that.

Tatiana had to focus on the twins because if she diverted her attention away from them, they got steaming mad. And speaking of mad, she had no idea what Jack, the mad scientist, was cooking up.

Finally, he turned on the blender to whip up his mysterious concoction.

The noise startled the twins. Ethan started to cry, but Everson held tough.

"It's just a gadget, honey," Tatiana said soothingly, rubbing the soles of his bare feet.

Ethan stopped and whimpered a little, uncertain but basically calm.

Jack poured the smoothie into a glass and presented it with a flourish.

The twins regarded her with thinly disguised jealousy.

Tatiana looked at Jack. "They want some, too."

He poured a smidge into their tiny Sippy cups.

This gesture thrilled them to no end. Ethan began kicking his legs excitedly, and Everson, overwhelmed with glee, started breathing hard.

Tatiana drank up, instantly won over by the sweet, fruity taste. It was obviously healthy but went down like a guilty treat. "This," she smacked after coming up for air, "is fantastic."

"It really shouldn't taste that good," Jack said. "But I had to improvise with what was available."

"You didn't plop in a raw egg, did you? Like in the *Rocky* movie?"

Jack nodded. "Half a dozen."

Tatiana stared at the glass in horror. She clutched her stomach. Was that really a sick feeling or just psychological?

"Relax. I'm kidding. No eggs. I promise."

She glared at him. "That was mean."

Ethan and Everson sipped their smoothies and giggled, as if in on the egg joke.

Tatiana gave the glass a suspicious look but turned it up anyway and finished the whole thing.

Jack placed his hands atop Ethan's and Everson's heads. "Are we going to use these two as dumbbells?"

"I thought we could take their playpen out by the pool and do the workout there. It's such a beautiful morning. And as long you're around, they won't fuss about a thing."

He shrugged easily. "Sounds good."

Tatiana heard someone coming through the front door and assumed that it was Enrique.

"Yes, it's me before noon. I brought smelling salts just in case you fell over," September said.

Tatiana's mouth dropped open.

September's gaze found Jack and locked on tight. "Who's he?"

Jack gently wiped a smear of mango off Ethan's chin.

"What are you doing here at this hour?" Tatiana asked, barely over the shock.

"I accidentally took a diet pill instead of a Xanax, and I couldn't sleep. One more time. Who's he?"

"Jack Thorpe, September Moore," Tatiana said. "He's my personal trainer."

September's eyebrows shot up. "Really? I'm in the market for a personal trainer."

"You already have two," Tatiana reminded her.

"Not exactly. One is a sex therapist and the other is more of a nutritionist." September gave Jack a lurid once-over. "Are you taking on new clients?"

"No, he's not," Tatiana broke in.

Jack looked at Tatiana. "I'm not?"

"I was lucky to get him," she went on. "He's very much in demand."

"I am?" Jack asked.

September licked already moist lips. "I can see why." She sighed and reached into her purse to fish a business card out of her Prada wallet. "Oh, well, let me know if you can ever squeeze in a new client. Maybe someone will break a limb or go into rehab. I'll come running." She slipped into one of the Pottery Barn chairs at the Pottery Barn kitchen table. "I would commit treason for a Bloody Mary right now."

"Enrique will be here any minute," Tatiana said. "He'll make you one."

September appeared shocked. "He's still working for you? I thought you would've slept with him and had to let him go by now. Wait a minute. That's my routine. Sorry. I really need that Bloody Mary. The kid's not bad, by the way. He's got the endurance but not the technique quite yet."

Tatiana set down her empty smoothie glass with a bang. "You slept with my personal assistant?"

"Remember when you sent him over to pick up that Vera Wang skirt you borrowed?" September arched her hand to inspect her nails. "And he didn't stay over, so technically we didn't sleep together. We just fu—"

Tatiana held up one hand to September and shielded the twins with the other. "They don't need to hear this."

"They can't understand me." For the first time since her arrival, September looked at Ethan and Everson. Doubt clouded her face. "Can they?"

"They might repeat something you say," Tatiana explained.

"Oh," September said, dismissing the notion with her

hand. "In that case, repeat after me, children, Greg Tapper is a prick."

Jack scooped up the twins. "Let's watch TV, guys. Something family-oriented."

September, unfazed by the sudden evacuation, said, "Yeah, turn on *The Constance Ann Show*." She glanced at the oven clock. "It's on right now."

"What channel?" Jack asked.

"Don't you dare let them watch that woman, that show, that . . . antichrist," Tatiana fumed.

The venom in her voice prompted a quizzical look from Jack.

"We were in acting class together," Tatiana explained. "We had . . . issues. Well, in all fairness to me, *she* had issues. I didn't have issues."

Jack grinned knowingly. "So who was the guy?"

Tatiana was instantly offended. "What guy? There was no guy."

Jack turned to September for confirmation.

"Greg Tapper was in the same acting class," September said.

"I see," Jack said.

"You *see?*" Tatiana challenged him. "There's nothing to see." She spun to face September. "And since when is he a prick? A few hours ago he was in your bed."

Jack made a show out of covering Ethan's and Everson's ears. "Watch your language. The children."

September giggled. "He's funny." She glanced around impatiently. "Where the hell is Enrique? I want my Bloody Mary."

"Do the two of you do *anything* for yourselves?" Jack asked.

September looked at Tatiana.

Tatiana looked at September.

"I don't know if you've heard," September said first, "but lately she's been forced to have sex on her own."

"September!" Tatiana screamed, mortified. She turned to Jack, no doubt red-faced, judging from the heat she felt emanating from her cheeks. "Don't listen to her."

September laughed. "For a sexpot, you can be so prudish. I'm sure Jack here is no stranger to pumping his own gas."

Now it was Jack turning red. "*The Constance Ann Show* is on," he said, starting out with the twins.

"Don't let them watch her," Tatiana called out. "I'm serious."

He doubled back. "She's the one with the lamb puppet who sings songs, right? What's the harm?"

Tatiana spoke in a grave tone, as if instructing Jack on the dangers of everyday household cleaners that are potentially poisonous. "It's a panda puppet, actually, not a lamb. The real point is this: Constance Ann and I are part of a mutual hatred society. With my luck, if the twins see one show, they'll get hooked, and I'll be forced to endure her on a daily basis. I would much rather be subjected to the sounds of Linkin Park."

"Who's Linkin Park?"

"A rock group," September put in. "Think Metallica only louder and more evil."

Jack grimaced. "That's not good."

"Just watch anything else," Tatiana went on. "*Sesame Street, Teletubbies, Bear in the Big Blue House,* or even *Maury Povich.*"

September nodded enthusiastically. "Maury's good. I think he's sexy."

Tatiana made a face. "Really?" She mulled it over. "Maybe he is. I've never really thought of him that way. But he is sensitive, the way he comforts the people who cry and everything."

Jack left the room without a word.

"I feel terrible about last night," September started in. "You must think I'm such a bitch."

"Well, of course, I do. That will never change." Tatiana started to clean up the breakfast mess, then decided Enrique should do it. Instead, she sat down at the kitchen table and sniffed the not-quite-fresh, almost dead flowers, hoping Enrique remembered to pick up a new batch—a move that would require forethought on his part, not her spelling everything out in mind-numbing detail, so all bets were on that no fresh-cut flowers would fragrance the air today. Rats.

September regarded the old flowers like highway litter and pushed the vase away. "You mean to say I'm an *impossible* bitch, right?"

"Absolutely."

"Not a *mean, backstabbing* bitch."

"Never."

September tilted her head in peaceful acceptance. "I can live with that."

"So what happened with Greg?"

"We're having sex in the shower, and he informs me that there's a closed short list for the role of Nikki and that casting is imminent. The sneaky bastard threw me a bone, though. There's a part as a psychiatrist he said I'd be perfect for. Needless to say, I didn't let him use my good shampoo."

"J. F. Lazartigue's White Orchid?"

September nodded.

"Excellent move. He's not worth it. But he's right about the supporting role. It's a meaty part, not like the cameo Faye Dunaway had in *The Thomas Crown Affair*. You'd have some heavy scenes."

September sighed. "I really want to do a comedy. I just did heavy in the Lifetime movie *Just A Few Bites, Jenny!*

Sorry. I always say it loud because of the exclamation point in the title.''

"This is a feature, though," Tatiana argued. "Big budget, big promotion. You'd be crazy not to do it. Who knows? Maybe we'd get the chance to act together."

September brightened. "That would be fun." She slapped both hands on the table. "Okay, I'll do it. Which means you *have* to get the lead. Courtney Love is on the short list, and I will not put up with her for three months. What time is your reading?''

"At ten.''

"I'll help you get ready. The key is showing up *in character*. That's how I got the part in *Postcards from Paris*. I won the Oscar for that, by the way. Have I ever mentioned that?''

"I think it's come up before.'' Tatiana grinned. September found a way to get her Oscar win into a conversation at least once a day. She kept it in the bathroom. That way she would always come face to face with the award several times a day.

September stared off into space. "I'm trying to put the Bloody Mary out of my mind and think about what Nikki Alexander would wear.'' She clucked. "For starters, definitely no underwear.''

Tatiana heard Ethan squeal in the next room.

"Not to worry,'' Jack called out. "He's just excited. The red one's dancing. I think it's Po. Let me know when you're ready.''

Tatiana bit down on her lower lip. "I'm supposed to be working out.''

"There's no time for that,'' September hissed. "Come on, let's go through your closet.'' She stood up.

Just then Enrique came bustling through the kitchen door

with a grocery bag but no Starbucks. Would she have to
hire him an assistant to get anything done?

"Thank God!" September exclaimed. "Drop everything
and make me a Bloody Mary."

Enrique froze. "I'm pretty sure we're out of tomato
juice."

September threw up her hands. "Fuck it. I'll take a Diet
Coke."

Tatiana marched over and slapped Enrique on the side of
the head.

"Ow! What was that for?" He shifted the sack and rubbed
the spot of impact.

"Is there one woman in my personal or professional circle
that you *haven't* gone to bed with?"

"Your new agent, Cleo Mars."

"She's a lesbian."

"Damn," Enrique murmured. "Do you think she's really
dedicated to the cause?" He laughed and began putting up
the groceries, tossing Tatiana her Secret deodorant.

She almost dropped it but managed to hang on.

"Good save," Enrique said.

September cleared her throat.

Enrique grabbed a Diet Coke from the fridge, flipped the
lid, and handed it to her. "Here. Baby can go night-night
now."

September turned to Tatiana. "You know, I'm having the
hardest time finding a new personal assistant."

"That's because you're on the list," Enrique said from
inside the pantry.

September registered alarm. "What list?"

"We have an association and get together once a month."

"All the personal assistants in one place?" September
asked.

Enrique nodded.

"How frightening. Is that legal?"

"You're the Murphy Brown of our industry," Enrique explained. "You've gone through forty-six assistants in three years." He shrugged. "People talk."

Tatiana couldn't help but laugh.

"I've never let anybody go without a damn good reason," September maintained.

"You fired a girl because she couldn't translate a letter written in Japanese," Enrique pointed out.

September shot back an indignant look. "I got a fan letter from Tokyo. I wanted to know what it said. She was useless."

Enrique stopped suddenly to survey the scene. "Where are the twins?"

"Jack's watching them," September said, taking another hit of Diet Coke.

"Who's Jack?"

"My new personal trainer," Tatiana said.

Enrique gave a vague nod. "Now all you have to do is find a nanny to put you through a workout, and you'll be set."

Chapter Seven

Constance Ann sat on the enormous pink pillow in the center of the floor, surrounded by a veritable United Nations of children—white, black, Asian, Hispanic, Arab—of all ages and shapes. As the cameras rolled, they sang along with the smiling songstress, whose Pappy the Panda puppet bounced to the beat.

Clap, clap, clap; clap, clap, clap
If you love peanut butter; clap, clap, clap
If you love one another; clap, clap, clap
Whenever you feel happy just
Clap, clap, clap; clap, clap, clap

"Crap, crap, crap!" Constance Ann screamed, ripping the Pappy puppet off her hand and flinging it several feet past the masking tape on the floor that marked the set parameters.

"Cut!" Will Hayes, the show's director, raked his hands

through a mass of wiry, prematurely gray hair. He gave the show's star a weary look. "What's wrong?"

"Are you blind *and* deaf? That fat kid in the red sweatshirt was off beat!" Constance Ann stood up, put on an insulting show of bad clapping that mocked the child, and stormed off the set.

Right away the young actor in question, a plump Latino boy named Chris, broke into heaving sobs.

Constance Ann halted and spun around. "Hey, crybaby! Toughen up, or you'll never make it in this business!" She stomped to her dressing room. Once there, she slammed the door, shaking the foundation. Her first and only cover of *TV Guide*, framed and hanging, crashed down into shattered bits.

Three soft knocks sounded on the door.

Constance Ann zeroed in on the broken glass. "Take off your shoes before coming in," she hollered. Whoever had the bad judgment to bother her now deserved to bleed.

"Why?" It was Will.

She rolled her eyes. "Never mind."

Tentatively, he turned the knob and poked his head inside. "We've only got the kids for another half hour. I need you to pull it together."

For a split second, Constance Ann considered snatching a piece of jagged glass and charging him with it. "Correction: Those no-talent brats need to pull it together."

Will sighed. "You should probably know that Chris— he's the eleven-year-old you just sent into years of therapy— happens to be Sam Taylor's nephew."

Constance Ann's face registered nothing. Sam Taylor owned Tycoon Productions, which distributed *The Constance Ann Show* to syndicates worldwide. "If he wants that retarded boy to excel, he should put him in the Special Olympics. This show is a place for professionals."

Will shrugged helplessly. "I'll pass that along."

"Give me ten minutes," Constance Ann said.

Will opened his mouth to speak.

With her eyes, she dared him to utter so much as a peep. "In the meantime you can work on getting those little shits in rhythm. I can do this song in one take."

Blearily, Will nodded his agreement and started to go.

"Wait. The skinny white girl who wears the ponytail. What's her name? Linda?"

"*Lacey.* She's been with us since the first show three years ago."

"Really? Is she some mucky-muck's niece or godchild?"

"No."

"Good. Fire her. She looks like a monkey."

Will appeared stunned. "Lacey is a sweetheart. And she gets more fan mail than any other kid on the show."

Constance Ann raised an eyebrow. "Even more reason, then. There's only one star around here, and that's me! No little monkey brat is going to hitch a ride on my wagon. I knew that chimp was trouble."

Will shook his head. "She's got a contract, Constance."

"Constance Ann! The name is Constance Ann! Goddamn it, I hate it when people leave off the Ann!"

Will surrendered a brief bow. "Apologies."

She glared at him. "Don't patronize me. You think you're better than this, don't you?" Her hand gestured around the room, as if to take in the whole sound stage. "If you were, Mr. Yale School of Tight-Assed Drama, then you would be someplace else. So get used to it. This is as good as it gets for you. Ha!"

Will swallowed the insult like the bitter pill it was. "Back to Lacey. We can't just fire her at your whim. She's under contract."

"Contracts are made to be violated. Plant a dime bag of pot in her backpack."

Will laughed.

Constance Ann just stood there, stone-faced.

"You're serious."

"If you don't like my solution, then come up with another. But do it today. And shut the door on your way out."

Relishing the few minutes of solitude, Constance Ann helped herself to a drink from the stash she kept hidden in her wardrobe bureau. Spiking deep, she smiled at the irony. What would her adoring public think if they knew that sugary-sweet, chocolate-covered, dusted-with-rainbow-sprinkles Constance Ann needed a stiff one (a drink or a man, sometimes both) to get through a show with *the children*. Christ. Her underage costars were nothing but bitches and bastards, just like the rest of the entertainment world, only smaller in size.

She flung herself on the sofa and picked up *Daily Variety*. Why did she continue subscribing to this rag? Oh, yes, to remind herself of the career that never happened. A headline caught her eye.

EMBATTLED TAPPER PROJECT SINS AHEAD WITH NEW LEAD

Constance Ann took in a sharp breath. She felt a stirring in her loins. All it took was the mere mention of his name. Greg Tapper. Oh, God! How many times had she fantasized about him in all his brooding rebel James Dean glory? At least thousands. She'd even nicknamed a vibrator after him. Two, actually. The first one had been left in a San Francisco hotel.

Thinking back to those desperate acting class days, she felt a tightness in her chest. The memory kept on tickling. . . .

I'm not feeling anything from you, Constance Ann. You're an empty vessel. Show me a tree that has a history. Show me!

Ugh! The voice of Eileen Beasley rang inside her head as if it were yesterday. That stupid, boozy hack! What had she known about teaching acting? Not a goddamn thing! And how the hell was someone supposed to act like a tree?

One of the few positive things to emerge from that experience was the fact that she and Greg Tapper were the only students actually to have made it. Granted, some would argue that she hadn't. But those assholes didn't know the finer points. Cynics could make fun of her sappy songs and even sappier skits, and late-night comics could rip her to shreds. She didn't care. Because at the end of the day, Constance Ann was cashing the checks. A long-term deal to keep her show going for years. Royalties from album and video sales. Merchandising points for Pappy the Panda toys. Huge booking fees for Constance Ann kiddie concerts and appearances at shopping mall openings. *Take that, critics! With your second mortgages and your high-interest credit cards up the wazoo. Take that, ex-classmates! With your waiter/waitress gigs and your exile to retail oblivion. "Welcome to the Gap." Ha!* She never had to mutter that pathetic phrase.

Feeling downright giddy now, she chased down some more liquor and settled in to read the details on Greg Tapper's latest triumph. She tracked his every move in the trades and columns, dreaming about someday running into him at a glittering, high-profile event. They would laugh about those old days in Eileen's torture chamber, agree that it felt like a lifetime ago, trade congratulations on their success and growing fortunes, and . . . ravish each other behind a curtain, all thrashing limbs and dirty grunts.

In fact, it almost happened once. She'd paid big bucks

for a VIP ticket to a black-tie affair sponsored by the Greg
Tapper Foundation for some disease that everybody had
been whining about. AIDS? Alzheimer's? Colon cancer?
She couldn't remember. Anyway, he'd shown up at the end
of the night for maybe five minutes, instantly surrounded
by throngs of sycophants. Just as she got close enough to
say hello, he'd been ushered away by a PR flack and a
security bozo. Balls! One thousand dollars a plate down the
drain. Good cause or not, what a rip-off! Charity sucked.

Constance Ann stole another hit from the bottle and
revisited the headline to prepare herself for the rest of the
story. . . .

EMBATTLED TAPPER PROJECT SINS
AHEAD WITH NEW LEAD

*Though once thought to be guilty of the ultimate Holly-
wood sin—development hell—the next Greg Tapper
vehicle,* Sin by Sin, *is officially on track. Tapper will
executive produce and star in the Univision picture,
with Kip Quick signed to direct and David Walsh
producing under his Star Bright banner.*

*After weeks of speculation about which A-list female
actor would come on board to star opposite Tapper
in what has been described as an edge-of-your-seat,
shockingly erotic psychosexual thriller, word came
down late yesterday that Tatiana Fox, a relative newcomer best known for her role in the straight-to-video*
Lady Cop Undercover *series, has accepted the role.*

*Agent Cleo Mars confirmed Fox's casting, pre-
dicting a star turn by her unknown client, and serious
on-screen sparks with Tapper. Reportedly, it is those
graphic lovemaking scenes that Mars obliquely
alluded to that ultimately precluded Nicole Kidman,
Ashley Judd, Cameron Diaz, and other bankable*

actresses from pursuing the project. The planets seem
to be perfectly aligned for Fox. Similar circumstances
were in place when Sharon Stone chipped away at
superstardom as the ice-pick-wielding seductress in
Basic Instinct.

In related casting news, Academy Award winner
September Moore has signed on for a supporting role.
Sin by Sin *begins shooting later this month and is*
scheduled for national release next May.

Constance Ann calmly put down *Daily Variety* and slowly
rose from the sofa. Only then did she clench her fists and
stomp her feet and scream her throat raw.

Will Hayes came bursting into the room. ''For Christ's
sakes, I thought you were being killed!''

''It's worse than that. Believe me.'' She stood there seeth-
ing, not knowing what to do, how to proceed. But one thing
was certain: something had to be done.

Will approached her gingerly. ''Can the meltdown wait
until after we shoot the 'Clap, Clap, Clap' song?''

A little girl appeared in the doorway, brandishing a gap-
toothed smile. She was the newest member of the cast and
already a favorite with viewers, a fact not lost on or appreci-
ated by Constance Ann.

Will's protective instincts kicked in. He bent down to
address the pint-sized *All About Eve* wannabe. ''Hello,
Hallie.''

''Hi, Mr. Hayes,'' Hallie chirped.

''Remember when we talked about rules on the set? One
of them was not to come to Constance Ann's dressing room.
She uses this time to get ready for her big part on the show.
It takes a lot of concentration.'' He spoke slowly in an
almost musical tone.

Undeterred, Hallie lifted the locket hanging around her

neck and presented it to him. "But I wanted to show Constance Ann the gold locket that the tooth fairy brought to me."

Constance Ann rushed the scene to intercede. "There's no tooth fairy." She fingered the jewelry and scowled. "Your parents put that junk under your pillow."

"It's not junk!" Hallie yelled. "And the tooth fairy gave it to me!"

"It's not eighteen-karat!" Constance Ann shot back. "And it was your mom and dad. Go ask them!"

Hallie slunk away.

Will stood there in horrified amazement. "She's just a little girl!"

Constance Ann shrugged. "She needs to learn. The tooth fairy, Santa Claus, the Easter Bunny—they're nothing but crass commodities."

Will surrendered. "You've got five minutes." He shot a glance at the liquor bottle. "Have an Altoid. Otherwise the kids might get drunk off your breath."

Constance Ann grinned. "That was clever, Will."

He beamed, pleased with himself. "Why, thank you."

"Don't let it happen again." And then she slammed the door in his face and stalked over to the sofa to retrieve *Daily Variety*, ripping the offensive story off the front cover.

Damn her! It was fine when that bitch made news but got buried in the back pages of some stinky tabloid. Especially when the headline screamed "OBSCURE SEXPOT." Ha! Constance Ann had loved that one so much she'd tacked it up on the fridge.

Shit movie after shit movie. Dumped by a fag husband. Saddled with two screaming brats. *That* was the kind of news about Tatiana she wanted to hear. But somehow the slutty so-called actress had fooled around and snagged a great agent and a star-making role in a real movie.

The enormity of the situation smoked inside Constance Ann's brain. Greg Tapper and Tatiana Fox. A steamy film. Graphic love scenes. The inevitable affair. Precisely the kind of Hollywood cliché the world could count on. Oh, God, it wasn't fair! She felt like popping a handful of Ambien tablets and sleeping for three days.

Suddenly, she got a wild hair to do something crazy, flung open the door, and shouted, "Where the fuck is my assistant? I've been fending for myself all goddamn day!"

"You fired her yesterday," a production assistant remarked casually as he passed by.

Constance Ann honestly couldn't remember doing that. "Well, I didn't mean it."

"The three stitches above her eye from the paperweight you threw say you did."

"Oh, yeah? Well, I should've picked up something heavier!" Constance Ann slammed the door again and dialed information for Cleo Mars's number. It took some artful bullshit to get past the receptionist, but soon the famous agent came on the line.

Without preamble, Constance Ann started in. Cleo Mars was a busy woman. No need to waste time on chitchat. "I'm looking to shake up my career a bit," she said. "*The Constance Ann Show* can't last forever, and I don't want to get typecast as the saccharine-sweet puppet lady. I was an actress first, you know. I'm open to anything: hookers, strippers, drug fiends, you name it."

Cleo started to laugh. "Who is this?"

"Constance Ann. Really."

"Oh, please. This has to be Sandra Bernhard." Cleo laughed again. "You have to use this in an act. It's priceless. And frightening when you think about it. Can you imagine Constance Ann as a *hooker?* Or as anything but a Pappy carrying goofball?" Still more laughter. "Oh, it'd be worse

than Kathie Lee Gifford's attempt to become an actress. I
don't think the industry would ever recover."

Constance Ann felt droplets of sweat form on her forehead. The level of humiliation went far beyond her compre-
hension.

Cleo paused. "Sandra? Are you there?"

Quietly Constance Ann hung up the receiver. She'd been
shoved alongside Kathie Lee while Tatiana earned compari-
sons to Sharon Stone. The injustice was paralyzing. The
need to strike out was burning. The plan was percolating.

Two knocks hit the door. "It's time," Will said.

Constance Ann gazed into the mirror. "It's not time yet,"
she whispered. "But it will be soon, Tatiana. Very, very
soon."

Chapter Eight

It could have been worse. To be back in London, for example, nursing an ale at a neighborhood pub, dealing with some well-meaning chap who comes along to say, "Hey, didn't you used to be Jack Thorpe?"

Nobody in Los Angeles knew about his former life—the games, the girls, the advertising profile. Generally speaking, he enjoyed not being recognized. But a little part of him missed the ego boost that accompanied mass love.

Better to be in another country, though, for the football jock had fallen far and fast. From sold-out stadiums and VIP treatment to diaper changes and part-time work as a glorified gym coach. Any producer for one of those lame "Where Are They Now?" shows would kill for his story.

Tatiana stopped swimming in the middle of the pool, and with heaving breath, begged, "Please let me stop! I'm *dying!*"

Jack shook his head. She'd gone maybe three lengths. He

made a fist and punched the air a bit. "This is just the warm-up. Keep going."

"I hate you!"

"That's okay. You'll love me when the movie comes out."

Tatiana flailed onward in a spastic freestyle stroke.

In each arm, Jack held the twins. He leaned back to regard them. "Your mommy is a terrible swimmer. I've never seen so much splashing to get to the other side of a pool."

Everson giggled, as if understanding every word. "Ma . . . Ma."

Ethan remained focused on the spatula that had captured his interest since breakfast.

The nanny issue was still unresolved, and all the excitement associated to Tatiana's big break in *Sin by Sin* had pushed it further down the priorities list. To be true, Jack really didn't mind, as long as his nanny duty wasn't official. He loved kids. Hugh had routinely signed him up for children's charity appearances, and Jack constantly badgered his sister to hurry up with a niece or nephew. Of course, she needed to find the right man and get married first.

Tatiana finished another lap and stopped, gasping for breath at his feet, peering up at him. "This is torture."

He grinned and worked Everson's little hand into a wave. "No, torture comes later, when we get to abs."

"I hate you."

"You said that already."

"It's a point that needs reinforcement." As she attempted to lift herself out of the pool, her arms nearly buckled, but she held fast and managed to negotiate the deck without falling over.

Jack tossed her a towel. "Dry off and join me at the mat for stretching."

"If you weren't holding them, I'd push you in the pool!"

He turned on her innocently. "Where is all this hostility coming from?"

"It started with that protein bar you gave me for breakfast. It tasted like bad gravel."

"As opposed to good gravel?"

"You know what I mean." She huffed and rolled her eyes, slipping on nylon shorts, an old U2 tour T-shirt, and Nike cross-trainers.

Jack plopped the twins into their playpen and presented each with a small cup of ice shavings. That would occupy them for at least fifteen minutes. He regarded Tatiana for a moment. "May I offer guidance on a matter unrelated to physical fitness?"

She looked up. "You're not a Jehovah's Witness, are you?"

Jack shook his head. "No."

Tatiana breathed a sigh of relief. "Good. What's on your mind?"

"You need to find a suitable nanny. I think you're letting the 'It Takes a Village' concept go a little far. Between you, me, Enrique, Kerr, and now Jaron, these kids have too many caregivers. It must be confusing for them."

Tatiana glanced over at Ethan and Everson. "They look perfectly content to me. You're the magic link, you know. They adore you. They merely put up with me. They mostly stare at Enrique. Maybe it's because he's so pretty. Babies love beautiful things. Kerr is like a big playmate. Jaron is like a great aunt. Oh, you forgot about September. Sometimes she pitches in. But it's minimal care. You have to just give her one directive, like, 'Don't let them drown,' or 'Keep them alive until I get back from the market.' " Tatiana stretched her arms over her head. "And there's also Dr. G. She's never seen them, of course, but she provides moral support. You know what? Swimming makes me hungry."

"Shooting on the movie starts soon," Jack said. "What do you plan to do?"

Tatiana gazed at Ethan and Everson with longing. "I don't know."

Jack stretched his neck, bending ear to shoulder.

Tatiana mirrored the move. "I was secretly hoping you'd be there for them, I guess."

Jack stretched his neck to the opposite side.

Tatiana did the same. "I'd hate to bring in a stranger, especially after they've grown so attached to you. What if they don't adjust? It could be traumatic for them."

"Don't do that," Jack said.

"Do what?"

"The emotional blackmail thing."

Tatiana pretended to be shocked. "I was just—"

"I know what you were doing," Jack cut in. He started the shoulder stretches. "We've already had this conversation. I'm not a nanny. I'm a personal trainer."

"With *one* client. It's not like a career."

"*You* squashed my business growth with September."

"For your own good. September goes through men like paper towels."

"So what? I'm not seventeen. I can handle being used and disposed of. Sometimes I even like it, depending on the circumstances."

Tatiana's eyes flashed angrily. "What is it about being a nanny that's so unappealing? Is it because it sounds like a girl job?"

Jack hiked a leg atop the wrought-iron table to stretch his hamstring. *"Sounds like?* It is."

Tatiana kicked up her leg right beside his. "Come on, men do it. There are lots of single mothers out there who hire guy nannies to give their kids a positive male influence. I read an article about it in *Redbook*."

"Oh, well, sign me up."

"Don't be sarcastic. I'm starving and exhausted."

Jack switched legs and leaned into the stretch. "You can have a smoothie at ten o'clock."

Tatiana made a face. "I couldn't eat such a feast with a clear conscience."

"Now who's being sarcastic?" He raised his knee and began rotating his ankle.

Tatiana didn't bother keeping up this time. She put both hands on her hips and zeroed in on him with a determined gaze. "No one I could find will be as good as you, Jack. They *love* you. I've never seen them light up like they do when you walk in the room. Well, there was a similar reaction to Barney. But it didn't last. He makes them happy, but you send them over the moon. It's like magic."

Jack glanced over at the twins, who were still busy with their ice shavings. So far they'd been no trouble at all. He did seem to have a knack for dealing with kids, especially these two. But they deserved more of a commitment than he was willing to give. "You need to find someone . . . you can count on long-term."

Tatiana practically jumped up and down in frustration. "I need someone right now! I need to know that they're well taken care of so I can concentrate on this movie!"

He bent over to grab a pair of free weights. "So this is really about you."

She hesitated. "Sort of. But only about, say, thirty percent. The rest is all about the children. I promise."

Jack demonstrated a hammer curl and passed the free weights to Tatiana. "I'm not a nanny. Don't get me confused with your husband."

"What does Kerr have to do with this?"

"He's an Avon lady."

"No, he's a Mary Kay girl . . . uh . . . representative."
She pumped her arms up and down, looking confused.

"I've been a professional athlete since I was sixteen. I
grew up in locker rooms. Do you even realize what you're
asking me to consider?"

"Oh, damn," Tatiana hissed. "I knew I was forgetting
something." She stopped after a few repetitions and gave
the weights back to Jack, heading straight for her cell phone.
"This won't take long." She pressed a button and impatiently waited out a few seconds. "Enrique! Major emergency. Well, not major, exactly. It has nothing to do with
me. Let's call it a minor emergency. Kerr's having a Mary
Kay party at the house tonight, and I completely forgot to
have you make arrangements for a caterer. Pop in Ralph's
for munchies and little sweets. I love the mini cheesecakes
with tiny little kiwi slices on top. And make up a huge batch
of your margaritas. If everybody's drunk, they're certain to
buy more, and I want Kerr to do well. He needs some
success. Another publisher rejected his poetry collection,
and he's feeling blah. Oh, and stick around so he can demon-
strate all the cleansers and moisturizers and masks on you.
By the way, I've got, like, one tampon, and you know I
start my period soon. I really wish you would at least glance
at that Hello Kitty calendar I gave to you. I spent all that
time writing my important dates in there. OK, that's it.
Bye." She slapped the phone back on the table. "I hate
voice mail."

Jack could only sympathize with the poor bloke on the
receiving end.

"Where were we?" Tatiana wondered. "Oh, taking a
nanny job will not make you gay, if that's what you're
worried about. Let's not even call you a nanny. From now
on, you're a *manny*. Hey, that's macho. *Manny*. Do you like
it?"

"No." Jack passed the free weights back to Tatiana. "Let's concentrate on your workout."

"What's your problem? Don't you need a job? I thought you mentioned something about losing all your money in a land mine."

"Land *deal*. And it was my manager who lost all the money."

"You should fire him."

"I did."

"I can pay you fifty thousand dollars a year. The average nanny—excuse me, *manny*—only makes about thirty-six, so I offer a very competitive salary. Don't tell Enrique, though. He'll get mad. I pay him by the hour."

Jack gestured for Tatiana to continue with the hammer curls.

She started pumping again. "You know, it's not just single mothers who need mannies. Think of all the new fathers out there who are old. Men like Michael Douglas and Don Johnson. They might hire a manny just to teach their kids how to ride a bike and play baseball. When you think about it, this is very important work. Quite manly. By comparison, a construction site manager is kind of prissy."

Jack didn't crack a smile. "Work your arms, not your mouth."

"You should move in, too," Tatiana went on. "Melina was great—she was the nanny before you—but I never liked the fact that she didn't live with us. She had this weird thing about wanting to be with her own family. I was offended but never let it show. Better not to have tension in the house." Tatiana struggled with the weights. "How many does this make? Can I stop?"

Jack nodded, moving in to retrieve the dumbbells, but Tatiana dropped them on the ground before his hands could reach their target. "The house has two bedrooms, yours and the twins'. Are you suggesting that we sleep together?"

Tatiana laughed. "No, but you'd love that, wouldn't you?"

"Not as much as you would."

She took in a sharp breath. "What's that supposed to mean?"

Jack grinned. "I didn't speak in code."

"Listen, Mr. Wonderful, you must have me confused with one of your teenage fans back in London."

Jack opened up his arms as if the world were embracing him. "Come on, Tatiana. You know you want some of this."

"Oh, my God!" She took a giant step backward, obviously unaware that she was inches away from the edge of the pool. "You are *so* in love with yourself. How did I not see it?"

"What can I say? Lust is blind."

"Okay, stop. Please. It was funny at first, but now you're just embarrassing yourself."

"Hey, you started this."

"Well, of course you want *me*. I was in *Playboy*. And you saw it. And most important of all, you remembered."

Jack took a few steps toward her, his gaze smoking with exaggerated desire. "You are a hot girl."

Tatiana flipped her hair. "How sweet of you to notice."

"A little too hot, I think. Maybe you should cool off." And then Jack gave her a playful shove that sent her sailing into the pool.

The look on Tatiana's face was priceless: shock, fury, frustration, and just a hint of delight.

Jack laughed harder than he had in weeks. Then, being a true gentleman, he leaned over the side and offered his hand to the beautiful wet seal.

She rebuked him, stopping to push the hair from her face and dry her eyes. "That was mean!"

Jack crouched down. "Come on. I was just having some fun."

Tatiana softened a bit. "At least help me out of the pool, you big bully."

Jack offered his hand.

Tatiana accepted it, and, in one fast and alarmingly strong move, she yanked him toward her.

The force of the pull caught Jack off guard. Unable to secure his footing, he went splashing into the pool. Coming up for air, he whipped his hair free of chlorine water and smiled like the good sport he was. "Impressive upper body strength."

Tatiana crossed her wrists Wonder Woman style. "You should see me dodge bullets."

He made his way toward her, laughing as she inched away from him. "Wonder Woman never runs from danger."

Suddenly, she came up against the pool wall and could go no farther.

Jack grabbed the deck on either side, trapping her between his arms. An unstoppable urge came over him. To kiss her. To taste her mouth. Slowly, he leaned in, his gaze teasing, his lips slightly parted, ready to claim her.

"Kiss me, and I'll scream," Tatiana blurted.

Jack hesitated but didn't back away so much as a millimeter. Cool as ever, he laughed at her. "Is that what you thought I was going to do?"

She seemed uncertain now.

He blew a quick stream of air just above her lip, then gently smoothed the spot with his index finger. "You had a little fleck of dirt on your face." He surveyed the water. "How often do you get this pool cleaned?"

"Every week," she answered sourly.

Jack released his arms and floated backward. "If you say so." He fought hard to keep a straight face.

"I *know* you were going to kiss me."

He gave her a quizzical look. Then he sighed, shrugging slightly. "If you have to make yourself believe that, I'm not going to argue."

"Ugh!" Tatiana clenched her fists and punched at the water. "You're infuriating!"

"No, kitten, I'm Jack Thorpe . . . your new manny."

Clumsily, she swam toward him and grabbed his hands. "Are you serious? Don't tease me!"

Jack had barely taken a minute to process the decision. His mouth came stomping out of the gate as fast as his mind had. For now, though, it just seemed like the right thing to do. He enjoyed the twins. He liked their crazy, terminally self-absorbed mother even more. The half-assed personal assistant was a kick, too. Ditto September Moore, the wacko actress. These kooks lived in a whole other place, and that was precisely what he needed right now: a brand-new world. Not to mention a job. That couldn't hurt, either.

Tatiana squeezed his hands, digging her nails into his palms. "Tell me. Are you serious?"

"Yes, I am."

She threw her hands around his neck and hugged him tightly, giving him a loud smack on the cheek with her lips. "I know this is great for me. It takes a lot off my mind. But it's also great for Ethan and Everson, and I'm happy about that, too."

Jack touched her cheek. "You're so selfless, like Gandhi."

Tatiana playfully slapped away his hand. "We have to agree on some ground rules."

"Such as?"

"No sex. It could ruin everything."

"You mean just us, right? I can have sex with other women."

"What other women?"

"Tiffany, April, Heather—whoever I might meet."

"If a woman has a name like that, she's either a stripper or still in high school."

Jack mulled this over. "Both work for me. But she has to be at least eighteen and a senior."

Tatiana rolled her eyes. "A man with high standards. I like that."

"Hey, I'm twenty-six. If you want a celibate manny, then may I suggest you post some flyers outside a *Star Trek* convention."

"Whatever. I really don't care who you wine, dine, and leave unsatisfied. But women in my personal and professional circle are off limits. Besides, Enrique has already slept with all of them. Ask him for the list, though. Just so you'll know." She pointed to the house. "And no hanky-panky under my roof."

"Of course not. I'll have all my sex right here in the pool."

Tatiana narrowed her gaze. "On second thought, I'm not sure that I want you around my children at all."

"This is very interesting," Dr. G said, scribbling at hyper-speed onto her yellow legal pad.

Tatiana sat there, legs crossed, alternately tense and relaxed. "Well, good. I'd hate to think that I bored my therapist. That might mean you weren't listening. Why should I pay you not to listen to me? I can get that for free from just about anyone in my life." She paused a beat. "Actually, I have people on payroll who don't listen, so it would be quite normal."

"I could never be bored by a patient, Tatiana," Dr. G assured.

"Not even a narcoleptic?"

Dr. G surrendered a brief smile.

"Again, thanks for seeing me on such short notice."

"As it happened, I had a cancellation."

"I know. I called Anita Jasper and told her that I needed her appointment today. She's going to take an extra Xanax and get a massage."

"You know Anita?"

Tatiana nodded. "I'm the one who referred her to you. She's a lovely woman. A bit of a doormat, though. I would've divorced Graham years ago after the first transvestite hooker incident."

"Asking someone to forego their appointment for you is inappropriate, Tatiana. I have to ask you not to do that again."

"Enough about Anita. Let's not eat up my fifty minutes dealing with her problems. Now, what did you find so interesting? I'm dying to hear."

Dr. G seemed relieved to go on. "Your news about getting the part in this big movie is very exciting."

Tatiana returned an exuberant nod.

"But you've spent most of the session so far talking about Ethan and Everson, how this might affect them, your concern about their quality of care, and your genuine affection for this Jack Thorpe."

Tatiana jolted in her seat. "I wouldn't call it *genuine* affection. I admire the way he interacts with the twins. That's all there is to it."

Dr. G made a quick note. "Your face lights up when you talk about him. Your eyes dance. I've never seen you react this way about any man. I think there's more here than you're willing to admit right now."

"Even if I did like him a little bit, we couldn't get involved. He's Ethan and Everson's nanny—*manny*! What if things ended badly? I'd lose him and so would the twins."

"What if the romance flourished?" Dr. G posed.

"No romance or relationship—or friendship, for that matter—has ever *flourished* for me."

"Why do think that is?" Dr. G tilted her head, which meant she would *really* be listening to this answer, deconstructing every syllable.

Tatiana hesitated. Why had she opened this door? She should have stuck to the easy stuff, like fear of failing in her first big-budget feature, or anxiety over how big her butt might look in the love scenes with Greg Tapper. Oh, hell! She just had to go down a meaningful path with her therapist. A huge mistake. But now she was forced to answer. "All my relationships are ultimately disappointing. Maybe my expectations are too high. I want people to be a certain way, and they rarely are."

Dr. G merely stared. Not a single note had been taken.

Tatiana was mildly offended. "You didn't write that down."

"No, I didn't."

"Well, I thought it was pretty insightful. It deserved at least a note in the margin."

"Don't concern yourself with my note-taking. It's a shorthand I've developed over the years. There's no science to it. Let's get back to you. What is your earliest memory of a disappointing relationship?"

"That's easy. My parents."

"And what was so disappointing about them?"

"Well, my father left us when I was a baby, remarried, had another family, and basically did a bang-up job of forgetting that I ever existed. And, of course, my mother is a deranged, psychopathic, emotionally distant freak of nature who, as far as living things go, should only be allowed to tend to an aquarium—under supervision, of course. All in all, a pretty disappointing pair.''

"How would you describe your relationship with them today?''

"My father? Nonexistent. I do try to keep the lines of communication open with my mother, which means I provide her with my phone number and address, and she rarely makes use of them. It's very Shirley MacLaine and Debra Winger, only without the cancer and constant arguing. I call it the silent movie version of *Terms of Endearment*.''

"When did you talk to her last?''

"I'm not sure, exactly. I know Clinton was president.''

Dr. G's brow lifted, and then her pen got busy on the pad.

"That was a joke. It hasn't been that long. Seriously, George Bush was president. Well, not technically. They were still counting votes in Florida.''

Chapter Nine

"This is it?" Kitty Bishop asked.

"I know, it's small, but—"

"Small? It's a closet. Honey, this is New York space, not California space." She stalked through the house, surveying the decor. "I like what you've done with it. A little too much Pottery Barn and Ikea, though." She waved a dismissive hand. "Doesn't matter. We'll rent a bigger place for the photo shoot."

Tatiana chased after Kitty. "But I thought this was supposed to be an at-home feature with the kids."

"It is. Don't worry. Stars rent fabulous homes for that kind of publicity all the time. There's a showcase mansion in Malibu that'll be perfect." Kitty marched on, ending up in the kitchen, face to face with Jack, who was busy chopping fruit for Ethan and Everson's afternoon picnic. She stopped. She did a double take. She practically salivated. *"Hello."*

Tatiana caught up with her just in time. "This is Jack Thorpe, the twins' manny."

Kitty kept her gaze locked on Jack. "What's a manny?"

"A male nanny," Tatiana explained.

Kitty snatched a slice of melon and popped it into her mouth. "We have to keep him out of sight. Don't bring him to the shoot."

Tatiana felt a surge of protectiveness. "Why not?"

"Two reasons. First, people want to see stars taking care of their own kids. Nannies or mannies or whatever you want to call them have no place in a photo opportunity." Kitty gave Jack another once-over. "Are you two doing it?"

Jack played dumb. "Doing what?"

Kitty grinned. "Honey, you've spent too much time watching that big purple dinosaur. What's his name? Bart?"

"Barney," Jack said.

Kitty raised an eyebrow. "You are watching too much. So, back to my original question. Are you two fu—"

"No!" Tatiana cut in. "He takes care of the twins. That's all."

"Hold on," Jack protested. He turned to Kitty. "I'm also her personal trainer."

Kitty bounced suspicious looks back and forth between them. "You two have got to be fu—"

"We're not," Jack insisted.

Kitty opened her mouth to speak.

"And no," Jack said, "I'm not gay."

Kitty shrugged. "Can't blame me for wondering. She did marry one."

Jack stared at Kitty as if she carried the head of Medusa. "Who are you?"

She pumped his hand firm and fast. "Kitty Bishop, celebrity publicist."

Tatiana cleared her throat. "What's the second reason?"

Kitty regarded her blankly.

"For Jack not being around."

"Oh, that. No one will buy that the two of you aren't banging each other. Just like I don't. With our plans for pushing the Greg Tapper romance, though, it's better to keep the hot *manny* out of sight."

Jack turned to Tatiana. "There's a Greg Tapper romance?"

Kitty grabbed a strawberry. "Cut your fruit, handsome. PR's my territory."

Before Tatiana could respond, she was pulled outside and onto the pool deck by Kitty.

"I've been rethinking the rock-star lover idea," Kitty began, checking off an item in her little red Hermes notebook. "You're not trashy enough to pull off the slut mom thing like Pamela Anderson, so you can keep boffing your nanny on the side until we unwrap the Greg Tapper affair."

Tatiana wanted to strangle her. "For the last time, I am *not* having sexual relations with that man."

"I just had a déjà vu. Where have I heard that before?"

Tatiana felt frustration building. "You know what, Kitty? I'm a little uncomfortable with this whole idea of image manufacturing. Using someone else's home to represent mine, fabricating a relationship with Greg, who barely looked me in the eye during my last audition, by the way. It's just not me. I want—"

"Honey, stop. There's something you have to realize. Tatiana Fox is no longer a person. She's a product. *You're* a product. Think of yourself as a box of detergent, preferably one with a color-safe bleach formula. It's a better value. *Cleo* decides which roles you accept and negotiates the deals, *you* get naked and dry-hump movie stars, and I carefully mold your image for the media. Don't stress yourself out and think you have to do all three jobs. You're part of a team now. We each play to our strengths."

Tatiana shook her head. "I don't want to be a box of detergent."

"Honey, be anything you want: a box of candy, a nice sweater, a Barbie doll. Just let me know so I don't mix metaphors."

"I'm not a commodity!" Tatiana said, raising her voice defiantly. "I don't have to hide behind lavish homes and fraudulent boyfriends—"

Kitty held up a hand to cut her off. "Yes, you do! Listen, honey, I'll take this shit from the Michelle Pfeiffers in this town because they've been around the block, but you're new to the game and nothing but a bit player. And if anyone needs the smoke-and-mirrors routine, it's you. How the hell can we go with the truth here? You're an ex-*Playboy* pinup with a string of shit movies to her credit who married and got dumped by a gay man who hawks Mary Kay! Even worse, your rebound guy was Stephen Baldwin! Jesus Christ. At least give me a chance. Already I've landed you a four-page photo spread in *In Style*, and you haven't shot frame one of your first real movie. Let me do my job."

Tatiana started to cry.

Kitty made an awkward attempt to hug her. "Honey, did I come on too strong? That's the way I talk to everybody in New York. Even the elderly. I keep forgetting things are more delicate out here."

Tatiana regained her composure. "I'm Okay. It's just . . . everything's happening so fast."

Kitty rubbed Tatiana's back. "Are you still seeing your shrink?"

Tatiana sniffled a bit and nodded. "Once a week."

"Maybe you should bump it up to twice a week. I'm not good at issues like this, and Cleo doesn't have the time.

Okay, all done with the breakdown? Good. Can I get a look at your kids? If they're too ugly, I know an agent who handles babies. He can get me a set of beautiful twins to pose with you. All it takes is a phone call.''

At first, Tatiana couldn't believe it. Until it dawned on her that anything, no matter how appalling or offensive, could come out of Kitty's mouth. "My children are gorgeous.''

"Still, I should take a peek. You know how mothers can be.'' Her voice took on a mocking tone. "Oh, look at my precious baby.'' Then she stuck her finger down her throat. "Meanwhile the rest of the world sees a troll. Happens all the time. I have an objective eye. Let's have a look.''

Tatiana led Kitty back into the house and quietly slipped into Ethan and Everson's room, where they were napping.

Kitty peered over the cribs and smiled her approval. "Even my agent friend couldn't do better than this.''

Tatiana beamed.

"And their little blond heads will photograph great against your red hair,'' Kitty gushed in a loud whisper. "The art director will be swooning.'' She widened her eyes. "Can they swim?''

Tatiana almost laughed. "They're not even two yet! But they do enjoy the water. No fear at all.''

Kitty scribbled a note. "I want to get a shot of you in the pool with them. That way we can show off your body without looking too desperate.'' She tapped her pen as if deep in thought. "I forgot to ask. Is your mother famous, by any chance?''

"My mother?'' Tatiana flashed back to the session with Dr. G, then forward to the task she'd been avoiding at all costs—calling the woman in question.

"Every angle helps. It never hurts to have a mother like Tippi Hendren or Janet Leigh.''

Tatiana put on a show of hopefulness. "Are they available?"

Kitty got the point. "That bad?"

"Trust me. We don't want to go there."

Kitty cackled. "Honey, one day we'll get drunk and swap family stories. Hundred bucks says I've got you beat."

"You're on," Tatiana said, ushering Kitty out of the room before one or both of the twins woke up.

As soon as the door closed, Kitty's cell phone jingled. "Kitty Bishop . . . Calm down, I can't understand you. . . . Is it the same scumbag? . . . Don't worry. . . . No . . . I'll take care of it." She sighed and hung up. "One of my lesbian clients is being stalked by a tabloid photographer hell-bent on outing her. He just got a shot of her in lip lock with a girlfriend. Again."

"Do I know her?"

"You probably watch her show every Thursday night."

"What are you going to do?"

"Get the film."

"How?"

"I used to date a mob guy. I've got my ways." Kitty started out in a rush. "I'll call as soon as dates for the shoot are firmed up. Good luck on the set." She waved to Jack. "Bye, John."

He looked up from the sink, visibly annoyed. "It's Jack."

"At least I tried," Kitty said. "Normally, I don't speak to the help." And then she closed the door behind her.

Tatiana saw the hit register on Jack's face and felt terrible. "I used to have a publicist," he said heatedly, his cheeks red. "And she never behaved like that. The woman's got no tact at all. You want her as your official spokesperson?"

"I know, she's a little rough around the edges."

"*Rough? Try jagged.*" He stepped into the pantry for the

animal crackers, vanilla wafers, and goldfish-shaped cheese snacks.

Tatiana smiled. There was something so sweet about the way he went to such lengths to prepare Ethan and Everson's meals precisely the way he knew that they liked them.

"And what's this about a romance with Greg Tapper? I thought the guy was a jerk."

"He is," Tatiana said softly. "But Kitty thinks going public with a relationship would be good for the movie and my profile in the press."

Jack said nothing.

Tatiana noticed the tension in his jaw. "You're not jealous, are you?"

He looked at her with blazing eyes. "Of a fake romance? No way. Not when I can go out there and get a real one."

"Oh, I have no doubt that you can. I don't know how *real* it will be. This is L.A. Would you tell a girl that you were meeting for the first time about being a nanny?"

"*Manny.*" Jack chewed on the thought. "Yes," he said firmly. "I would. In fact, it could be quite the babe draw. Think about it. A man who nurtures and protects children for a living. Women will go wild for that. It's sensitive. And much better than a puppy. You know how girls go crazy for a guy with a six-week-old chocolate lab. I need a picture for my wallet. Do you have a recent shot of the twins?"

Tatiana wanted to deck him. "Ethan and Everson are not going to pimp for you. That's disgusting."

Jack laughed.

"What's so funny?" Enrique asked, just joining the fray. He presented Tatiana with a white pharmacy bag. "Is nothing sacred to you?"

She peeped inside. "Birth control pills? What's the big deal?"

Enrique smirked. "Yesterday I picked up your tampons. I'm beginning to feel like your gynecologist."

"Which reminds me—see if you can get me in for a bikini wax. Shooting starts in a few days, and the big love scene is up first. Oh, and take all that food you bought for Kerr's Mary Kay party back to your place. It's crowding the fridge. I figure your roommates will appreciate it."

"Kerr's thing was a disaster," Enrique said. "Only six showed up. I've had more people in my bed."

Tatiana and Jack gave him a strange look.

"After *a lot* of tequila." Enrique slapped his cheek. "But my skin looks great." He winked. "Kerr gives good facial."

Tatiana grinned. "Maybe you can steal him away from Jaron."

"That could be complicated," Enrique said. "Because technically he's still married to you."

Jack laughed.

Tatiana stewed good-naturedly. "The divorce will be finalized soon, and I'll be a free woman." She cut a teasing glance at Jack. "Free to marry Greg Tapper, perhaps."

"Greg Tapper?" Enrique balked. "Better keep that divorce lawyer on speed dial."

"Go see about getting me in for that bikini wax," Tatiana snapped.

Enrique shrugged diffidently. "Okay."

"Enrique," Jack started in a friendly but, to Tatiana's keen ear, conspiratorial tone, "maybe we could go out for a drink sometime. I'm in the market for a beautiful girl, and I get the feeling you know the best hunting grounds."

Tatiana glowered.

Enrique nodded with self-satisfaction, loving the idea, loving even more the acknowledgment of his stud status. "I can definitely show you some awesome scenery."

Tatiana decided to bust up this male-bonding moment.

"Jack thinks that telling women he's a manny will make him irresistible."

Enrique gasped. "Brilliant, dude! You'll get more action than you can handle. That's almost as good as being a fireman."

Tatiana's mouth dropped open.

Jack beamed. "I was thinking I could even take along the twins' diaper bag. You know, really play it up."

Enrique gave Jack a quick bear hug. "You are my new idol, man."

The two guys high-fived each other, then engaged in some kind of complicated press-grab-pull handshake, just the sort of macho routine that other men with limited brain cells engaged in.

Tatiana left them to it and sashayed off to watch *The Bold and the Beautiful.*

Retail therapy. Sometimes it was the only answer.

"We're sold out of the black, but we do have that style in brown, red, and white."

Constance Ann scowled at the Prada sales bimbo, tall and gaunt, a sickening size zero. Someone should strap her down and force-feed her a Big Mac and fries. "Fine."

A vacant smile. "Which color do you prefer?"

"All *three,*" Constance Ann snarled. Stupid twit.

A bigger, dumber smile. "They must be gifts. Would you like them wrapped?"

Constance Ann slapped a platinum American Express card on the counter. "No. They're all for me."

A dim nod of approval. "It's important to treat yourself."

"It's also important to eat more than a Tic Tac for dinner, Calista."

The idiot smiled. "Actually, it's Krystle. With a *K.* My

parents named me after Linda Evans on *Dynasty*." She stood
there with a blank stare for a moment. "Did you decide on
a color yet?"

"I want all three."

Krystle appeared confused.

"Brown, red, and white," Constance Ann hissed through
clenched teeth.

Krystle tilted her head. "I'm surprised you're not getting
the black. It's our most popular color."

"On second thought, fuck it." Constance Ann snatched
her credit card and stormed out of Prada and onto Rodeo
Drive, the street that was the heartbeat of Beverly Hills. She
turned and headed for Louis Vuitton. Hopefully, she could
find a sales girl there who hadn't undergone a full frontal
lobotomy.

Passersby looked twice but didn't stop her. Without Pappy
the Panda and her trademark blue frock, she looked less like
her famous self and more like an old acquaintance that you
couldn't quite place.

She walked on, feeling her open hostility downgrade to
low simmering rage, wanting a drink, needing a man, preferably a dumb and strong one, like a street cop or a military
drone on weekend leave. Suddenly, she froze in her tracks
at the sight up ahead.

Tatiana Fox, two brats in a double stroller, and a hot man
in his midtwenties were coming straight at her.

Constance Ann wanted to cross the road to avoid an
encounter, but a line of expensive cars was cruising down
the busy lane. It would mean taking on a Range Rover at
thirty miles an hour. Briefly, she considered the challenge.

And then she made eye contact with Tatiana, whose reaction went something like this: surprise, bitter memories,
hatred, fake smile, decision to offer artificial niceties like a
grown up.

"Constance Ann!" Tatiana squealed, sorority-girl style. "You look great! How long has it been?"

"Oh, just a week. I saw you in the tabloids," Constance Ann said, punctuating the dig with a laugh to soften the edge. No reason to come off too bitchy in front of the sexy stranger.

"You shouldn't read such trash," Tatiana said, dismissing the scandal with a giggle and a wave of her hand. "Lies, lies, lies. If you want to read the truth about your old classmates, pick up *Daily Variety.*"

Constance Ann swallowed the subtle dig with an icy glare. The plural usage of classmates—the tramp's clever, oblique reference to Greg Tapper—stung the most. Glancing down at the twins, she gushed, "What gorgeous children! They look nothing like you."

Tatiana's grip on the stroller tightened, her white knuckles turning whiter.

"Aren't they adorable?" Constance Ann went on with faux innocence. "I really admire women who open their hearts to other children when unable to have their own."

Tatiana bristled. "There's nothing wrong with me. I can have children whenever I want."

"Oh, of course. I didn't mean you. I was speaking in the general sense." Constance Ann smiled at the delicious man. "Open mouth, insert . . . *foot.*" She laughed and gave him a dirty wink. "I'm Constance Ann. But you can call me Constance Ann."

"Jack Thorpe," he replied, offering a large, tan, neatly manicured hand. "But you can call me Cindy."

She accepted with an appropriately effusive laugh, took note of his skin's smoothness and warmth, and reluctantly let go. "You're not the gay husband, are you?"

"No, I'm the straight manny and personal trainer."

"Manny?" Constance Ann inquired rhetorically, touching his arm for emphasis. "A male nanny? How brilliantly unconventional."

"Thank you," Jack said, clearly relishing the instant appreciation.

Tatiana took a bold step forward, practically coming between them. "It was my idea."

Constance Ann ignored her so loudly that eardrums should have been damaged. "Jack, I could benefit from some one-on-one attention. I'm a fiend for exercise, but I fear that I'm not pushing myself hard enough." She paused a beat. "Do you push hard?"

Tatiana's face was a masterpiece of disgust.

Jack played along, ever the flirt. "I've been known to leave women totally exhausted but feeling great."

Constance Ann reached into the side pocket of her handbag and pulled out a business card. "Here's my private number. Call me."

"I will," Jack said.

"Jack is very busy," Tatiana cut in desperately. "Between taking care of the twins and getting me in shape for the movie . . . Oh, did I mention that I'm starring opposite Greg Tapper in *Sin by Sin*? No, I don't think so. Well, I am. It's amazing. The catering budget for this film is bigger than the entire budget for all those *Lady Cop Undercover* movies I did."

Constance Ann put on a show of surprise. "I had no idea that you've been starring in movies! *Lady Cop Underwater*? Never heard of it. Someone told me you were working the perfume counter at Neiman Marcus. I just assumed that you'd given up acting."

Tatiana seethed. "*Undercover*, not underwater. And I worked at Neiman's for one Christmas season—seven years ago!"

"There's no reason to be ashamed," Constance Ann said. "Retail is honest work."

Tatiana practically jumped up and down. "I'm not ashamed!"

Constance Ann regarded her strangely. "Well, don't get a big head, dear. Being seasonal help is hardly one's finest hour." And then she turned to Jack again. "I don't give out my number to just anybody. You better use it."

"Like I was saying before," Tatiana began. "Jack is—"

"On salary and not under house arrest," he cut in. "I'll find the time."

Tatiana was clearly taken aback.

Constance Ann relished the moment. Just then, several yards away, she noticed a little girl pointing at her. Next, the face of the girl's mother lit up as they both picked up speed. Christ. A fan. Nothing more annoying and predictable. She searched for a pen to sign the inevitable autograph.

The mother-daughter team rushed the scene without so much as an "excuse me." Roadside whores had better manners. "Oh, gosh, they're even more beautiful up close!" the mother exclaimed.

Wait a minute. *They?* Constance Ann sized up the situation. These freaks were going mad over the stupid babies!

"Thank you," Tatiana said sweetly, smiling as if she actually had something to do it. Then the joke of an actress bent over to address the enchanted girl. "What's your name?"

"Kelly," she answered shyly, with a crooked grin that pointed out a serious need for braces. What the hell were they doing on Rodeo Drive? Get this runt to an orthodontist!

"That's a pretty name," Tatiana said softly. "My babies are named Ethan and Everson."

The mother put her hand over her heart. "Angels. Absolute angels." She looked over at Constance Ann. "Have you ever seen such beautiful children?"

"Actually, just yesterday I—"

"You're that yucky lady from the TV show!" the little girl roared.

The mother's face turned scarlet. "Kelly!"

Tatiana put hand over mouth to conceal her laughter.

Constance Ann wanted to push the little snot into traffic.

"Pappy the Panda is dumb, and you're a big stinky-face!"

"Kelly!" the mother shouted, horrified, yanking her by the arm and pulling her into the nearest store, leaving a trail of overwrought apologies in her wake.

The situation left Constance Ann unnerved. First, to be shoved into the background in favor of Tatiana's brat brigade. And then to be accosted by some ill-tempered street urchin with lousy teeth!

"Don't feel bad," Jack said. "A boy from Essex spit on me once for missing a goal."

Constance Ann merely looked at him.

"I played professional football in England."

Hmm. A real athlete, not a gym robot. Even better. She liked this one. "Is there anything that you don't do exceptionally well?"

"Choose managers wisely," Tatiana offered quickly. "He lost everything in a land mine. That's why he works for me now."

Constance Ann turned to Jack for confirmation.

"It was a land *deal*." He turned on Tatiana. "A land mine is what I'd like you to step on right now."

Tatiana sniffed the air. "I think Ethan needs changing."

"His diaper's not the only thing that smells," Jack grumbled, pushing the stroller forward. A few steps later he called back, "Expect my call, Constance Ann. I know just what to do with a body like yours."

Tatiana pursed her lips.

Constance Ann smiled. "You're so lucky to have good help."

Tatiana seemed to be willing herself not to react. "It is a blessing, especially with so much going on. *In Style* is doing a four-page spread on me and the twins, and it has to be done before shooting starts."

Constance Ann kept on smiling. Normally, this kind of news would drive her crazy. But today she was pleased as punch.

Because it fit perfectly into her plan.

Chapter Ten

Tatiana ducked into two boutiques before finding Jack in shop number three. Once her foot hit the sales floor of Shimmer, all she had to do was follow the sound of oohs and ahs.

"You do that *so* good," one woman praised.

"If I handed my husband a diaper, he wouldn't know what it was," another woman griped.

Stomping her way to the scene, Tatiana huffed impatiently. "Don't ever take off like that again! I've been in and out of practically every store on this side of the street!" She held up a small bag. "And I didn't even need this bracelet. I'm taking three hundred dollars off your salary."

The women fired off dirty, possessive looks.

Jack completely ignored her.

"May I help you?" the second woman asked. The subtext of her delivery was, "Get out, bitch." Apparently having a husband who knew nothing of Pampers made you extremely rude.

Tatiana kept her eyes on Jack and the twins. "I'm with him . . . *them*," she corrected tightly, but not before the pronoun slip had hit the airwaves.

"Oh," the first woman began, her tone fawning, "you are so lucky to have an attentive man in your life. My hus—"

"He's not my husband," Tatiana said.

"That's right," Jack added. "I'm straight. She only marries gay men."

The women tittered.

"I've been married *once*," Tatiana said. "He happened to be gay. That makes it an incident, not a habit." She halted. "Wait a minute. Why am I explaining this to you?"

The women shrugged.

"Could you give us a minute?" Tatiana half asked, half demanded. "Your window display is far from enticing. Maybe you could work on that while we have a word."

The women started off. "I told you it needed more color," one said to the other.

Jack finished fastening the diaper tape and effortlessly got Ethan back into his pants.

Tatiana experienced an odd build-up of frustration. "I thought we had an understanding about Constance Ann. You know how I feel about her."

Jack looked at her as if she'd just suggested that Cybill Shepherd was a really good singer. He rose to face her. "What does that have to do with me?"

Tatiana sighed. "September Moore will testify to this: I stood in my kitchen and forbade you to have anything to do with Constance Ann."

Jack laughed at her. "You are unbelievable!"

"I pride myself on a very detailed memory."

"Me, too. And the only thing forbidden was the twins

watching her show. You never said anything about me training her or dating her or just meeting her in the middle of
the day to have incredible sex.''

Tatiana felt a flush of heat rise up her neck. ''The implicit
message was to stay away from her no matter what the
circumstances.''

''Funny, I didn't get that.''

''Well, now you do.'' She checked her watch. ''We should
go. I have a session with Dr. G later today.''

Jack reached into his pocket to retrieve Constance Ann's
card. He fingered it meaningfully. ''I'm going to call her.''

She fought hard to conceal her irritation. ''To prove what?
That you have no taste?''

''Don't put me in the middle of your hair-pulling fight
with Constance Ann.'' He winked suggestively. ''Unless
you want to.''

''You're disgusting.'' She reached out and snatched the
card from his hand, ripping it to shreds. ''And you're not
calling her.''

''Hey!''

''Constance Ann is off limits. Date anyone else. Carmen
Electra, Tonya Harding, Heidi Fleiss . . .''

Jack pulled a face. ''These are my options?''

''Tatiana?''

She turned in the direction of the girlish voice. There
stood Tori Valentine. Lurking behind her was a zoned-out
Mookie. Enrique had mentioned a break-up. The two were
obviously going for that whole are-they-or-aren't-they
Pamela-and-Tommy-Lee thing. ''Oh, hi, Tori.'' She gave
her greeting zero enthusiasm, a half smile, no teeth.

Tori rushed her for a quick hug. ''Gosh, I've been meaning
to call you to tell you what an honor it is to be the new
Lady Cop Undercover. You left some big shoes to fill.''

''Don't you mean G-string?'' Tatiana countered. ''The

Dobsons like to keep wardrobe to a minimum. It saves them a trip to Target."

Tori took a moment to process the humor. It fell to the bottom of her empty head with a clink. She reached for Mookie's hand and pulled him forward. "This is my boyfriend, Mookie."

"Yes, I recognize him from his mug shot."

Tori looked puzzled.

"It shows up frequently on *Entertainment Tonight*."

Mookie chuckled. "I plead guilty to partying my ass off. Throw the book at me. Fuck, yeah."

Tori giggled and nuzzled him closer. "He's such a bad boy. Anyway, I just wanted to say hi. Yesterday I shot a scene where I had to look in a Dumpster and pretend that you were in there dead, so it's wild to see you in person."

Mookie lit up a tiny cigarette and took a deep drag.

One whiff and Tatiana knew it was marijuana. Urgently she turned to Jack and gestured for him to get the twins out of the store, then spun on Mookie. "Are you crazy? My kids were just a few feet away."

Mookie shrugged and laughed. "Relax, baby. Hey, you could definitely use a hit of this." He offered her the joint.

"I'm sorry, sir. No smoking in the boutique." It was the bitchier sales associate ... until she recognized the drug fiend. Then it was fawning fan central. "Oh, *Mookie*, let me get you an ashtray."

Tori beamed. "Everybody loves Mookie."

Tatiana started to leave in disgust.

"Wait!" Tori called. "Could we have lunch sometime? I'd love to get some advice. I mean, I still want to be working when I'm your age."

Tatiana froze, instantly plotted out a payback, and smiled sweetly at Tori. "Now that you mention it, I'd love to chat more. But first I need to pick up something around the corner. Sit tight right here. I'll be back in a flash.''

Tori nodded excitedly. "We won't move!"

The moment Tatiana stepped outside, she called 911 and reported a pothead lighting up at Shimmer. Then she made a mental note to watch *Entertainment Tonight* later that evening.

''It strikes me as odd that the personal life of your nanny could ignite such strong emotional feelings,'' Dr. G said. She raised an eyebrow. "You do realize that there's more here than you choose to be aware of.''

"I realize how much I hate Constance Ann! I would be this worked up if my *mail carrier* wanted to date her.''

Dr. G scribbled something onto her legal pad. "She's the colleague from acting class?''

Tatiana nodded impatiently, hating all the work that went into setting up a problem. She just wanted instant insight. Was that too much to ask?

"Tell me about her.''

"Imagine the most vile person you can.'' Pause. "Are you with me?''

"Yes.''

"OK . . . Constance Ann is worse.''

Dr. G merely looked. "I was imagining Saddam Hussein.''

Tatiana didn't blink. "A monster, yes, but not so bad when you put him up against Constance Ann.''

"Why don't you tell me what happened between the two of you. That might help me put this animosity into perspective.''

Tatiana shook her head. "I'm not going to spend the next four sessions talking about *her*.''

"Four sessions?"

"At least. It could take more." She shook her head. "Let's not even go down that road."

Dr. G pursed her lips. "Have you spoken to your mother?"

"No. I've thought about calling, though. Does that count?"

"It's a start."

"Are you being facetious?"

"Is that what you think?"

"I refuse to answer on the grounds that it may incriminate me."

"You're not on trial, Tatiana."

"Really? Sometimes therapy is like a fifty-minute cross-examination, minus F. Lee Bailey, of course, but with the added bonus of prescriptions. By the way, I'm on my last refill of Klonopin. My pharmacist gave me that look. Actually, he gave my assistant, Enrique, that look."

Dr. G put pen to lip for a moment, then scratched furiously on the pad as if the secret to Tatiana's psyche were spilling out of her Columbia-educated brain. Finally, she spoke. "What bothers you more? The fact that Jack has announced plans to date Constance Ann or the fact that you can't control him?"

Tatiana stiffened. She tried to laugh off the suggestion. "I have no interest in *controlling* Jack Thorpe."

"No interest in controlling him or no ability to?"

"I thought we were talking about Constance Ann."

"Are you ready to discuss her now?"

Tatiana narrowed her gaze. "I'm not a control freak."

Dr. G stared impassively.

"I'm not!" Tatiana glanced at her watch. God! She was so ready for this session to be over. Her favorite ones were when she got to complain a lot and Dr. G said supportive things that reinforced the notion that everyone around Tatiana was crazy, selfish, and unworthy of her. The challenging times on the couch, those moments of intense self-analysis, were, well, annoying.

"There's a distinct pattern in your relationships with men, Tatiana," Dr. G began.

"Yeah, it's called 'terribly unsuccessful.'"

Dr. G pressed on. "Hear me out. This needs to be explored. You chose Kerr as a husband, a man who didn't work and had no marketable skills, a situation that put you in the position as man of the house, as it were, the sole breadwinner of the relationship unit. You currently employ Enrique, a young, single, and by all accounts vibrantly sexual man, as little more than an errand boy. And now you've brought Jack Thorpe into the fold as a caregiver to your children."

Tatiana sat quietly for a moment. "So what's your point?"

Dr. G gave a thin smile. "My point . . . is that all the men in your personal orbit are in positions that emasculate them. And I don't think that's a coincidence. I believe it goes back to your feelings about your father and the way that your mother reacted to his cruel departure."

Tatiana rolled her eyes. "Can't a rose just be a rose? Why does everything have to be about the inner child?"

"Because everything usually is." Dr. G leaned forward and offered Tatiana a comforting smile. "And this is a safe place to talk about these feelings."

She hesitated at first, but then she started to think about opening up, *really* opening up, and suddenly she was. "My mother lived for any sign that he might come back—a phone call, a letter, hearing about his whereabouts from a mutual friend. I hated her for missing him. I swore to myself that I'd never let a man break me like that." A tear cascaded down Tatiana's cheek. She killed it with her knuckle. "It was like she looked at me and thought of him and resented me for being a reminder. . . . Sometimes I think about the

things she used to say to me . . . the way she made me feel
. . . and I get this ferocious determination, you know . . . to
never, I mean *never* . . . make Ethan and Everson feel like
that. I will always be their biggest fan. Always.''

Dr. G reached out and took her hand. "That's a beautiful
thing to feel.''

Tatiana tried to hold them back, but more tears came.
Ultimately, she just gave in to the onslaught.

Dr. G grabbed a few tissues and passed them to her,
keeping one to dab her own tears.

"God, look at us,'' Tatiana said, laughing a little. "It's
just like it would be if we were sitting at home watching
Providence.''

Dr. G squeezed her hand tightly.

Tatiana wiped her eyes and took a deep breath, desperate
for some levity. "So . . . are you suggesting that I give
Enrique a raise?''

This time Dr. G actually laughed. "No, that's entirely up
to you.'' She allowed a few moments of silence to pass.

Suddenly Tatiana blurted, "You think I'm attracted to
Jack.''

"That sounds like an accusation.''

"Maybe it is.''

"Let me say this: I think Jack dating Constance Ann
would be very difficult for you to accept.''

Tatiana sneered. "It's still a slow news day. I know her.
I think it would be difficult for *Jack* to accept.''

Dr. G paused. "Let me put it this way: I think Jack dating
anyone might be difficult for you.''

"Why? Because I want him barefoot and pregnant?''

"This situation has brought some jealous feelings to the
surface.''

Tatiana shifted in her seat and jutted out her chin defiantly.
"Please.''

"That's not a value judgment, Tatiana. If properly used, jealousy can be a very positive emotion. It can deepen a relationship, spark passion, and strengthen the idea of commitment. The fact that *you* are jealous, that *Jack* is jealous of this imminent media romance with Greg Tapper, tells me one thing: There's an emotional richness between the two of you."

"Yeah, it's called fifty thousand dollars a year."

Dr. G soldiered on with a steely glint in her eyes. "That's a load of crap, and you know it."

Tatiana looked around. "Did Dr. Laura just walk in?"

"Melina was your nanny for over a year, and you barely mentioned her in our sessions. Jack has been on the job for a short time, and he's the center of your universe."

"He is *not* the center of my universe. Acting is. I'm about to start the biggest movie of my life."

"I realize that. But even with all that excitement, you're still more interested in what's going on at home. Jack represents everything that you wanted with Kerr but didn't have." Now Dr. G checked her watch. "We have to stop. Our time is up."

Driving home, Tatiana decided to call her mother. No more procrastination! How bad could it be? Well, pretty awful, but it had to be done. Besides, it sure beat reflecting on her session with Dr. G.

Actually, it made perfect sense to ring up Justine Bonner. The last fifty minutes had been heavy-duty psychological work, and a conversation with Justine was no Sunday brunch. Why not pack all emotional upheaval into two tidy hours?

Calling from the car would be a great move, too, as it opened up speedy escape options. "Mom, I'm going under a bridge. I hope we don't get cut—'' Or the more dramatic, ''I've just been shot in a road rage incident. Gotta go!''

Tatiana twisted down the volume on the radio, sucked in her gut, and dialed.

''Hello.'' Of course, her mother answered on the first ring, leaving Tatiana even less time to prepare. Bad sign number one.

''Hi, Mom.''

''Hello? Is anyone there?'' An old trick of Justine's— pretending not to hear on the phone (perfected during the pesky creditor years). Bad sign number two.

''Mom, it's Tatiana.'' She spoke louder. Might as well give her the benefit of the doubt.

''Who?''

Tatiana thought about hanging up, but then star sixty-nine would give her away. Damn the bastard who invented that! ''Come on, it hasn't been *that* long.''

''Tatiana? I can barely hear you.'' Totally unconvincing. Even Tori Valentine could do better.

''Can you hear me now?'' Same voice level, same solid connection.

''Yes, that's better.'' The little play over. On with the guilt! One thousand one . . . one thousand two . . . ''I thought you'd written off your family to live the big Hollywood life. To what do I owe this honor?''

''Mom, you can't just wait for me to call. You have to get one of those new phones. You know, the kind that dial out.''

''Why call when I can just rely on my neighbors to bring me tabloid clippings? Alec Baldwin and Kim Basinger were such a happy family. Nice work.''

''That's not—'' Tatiana braked fast to avoid hitting a Federal Express truck. Her body lurched forward, the cell phone practically crushing her lip. She cursed silently. ''Alec and Kim imploded a long time ago. Besides, the rumor is that I had a fling with *Stephen* Baldwin, which is a total lie. I've never even met the man. But the part about Kerr is true. We're divorcing.''

"I knew that wouldn't last. You were a fool to marry him.''

"Oh, Mom, I miss this kind of support. Why don't I call more often?''

Justine cleared her throat but said nothing.

"I have some exciting news. I got a movie—a big movie playing opposite Greg Tapper.''

"Let me guess. They want you to take your clothes off.''

"Well, there is some nudity required, but—''

"Another porno.''

"I've *never* done porno.''

"If you get naked and roll around on a bed with a guy while a camera's on, that's a porno in my book.''

"Did Pat Robertson just pick up?''

"Porno, porno, porno.''

"What I'm doing is an R-rated feature. If you want to see real porno, then check out your second husband's stash in the garage. I think you'll find the box marked 'Bonner home movies' a bit misleading, unless Ron Jeremy happens to be his brother.''

Justine stewed in a cauldron of silence.

Tatiana remembered that trip home for the holidays. She'd been trying to lift a box of Christmas ornaments off a shelf in the garage when stepfather Ned's XXX stash came crashing down. "Enough about Ned. How's Kristin?''

"Impossible. She just got suspended for skipping two periods to go eat lunch with a college boy.''

Tatiana giggled. "That doesn't make her Pinky Tuscadero. She's seventeen. I skipped school with a college boy when I was that age.''

"You skipped school with a college *professor!*"

"He was a graduate student!" Pause. "But he did teach Freshman English." Tatiana thought of Eddie Vaughn, smiling at the memory. Amazing kisser. They used to make out for hours. "Just go easy on her. I can't imagine being seventeen today. It's so much harder for girls now. I used to think that I was living in some tragic Shakespeare play, but, God, today must be like the first half hour of *Saving Private Ryan* over and over again."

Justine clucked. "Well, since you're so sympathetic, maybe Kristin should come live with *you* for a while."

Tatiana shook her head. "Okay, that was so not the goal of my commentary. I just wanted to give Kristin some good PR and make you see that this probably isn't a teenage version of *The Omen.*"

"You think that you can do better?"

"I didn't say—"

"What do you know about Kristin anyway? You see her once a year if that much."

Tatiana sat there in guilty silence. Justine had met and married Ned, a finance manager for a used (sorry, *previously owned*) car lot during Tatiana's senior year of high school. Kristin had arrived a year later when Tatiana was away at college. Then it was off to Europe to model, then to Los Angeles to act. The truth was, she really didn't know Kristin. They were half-sisters yet virtual strangers. Having both grown up with Justine as a mother, though, they were at least de facto war buddies.

"You've been a mother for five minutes, so I guess you're an expert now," Justine said.

"The twins are fine, Mom. You're so sweet to ask." In a perfect world, Dr. G would be mediating this call from a third line. Actually, in a perfect world, Tatiana would have put off calling another day and gone shopping at Fred Segal.

"I take it you still have them."

"They're not sweaters, Mom. I can't very well return them for a refund or store credit."

"Do you have to be such a smart-ass all the time?"

Suddenly, Tatiana remembered a strategic move that Dr. G had suggested once to diffuse hostile conversations. Of course, this one had careened way past hostile and entered a radioactive zone. But still, it was worth a try. "Okay, let's call a truce and try to have a nice chat." She took a deep breath. "Tell me something fun or interesting that's going on in your life right now."

"*Judge Judy*'s on."

Tatiana concentrated on sounding upbeat. "See, we're talking like normal people now. I've never watched that show. Is it one of your favorites?"

"They're introducing the first case. I have to go." *Click.*

"Mom?"

Nothing but dead air. Tatiana turned the radio back up and played bongos on the steering wheel to the beat of Santana's "Smooth." Suddenly, it hit her. Justine hadn't run off to watch *Judge Judy*. She'd gone straight into the garage to rifle through Ned's 'Bonner home movies' box.

Laughing, Tatiana floored it all the way home.

Chapter ELEVEN

Jack grinned as he dialed the forbidden number.

Tatiana had been busy with Tori and Mookie when he bent over to stealthily scoop up the eight scraps that had once been Constance Ann's business card. A little tape, a little puzzle play, and now he was back in action.

He kept his eyes on Ethan and Everson, who were playing with a Fisher Price parking garage. Occasionally, he had to step in as umpire when Everson decided she didn't want Ethan touching any of the little people, which took place about every five minutes.

Voice mail clicked on. *Bloody hell!* Right now he felt downright charming. What a waste. No matter, at the tone, he gave it a go. "Constance Ann, this is Jack ... Jack Thorpe. We met on Rodeo Drive. Listen, I'd love to get together to talk about your fitness needs ... or any other needs you might have that I could help address." He laughed a little. "That was a joke. A bad one, I know. I don't do my best work on these machines. Call me. I can be reached at Tatiana's."

Suddenly Everson wailed at the top of her lungs.

"Gotta run!" He hung up and started over to play boo-boo medic.

Everson had tumbled backward and bumped her head against the corner of a bookshelf. She was crying hard tears, her little face tomato red.

"What happened?" Jack asked, keeping his voice soft. He knew this much already: bumps and falls were made much worse by rushing over in heightened alarm. He rubbed her head, feeling a tiny knot. "Ouch," he whispered, then pulled her in for a quick hug.

Everson's tears subsided quickly. "Da . . . Da."

He froze. "It's okay, Ev, *Jack*'s here."

She shook her head in stubborn disagreement. "Da . . . Da."

He worked hard to divert her interest back to the parking garage. "Look at this pretty lady. I think she wants to drive the fire truck."

Thankfully, Everson took the bait.

Jack sighed deeply and wondered why he hadn't seen this coming or, even more important, worked out how it would make him feel.

"Dude!"

He turned to see Enrique strutting through, heading toward Tatiana's bedroom, his arms full of Saks Fifth Avenue bags.

"How are you, mate?"

"Excellent. I was shopping for baby clothes, and this hot sales girl went down on me in the dressing room."

Jack laughed, thought about how long it'd been since a woman had gone down on him, and then stopped laughing altogether.

"Tonight we hit the clubs," Enrique announced. "With my pick-up skills, your accent, and a little baby book, it'll be like a party at the Playboy Mansion."

Jack had to admit that it sounded like a plan, but he had two charges to see after. "I don't know Tatiana's shooting schedule."

"Hey," Enrique said, dropping the bags on the big chaise and splaying out his hands. "You're talking to her personal assistant. I know her shooting schedule as well as I know her menstrual cycle—like the back of my hand. She'll get her period next week, by the way. So it's a good thing they're shooting the big love scene this week."

Jack experienced a twinge of jealousy. He felt his temples pulse. "What do you know about this Greg Tapper?"

"His movies are cool, but I hear he's a jerk. So . . . are you game? Tatiana will be home by seven."

Jack shrugged, trying to put the thought of Tatiana and Greg out of his mind as he gestured to the sofa. "Sleeping there kind of cramps my style, mate."

"Not a problem. We'll go to a swanky club with nice bathrooms. The right stall can be the perfect seduction spot."

Ethan toddled over and hugged Enrique's leg.

Enrique rubbed the boy's mop of blond hair. "What's up, champ?"

Ethan grinned. "Ree . . . Ree."

Jack looked at Enrique.

The personal assistant shrugged. "Enrique's quite a mouthful, so they've come up with Ree Ree. As a matter of fact, that story sealed the deal with the girl at Saks."

Jack zeroed in on Everson. She was a smart little girl who knew that not every man in her life was a daddy. If she started to think of him as one, what would she do when it was time for him to move on? His heart ached at the thought.

* * *

Tatiana stared at the storyboards for the climactic (no pun intended, but okay, let's go with it) love scene. She viewed them right side up, upside down, sideways, and from several obtuse angles. Then she looked at Kip Quick, the wonder boy director, key emphasis on *boy*.

"Kip, honey," Tatiana started in her best big-sister voice, "I hate to break it to you, but except for the girls in Cirque du Soleil, women can't have sex in these positions. It's anatomically impossible."

One of the line producers cracked up.

Kip shot him a dirty look.

Tatiana fought against an involuntary laugh. "I'm not trying to be cute."

There was an uncompromising glint in Kip's eyes. "Greg has already approved this scene."

Greg Tapper, he being the star and the joke of an executive producer, and, if Kitty Bishop had her way, Tatiana's pretend boyfriend for the press, was still in his trailer, waiting to be called to the set mere seconds before the yelling of "Action!" Tatiana huffed. "Well, Greg is not being asked to contort his body like a Chinese acrobat."

"I realize that you're nervous, Tatiana, but I can't indulge a diva tantrum. There's a tight shooting schedule to keep. Don't worry. Greg's a professional, and I've asked for a closed set."

"Is that so?" She glanced around the sound stage. Yesterday's *open* set for the scenes when she didn't appear naked hadn't drawn half this crowd. Did the caterer's assistant really need to be here? And the transportation insurance guy, too? Not to mention the three lesbians in the corner.

Tatiana gestured to the storyboards. "People do not have sex like this, Kip." She paused. "Do you have sex like this?"

Kip's cheeks instantly flushed.

"This is the kind of fantasy that lives only in the minds of men. Greg's audience skews largely female. Remember when Elizabeth Berkley and Kyle MacLachlan did it in the pool in *Showgirls*? Adam Sandler would kill for the kind of laughs that generated. Is that what you want for this movie?"

"I've had sex," Kip said defensively.

Tatiana regarded him strangely. "I wasn't suggesting—"

"Six times!"

"OK, I think we're on different channels—"

"If you want to change the scene, go talk to Greg!" Kip flicked off his Creed cap, smoothed his hair back, slapped the hat back on, and stomped away.

Tatiana left the set for Greg's enormous trailer. By comparison, she had a cigar box to retreat to. Oh, to be a real star . . .

Shannon, his pushy assistant, answered the door. "What do you want? Greg's preparing for his scene."

"That's why I'm here. To talk with him about it."

"He can't be disturbed."

Someone needed to pass a note to this high-strung beast that said something along the lines of, "Sweetie, you are not an aide to the president."

From inside the trailer, Tatiana heard the sounds of a video game. She jockeyed for a better look.

Shannon moved to block her line of sight. *"He can't be disturbed."*

"Since when is playing Grand Theft Auto Three a method-acting exercise?"

Shannon blanched.

"*My* assistant, Enrique, plays it all the time. I think all fourteen-year-old boys do." And then Tatiana pushed her way inside to find Greg in his underwear (nice silk boxers) with his hand on a joystick (not his own, thank God).

Shannon trailed her in an absolute tizzy. "I tried to stop her, Greg!"

He ignored her and leered at Tatiana. "I like to keep love scenes fresh, but if you want to practice . . ."

"Oh, please," Tatiana scoffed. "Just keep your tube sock on." Most actors cut the back off a thong and adhered the remaining fabric with skin-tone-matching tape to cover their unmentionables. But Tatiana had it on good authority (September Moore, practically a walking wire service for Hollywood gossip) that Greg Tapper preferred the old-fashioned tube sock approach.

He moved his eyebrows up and down. "When I get excited, it's like watching a puppet show." A self-satisfied laugh. "Can Shannon get you anything?"

Tatiana turned around to find the assistant glowering just inches away. "Yeah, some space, for starters."

"That'll be all, Shannon," Greg said dismissively.

She skulked out of the trailer.

Tatiana lit into him without preamble. "Greg, the storyboards for this love scene are ridiculous. I couldn't get my body in those positions even if I were the Incredible Bendable Woman."

He smirked. "Does that mean you've tried?"

Tatiana gave him a playful glare. "No." She sighed. "Listen to me. This scene could be so hot. It could be Julie Christie-and-Donald Sutherland hot from *Don't Look Now* or Tom Cruise-and-Rebecca De Mornay hot from *Risky Business*."

Greg's eyes brightened. "Or orgy-scene-hot from *Eyes Wide Shut*."

"Thank God you're famous. Otherwise, you'd never get beyond a third date." Deep breath. "Did you ever see *The Lover* with Jane March and Tony Leung?"

He mulled this over. "I don't think so. But I did see *Angel Heart* with Mickey Rourke and Lisa Bonet."

"Yuck! All that voodoo and chicken blood!"

He grinned broadly. "Kind of wild, huh?"

"We don't want *icky*. We want *erotic*."

Suddenly, Greg rose up. "*You* need a couple of drinks." He started for the bar. Yes, his trailer had a bar. Tatiana's had a dirty sink that coughed out muddy water.

"It's not even ten o'clock."

"What's the old saying? 'It's eleven o'clock somewhere'?"

"I believe the saying goes, 'It's five o'clock somewhere.' "

"Who waits until five?"

"People who don't have the Betty Ford Clinic on speed dial."

He poured an expensive Scotch into two equally expensive rock glasses. "Just have one. It'll take the edge off."

What the hell. In an hour or so she would be naked (save for the strategically placed fabric triangle) in front of seventy-five people. A little sauce couldn't hurt. She downed a generous sip. "You can try to get me drunk all you want. I'm not doing a back-bend on your lap."

Greg put down his drink. "Then why don't you show me how you want this love scene to go?"

Tatiana simply stared. Years ago, in Eileen Beasley's acting class, before Greg Tapper morphed into a Hollywood dick-head, back when he was poor and brooding and so sexy you had to bite down on your knuckle to contain the hunger, she would have given up her first born for the chance to practice a love scene with him. Right now, though, it didn't seem like such a great offer. In fact, she could just about choke on the smarm in the trailer air.

"I've got a better idea," Tatiana said. "Let's call David Walsh."

Greg's eyes hardened a little. "Suits me." He grabbed his cell and punched in a number. "David, it's Greg. Listen, I'm here with Tatiana, and she's got some issues about the love scene we're shooting today. . . . My pleasure." Greg held out the phone, his body language talking easy win. "He wants to have a word."

Tatiana experienced a minor panic but put up a calm front. "Hi, David."

"How's my new star?"

She smiled. "Being difficult, I guess."

"Already? I wasn't expecting this until the second picture."

The kindness in his voice gave her confidence. "I've been telling Kip and Greg that the choreography of the love scene is ridiculous. I might need a stunt double to get into those positions." Tatiana laughed.

David didn't. "This should be a cakewalk for you, Tatiana. In the *Lady Cop* movies, you'd get naked to brush your teeth."

Tatiana felt the blow right in the center of her gut. "It's not—"

"Don't worry about how you're going to look. On screen you'll be flawless. Digital editing can do wonders."

"I'm not—"

"Everybody has a job to do," David said tightly. "Yours is to act. Just play the scene." Click.

At first Tatiana couldn't believe it, but the line was dead. Stunned, she passed the phone back to Greg.

"Changes mean delays; delays bust the budget, and David is very budget conscious. Don't let the nice-guy act fool you into thinking he's a pushover."

Tatiana nodded, staring vacantly into space. It was all so eerily familiar: the curt orders, the sexually exploitative atmosphere. The only difference: this was supposed to be the big time. So why did she feel so small?

"Last year I had a speaking part on *C.S.I.* I played a bitchy showgirl."

Jack nodded and raised his eyebrows to Kara, an aspiring actress just out of UCLA.

"The young guy—I think his name's George Eads, but they call him Nick on the show—asked me what I knew about another showgirl who got stabbed, and I got to say, 'I borrowed lipstick from her once. She had bad taste in colors.' "

"Somebody get this girl an Emmy!" Enrique shouted, his arm wrapped tight around Kara's friend Mandy, who worked the sales floor at an Armani boutique by day and sang in a rock band called Restraining Order by night.

Everybody laughed and kicked back on their caramel-apple martinis.

Kara leaned in seductively, giving Jack the full benefit of her cleavage. "You know, I think you're pretty hot," she whispered.

Jack pulled away a little, as if offended. "*Pretty* hot? Bollocks. I'm hot. Period."

Kara giggled and moistened her lips with a slow sweep of her tongue. "You'll get no argument from me."

The others didn't hear any of this. The fact that Enrique had his tongue down Mandy's throat might've had something to do with it.

"So . . . *Jack* . . . What is it that you do?" She gestured to Enrique. "He's an agent."

Jack's smile almost turned into a laugh.

"You must be a big-shot lawyer or some kind of talent manager."

"Actually, Kara, the work I do is even more important than that."

Her eyes widened. "You're a producer?"

Jack wavered a moment. "In a sense. I do stage small plays and puppet shows on occasion—for children."

"You know, I came close to getting signed as a pink Power Ranger once. They called me back three times, but they gave the part to some girl who'd taken karate lessons."

"Tough break."

"Whatever." Kara bopped along to the turgid rock music, feeling no pain.

Jack wondered what the hell he was doing here, at the Abbey, the third trendy hot spot of the night, trading come-ons with yet another aspiring actress. First Danielle (turned out to be chemical-friendly), then Cissy (ditched him for a sitcom stud), now Kara (appeared promising). Still, the only thing on his mind was Tatiana, who'd arrived home in a blue funk, barely exchanging a word. She'd even telegraphed a hurt look when he announced plans to go out.

Kara's hand found his thigh under the banquette.

A few inches higher, Jack felt the law of sexual gravity.

"You never told me what you do exactly," Kara said, "or even what kind of car you drive."

Jack shifted a glance to Enrique, still playing tonsil hockey with Mandy. Unlike the *agent* over there, he couldn't make up a life to score with a girl. Never had to before, wasn't about to start now. "Would you believe me if I told you that I was once a sports star in the U.K. and drove a BMW Z8?"

Kara practically writhed in ecstasy. "Of course I would."

"Notice I used the past tense. I injured my knee, lost every penny I ever earned, and now I drive a rented Taurus and take care of an actress's twins for a living. You've heard of the nanny? Well, get a load of the *manny*."

Kara laughed, sort of, unsure whether she was supposed to or not. "I can't tell if you're joking."

Jack reached out and put his hand over hers. "I'm bloody serious."

Surprisingly, Kara didn't recoil. "This is freaky. Nobody in this town tells the truth, especially in a club."

"I can't lie to you, Kara. You're too special."

She leaned back a bit, no biochemist but no fool either. "Now, that's a lie."

Jack held his thumb and index finger a few centimeters apart. "A tiny white one. I'm sure you're special to someone—your mum, maybe. I barely know you, so I can't really say. But it seemed appropriate for the moment."

Kara eyed Jack quizzically, as if still not sure what to make of him. She threw a glance at Enrique. "I don't get it. What's a babysitter doing hanging around with an agent?"

"First up, I'm not a babysitter. That would imply that I just sit watch while my employer goes out to dinner and a movie. A manny is much more substantial. I'm a critical part of the children's overall development. Secondly—and this is against all covenants of male bonding, but I simply can't be party to a fraud—Enrique is not an agent. He's a personal assistant."

"I thought he looked too young to be representing the likes of Harrison Ford and Tom Hanks." Kara shook her head. "Mandy will believe almost anything a guy tells her."

Jack glanced over at the randy couple, pressed deep against the banquette, canoodling like mad. He shrugged. "It appears to be a fairly victimless crime."

Kara inched closer, practically on his lap now. "Let's go back to your place." She touched a finger to his lower lip. "You can read me a bedtime story."

He groaned a little, lamenting his current living situation. "I don't have a place, exactly. I have a sofa that folds out."

Kara traced her finger down to his chest. "At least yours folds out."

"You, too?"

"I got in this horrible fight with my roommate and had to move out. I'm crashing at Mandy's place until I find something else."

"Enrique maintains that the loos here are quite lovely," Jack said.

Kara laughed. "What's a loo?"

Jack perked up his brows. "A bathroom."

"Talk about a cheap date!"

"I was once a very generous chap, before my personal Enron, of course. Under normal circumstances I would squire you off to a lavish room somewhere."

"At the Beverly Hills Hotel?"

"Indeed. A bungalow, no less."

"Hmm . . ." Kara murmured, appearing almost ready to say yes to the loo. "Who do you work for? Anybody famous?"

"Tatiana Fox."

"Never heard of her."

"You will soon enough. She's poised to become a major star."

"Is she beautiful?"

"Very."

Kara glanced down, then up again. "More beautiful than me?"

Jack definitely had to lie convincingly on this one. Even as pretty as Kara was, she didn't come close to measuring up to Tatiana's level of enchantment. "She falls a tenth of a point short."

Kara seemed to buy it, because she stood up, took his hand, and led him away from the banquette, through the crowded club, past Janet Jackson and her large, slightly rowdy entourage, and toward the coveted sanctuary of the bathrooms. She pulled him inside a vacant stall and secured the steel lock. "I've never done anything like this before."

Jack smiled, resting his hands on Kara's slender hips. "That's funny. You don't act like a novice." He made his move, their lips touched for a fraction of a second, and then Kara drew back all of a sudden.

"How old are the kids?"

"Mine?" Bad Freudian slip. "I mean, Tatiana's?"

Kara nodded.

This wasn't exactly his idea of pillow talk, but he could be flexible. "They're twins. Sixteen months, I believe."

A look of inscrutable sadness clouded her features. "Do they know that she's their mommy?"

Something about Kara cried out for comfort. Jack gently cradled her face with his hands. "What's this all about?"

Kara swallowed hard. "I have a baby. She's three years old." She started to sob quietly.

Jack pulled her into a warm embrace. "It's okay."

Kara gripped him tighter, crying harder. "She stays with . . . my . . . mom most of the time, and she . . . barely knows who I am."

Jack patted her back softly in an attempt to calm her. "Where does your mother live?"

Kara took in a gulp of air. "The Valley."

"As in the San Fernando Valley?"

Kara nodded. "I can't give Claudia what she needs and concentrate on my career, too." She pulled away to face him, her eyes puffy with tears. "My schedule's insane. I have to go to the gym, go to the tanning bed, and then it's noon, and I'm dragging myself to audition after audition. Plus, there's always some guy who wants to meet me out for a drink. I think it might lead to a part, so I almost always go."

Jack sighed, slightly defeated. If he'd gone with the lie and pretended to be a studio executive, they'd both be smoking a cigarette right now. Oh, well, it wouldn't be the first time that his tendency to morph into every woman's wise and protective older brother had cost him a night of passion. He gestured to the toilet seat and asked Kara to sit down.

She slumped onto the pot. "I'm sorry to be such a drag. We were supposed to come in here and fuck, weren't we?" With smeared mascara eyes, she peered up at him. "Do you still want to?" Before he could answer, Kara started to take off her top. "Come on, let's do it."

Gently, Jack pried her fingers away from the buttons. "It's a lovely offer, Kara, but I think that moment has passed." He began to massage her shoulders. "Let's talk about this madcap schedule of yours."

Kara relaxed and took a deep breath. "Okay."

"You're going to the gym every day?"

She returned a resolute nod.

"I could design a more efficient program that would only require you to go four days a week *and* keep you in better shape."

Slyly she gave Jack's body a closer inspection. "Really?"

"Really. As for this tanning bed business, you need to stop that altogether."

"But—"

"How old are you?"

Kara opened her mouth to answer.

"According to your birth certificate," Jack said severely. He knew all about Tatiana and her Hollywood age.

"Twenty-four."

"I was going to say twenty-six."

Kara gasped.

"No more tanning bed."

"But I look better with—"

"Tatiana's ex-husband is a Mary Kay rep. I'll give you his number. He can set you up with a self-tanning cream."

A puzzled expression skated across Kara's face.

"Now you have three mornings a week completely free to spend quality time with Claudia, and with no tanning bed on the schedule, you can pop in the other four days for an hour or so before going off to auditions."

Kara beamed. "You're absolutely right!"

"It's all about organization," Jack reasoned. "Twins make for a busy household, so I've had a crash course."

She spun around to face him. "What are their names?"

"Ethan and Everson." Jack smiled just thinking about them. "Gorgeous creatures. And smart, too."

Kara looked up at him with nothing less than adoration. "You sound like a proud father."

"Oh, no," Jack said quickly, dismissing the notion. "It's better not to get too attached." But as a wave of emptiness tugged at his heart, he knew that he already had.

"I've missed so many moments with my little girl," Kara whispered. "And for what? Some stupid audition for a part I never got? Some jerk with a Nikon who promised to get my pictures to a studio head?"

"Don't focus on the lost moments. Just grab the ones you still can."

Kara jumped up and kissed him on the cheek. "Sweet *and* wise. Where can I find a manny just like you?"

Jack tried to smile, but the sadness that had crept up on him was still there.

Chapter Twelve

DEAR ASSHOLE,
CONSTANCE ANN RETURNED YOUR CALL.
                    T.

Jack found the note taped to the bathroom mirror. He left it there and began to floss.

Suddenly the passive-aggressive author appeared in the doorway. It was after midnight. He couldn't tell whether her eyes were red from hard sleep or hard tears.

Tatiana pointed at the note as if it were litter on the White House lawn. "The last thing I needed to deal with tonight was a call from her." She delivered the blast in a loud whisper.

Jack found himself employing the same hiss when he fired back, "Give me some room to have a bit of a life here. The phone doesn't exactly ring off the hook for me."

"Constance Ann constitutes a life? Honey, you are in serious trouble."

Jack snatched the note off the mirror, crumpled it into a ball, and took a shot for the stainless steel wastepaper basket. He missed. How lame! He chalked it up to the late hour, the caramel-apple martinis (two, to be exact), and the fact that his intended night of wanton sex with Kara had become a Heloise-inspired pep talk on time management and better skin care. Jesus, his mates back home would never recognize him. "You were pissed off long before Constance Ann rang up. What's the real issue?"

Tatiana narrowed her eyes. "That's what I pay Dr. G for. I need people like you around to shoulder misplaced blame. Let's not confuse our roles."

Jack went back to flossing. "I didn't sign on for this. We need to talk about a raise."

Tatiana sat down on the toilet and crossed her legs. "Where did you go tonight? Not that I care. It's just that I can't sleep. My book is boring. Anne Heche can't make being crazy interesting. And there's nothing on television. I tried watching Sheena Easton sell her doll collection on QVC, but that just got depressing." She sighed. "So here I am."

Jack tossed a glance her way, then started on his upper teeth. "I don't know if I can compete with Ellen's ex-lover and the singer of 'Morning Train,' but Enrique and I went clubbing. Three spots, as a matter of fact."

"And my sex-crazed assistant went home with . . ."

"Mandy. Lovely girl. She works at Armani and has already promised him a discount."

"He better buy over the next three days." She gave Jack a once-over. "And you're here practicing good oral hygiene."

"It's not as pathetic as it sounds. In all truth, I had a very promising conquest hanging on every word, but things took a complicated turn. The upside: Kerr probably has a new client for his Mary Kay business.''

Tatiana laughed, shaking her head, her eyes glowing with genuine amusement. ''I thought you and Enrique were supposed to show up at these places with a baby book and have women chasing after you like the Beatles.''

Jack fumbled around for the toothpaste. ''We tried that. It doesn't work in L.A. Women here want to see pictures of your pool, not your baby.''

Tatiana watched him apply the Crest (with an improved whitening formula, mind you) to his brush. ''Don't squeeze from the middle.''

He looked at her. ''Perhaps you were too quick to dismiss the work of Anne Heche.'' Then he silently obliged and kneaded from the bottom of the tube.

Abruptly, she stood up. ''I'm sorry. I should leave you alone.'' She started to go.

Jack reached out to stop her, catching her fingers. ''Come on, I was kidding. Since when are you so sensitive?''

Tatiana glanced down at his hand but didn't let go of it. ''I had a really bad day on the set.''

''What happened?''

''I shouldn't bother you with this. You've got your own problems. I mean, your bum knee rules out any return to sports, you don't have any money, you—''

''*Please,*'' Jack cut in. ''Burden me. I need the distraction.'' He turned on the faucet and proceeded to brush his teeth.

''I thought I was moving up in the world, you know? Graduating from the dime-store budget movies I used to make. There's a lot more money on the table, the people involved are definitely a few notches up on the food chain, but at the end of the day, it's the same bullshit. I'm the chick. I get naked. Even if I have a *brilliant* idea, nobody wants to hear it. Not the star, not the director, not the producer—*nobody*.''

Jack spit into the sink. "That sucks." He went back to brushing.

"I'm *great* at movie sex."

Jack perked up his brows.

"Oh, it's true. I can't say the same for real-life sex. That's because I've spent the last several years faithful to a gay husband. But movie sex—I'm a pro. Did you see *Lady Cop Undercover III: Escort Service*?"

Jack nodded. He felt pretty certain that he'd watched all the tapes. Of course, all the plots ran together—she takes off her clothes; she chases a killer; she takes off her clothes again; she catches the killer. Well, they didn't exactly run together as much as they just repeated themselves over and over.

"I choreographed that scene with me and the detective in the hot tub. Pretty steamy, huh?"

"Uh . . . yeah." That's all Jack could manage with a mouthful of Crest.

"By comparison, the love scene I'm filming for *Sin by Sin* is a joke. But what do I know? I'm just a bimbo with nice tits."

Jack spit into the sink again, clearing his throat and smacking his lips, finished now. "Don't sell yourself short. You also have a great ass."

She smiled a little. "Don't forget fantastic legs. All those Pilates classes, you know."

He fixed an intense gaze on her. "And dazzling eyes."

Boldly she held his stare. "What about my mind?"

"Magnetic. I've always found insanity wildly attractive in a woman."

"If that's the case, you will *love* Constance Ann."

Jack took a seat on the edge of the garden tub. "What's the story with you two?"

"We knew each other a lifetime ago. The Beasley Acting Workshop. Greg Tapper was in our class. Every girl, and quite a few of the guys, wanted him. But he was already into second-tier starlets at that point. He couldn't be bothered with aspiring actresses." Tatiana laughed a little. "Anyway, our class staged a three-night production of *A Streetcar Named Desire* as a showcase. I understudied for the role of Blanche. Constance Ann did the same for the Stella part. Lucky for me, the girl playing Blanche got sick, and I went on in her place for two nights. Poor Constance Ann was shadowing a very healthy actress and never got the chance to go on. She's despised me ever since. Likewise. I mean, if someone hates you, you have to hate them back. It's only fair."

Jack shook his head. "That's ridiculous."

She gave him a dumb look. "We're women; we're actresses; we live in L.A. It's not ridiculous at all. Now I can look back on it and laugh. Back then, though, it was heart-wrenching drama, worse than the hospital scene in *Steel Magnolias*."

Jack propped his elbows on his knees, held his face in his hands, and just smiled at her. "Do you have any idea what goes on outside your little world?"

Tatiana sighed. "A lot of fried foods and bad clothing, I imagine."

It suddenly dawned on Jack that for the second time in one night, he was huddled up in a bathroom with a beautiful but troubled woman, yacking back and forth, extracting secrets as if he were subbing for Montel Williams. "I won't see Constance Ann if it's going to upset you."

"Upset *me?* It'll be far worse for you. Trust me on that."

"How can I? You're in no position to be objective here. You hate the woman."

"Only on a reciprocal basis. I don't hate her directly."

"So you return feelings in equal measure?"

"Generally, yes. It's the polite thing to do."

"Suppose I were to announce that I'm in love with you."

Tatiana bent forward to pat his knee. "Happens with every guy who works for me. Ask Enrique. He had a huge crush once. Now I can change in front of him and he barely notices. The gardener actually proposed. I had to fire him. He didn't speak good English and thought I'd said yes. Things got awkward. Nice ring, though. It was diamonique, but still. Who would know but God and a fine jeweler? Anyway, don't book the church. This will pass."

"I'm not in love with you, Tatiana," Jack said. "I was just—"

"See, gone already. Wow. Are you fickle or what?" She glanced around the bathroom. "We should paint in here. Something wild. A deep red, maybe."

He smiled at her. "It's late. Don't you need your sleep for tomorrow?"

"Ugh. Another day of being pawed and licked and thrown around the bed by Greg Tapper. They had to grease me down with Vaseline and baby powder so I wouldn't get a rash. Then I had to listen to Greg bitch because the creme rouge they used on my nipples tasted bad. He should try kissing himself after one of his Marlboro Light breaks. The asshole didn't even bother with Listerine."

"Won't it all be worth it? This movie is setting you up to be a big star."

Tatiana rolled her eyes and waved a finger in the air. "Whoop dee doo."

"I thought that's what you wanted."

"It is . . . It was . . . Oh, Christ, I don't know anymore."

She stood up and faced the mirror. "The light in here is so unforgiving." Peering closer, she murmured, "I wonder if I should get Botox injections." Then she sighed and dabbed on two thick globs of La Mer eye cream.

Jack couldn't stop staring at Tatiana. Her wild red hair was pulled back with a scrunchie, her brick-house body camouflaged by loose-fitting pajamas embroidered with little teddy bears, her scrubbed-clean face slathered with expensive goo; yet she was more beautiful to him right now than in any shower scene from one of her terrible movies. He smiled at the white smears under her eyes. "What exactly does that stuff do?"

Tatiana parked her body on the side of the tub right next to him. "It helps me get away with my Hollywood age."

"You don't look a day over . . ."

"Careful," she warned playfully, then threaded her fingers through his and clasped tight in a surprising gesture of intimacy. "I'm glad you're here, Jack. I don't worry about the twins when they're with you. It's a huge relief. You have no idea."

Jack brought their joined hands up to his mouth and kissed the top of hers. "What can I say? You get what you pay for."

She turned to him earnestly. "Promise me you won't leave until they're at least eighteen and on their way to college." Tatiana tried to laugh, as if to dismiss the comment, but there was a subtle emotional timbre to her voice, a sudden vulnerability, a certain truthful desperation, the kind that so often comes in the middle of the night.

Jack considered making a joke but thought better of it. This concerned Ethan and Everson. He had to be serious. Feeling uncomfortable, he released Tatiana's hand. "I can't promise that."

"I know you can't. Did you think I was serious?"

He glanced at his watch. "It's two o'clock in the morning, and you're not drunk. Of course you were serious."

Tatiana looked away. "Well . . . maybe just a little . . ."

"I'm not going to stay on your payroll for the next eighteen years. This was supposed to be a temporary solution for both of us."

"But they love you, Jack. You're like this magical force in their lives, and they need a strong—"

"They have a father, Tatiana."

She scoffed at the notion. "Ever since Kerr took up with Jaron, he's hardly been around. I got dumped and left with two kids, but I'm still taking care of him. I let him host that stupid Mary Kay party in my house. And having you here gives him an out on taking care of the twins. Kerr just blows in for a visit every now and then like some famous uncle. God, I've *got* to get married again. He can't be the only husband I'll ever have. He just can't."

Jack nudged his shoulder against hers. "We were talking about the twins."

"Oh, right." Tatiana looked at him, embarrassed. "Be patient. I'm so used to only focusing on me. That's why you're such a necessary part of this household. You call me on it. Kerr never would. He'd just complain that we weren't talking about him. And Melina—she was the nanny before you—all she did was fuss at me about doing nude scenes. One day I got so sick of it that I flashed her. I opened my blouse right there in the kitchen and said, 'Honey, these boobs pay your salary!' That shut her up. But then she quit a few weeks later." Tatiana leaned her head against Jack's shoulder and stared into space for a moment. "I want some ice cream. Split a pint of Haagen-Dazs with me."

"No, thanks."

"Then I'll eat the whole pint and get fat and people will think you're a terrible personal trainer."

"How many people even know that I train you? Correction. *Attempt* to train you. You're an impossible client."

"I bragged about you in the *In Style* article that comes out next week. You're going to be famous."

"Again? It's already happened to me once. I don't recommend it before the age of thirty."

"You're only twenty-six."

"I know. I'm still not ready."

"Do you miss it?"

"Being famous?"

"No, I mean home. England."

Jack took a deep breath. "I miss my parents, a few of my mates. But it's been good to come to a place where nothing reminds me of my former life. I don't feel as much like a broke has-been here. I'm just a guy with a job. And that's okay. Success for me used to be a call from my manager about a new endorsement deal. Now it's getting Ethan and Everson down for a nap at the same time. Who would've guessed that could feel so good?"

"How does hearing Everson call you 'Da Da' feel?"

Jack just looked at her, stunned.

"She was carrying around your T-shirt tonight and saying 'Da Da' over and over again. Ethan only has one *Da* down, but it won't be long. I'm sure you've heard it."

"Yeah," Jack said quietly. "Not Ethan. That's new. But I've heard Everson say it."

"Getting them to go down wasn't easy. They like you to put them to bed."

"Did you read them *Baby Bop's Purse*?"

"No, *Mrs. Spider's Tea Party*."

"They like that one after they get up from their afternoon nap. *Baby Bop's Purse* is part of the nighttime routine."

"See, I don't know this stuff."

"I wrote everything down and posted it on the fridge."

"Is that what that was? September called and went on and on about whether or not she should take a regular role on a TV series. I was bored out of my mind and doodled all over the paper. By the time I hung up, I couldn't read a single word." Tatiana sighed. "I still want some ice cream. Come on, be bad with me. Two big spoons, one pint of chocolate chocolate chip. It'll be fun."

Jack shook his head. "That could come back and kill me in the morning. I'm still a little bit drunk, you know."

"Really? Hmm ... Maybe I should take advantage of you." She gave him a campy seductive gaze and pulled her pajama top to the side to reveal a little shoulder.

Jack laughed. "It's been so long since I've had sex that, even with all that gunk on your face, your offer is tempting."

She playfully tugged on his sleeve. "How long has it been?"

He shook his head. "You first."

"Months and months. I won't say years, although the months have turned into at least one, going on two, maybe three." She paused. "How many months in a year? Don't tell me. I'm hoping eighteen."

Jack couldn't believe it. "Bollocks."

Tatiana gave him a strange look, then mocked his accent when she said, "I don't bloody know what that means."

"Then let me Americanize it for you. Bullshit."

Tatiana giggled. "It sounds more dignified when you say it. But I'm telling the truth. I was never unfaithful to Kerr. Not once. And I could've had a go with Matt Damon. He wanted me bad. It'd been a long time even when I was shooting *Lady Cop Undercover IV: Red Light District*. In fact, whenever I see the movie, I say to myself, 'That is some good acting. You look like you actually know what to do with a guy.' So that's my story. How long has it been for you?"

"A total drought since I've left the U.K."

"Oh, please, that's no time at all. Compared to me, you should still be smoking a cigarette. I've asked at least two different Santas at the Beverly Center to bring me a man on Christmas. Still nothing."

"You must've been naughty."

"Well, he did bring me Ethan. Maybe I wasn't clear enough. I never specified age."

"What if we were to fall into bed together?" Jack mused. "How would that work?" It was late; the martinis were still doing their work; this was a perfectly normal thing for a guy to ponder.

Tatiana shifted her weight and crossed her legs, turning toward him quite seriously, as if they were engaged in a serious political discussion—say, campaign finance reform. "Well, I suppose you should know that I like to be on top. It's a control issue, I know. Dr. G is helping me work on it, but for now, that's my position of choice. Just so you—"

"What happens *in* bed is easy to figure out," Jack cut in. "Besides, once a girl sees my body and experiences my mouth and hands, she doesn't care what position she's in, just as long as she's in one."

Tatiana was clearly amused by his arrogance. "A shag with you is that good, is it?" she asked, mocking his accent again.

"It bloody well is!"

She laughed and reached out to touch his knee. Her hand lingered there.

"It's what happens *out* of bed that's so devilish," Jack said. He stroked his chin thoughtfully. "Take the day after, for instance. Am I back in your bed or back on the couch? We would have to determine whether this was a one-night stand or an extended thing. Then there's the whole sexual harassment issue to consider. I am under your employ. If we do give it a whirl and it ends badly, as most romances do, what then? I live here. I suppose I'd go back to the sleeper sofa, but things could get frightfully awkward. Which one of us would start dating first? How would the other one deal? And don't even get me started on the effect this could have on Ethan and Everson. Children are incredibly intuitive. They would certainly pick up on the hostility, perhaps even internalize it and think that it's something they've done wrong.'' Jack sighed. ''And what about—''

In one rapid-fire movement Tatiana reached out for him, grabbing both shoulders.

Jack, caught off guard, lost his balance and fell backward into the tub, taking her along. He hit the bottom hard and knocked his head on one side.

Tatiana landed right on top of him, suffering not so much as a bump. ''There are a million reasons,'' she whispered, ''but let's not go over every single one.'' And then her mouth came down on his in a frenzy of crushing passion.

Jack resisted at first, his lips tight, unyielding, but soon he just relented, opened up to the moment, and kissed back with equal fervor. Tatiana's lips were full, soft, and pliant, her tongue a honey velvet dream, conjuring up a moan from within him that belied his practical reluctance. He cradled her face in his hands and slipped the scrunchie out of her hair.

She pulled away a few inches, smiling as her wild mane fanned out, cascading over both of them. ''Are you okay? Anything broken?''

''I don't think so. Although there's no feeling in my back. Is that normal?''

She returned a dirty grin. ''You seem to have feeling down here.'' Her hand moved south to stroke the erection tenting his pants.

Jack groaned at the touch, his arousal increasing by the millisecond.

"So, Jack," Tatiana breathed seductively, "are we gonna talk this thing to death, or are you gonna give me some action? Because celibacy is for shit."

Jack turned away, feigning hurt.

"What?" Tatiana demanded, a hint of alarm in her voice.

Jack looked at her. He made his lip quiver. "I'm not just a stud. I've got feelings, dreams. Don't you want to hear my dreams?"

She smiled, catching on, liking the game. "Not really. I'm sure they would bore me to sleep."

"Then I guess I'll have to get used to the fact that you're using me for my body." He started on the top button of her pajama top. "Apparently, I'm nothing more than a hard dick to you."

Tatiana winked. "I hope you're okay with that."

"Only because it's late. At least take me out to dinner next time." And then Jack ripped open the rest of her top. The remaining buttons went flying, clattering against the tub, skating this way and that.

The shock on Tatiana's face was total.

His hands slid down her silky back and deep into her pajama bottoms to squeeze her tiny, soft buttocks.

Tatiana tried to tear open his shirt but didn't possess the strength or elbow room to pull it off. Frustrated, she struggled, button by button, huffing and puffing to get to his skin. Once there, she feasted on him with little kisses and licks and bites that drove him absolutely crazy.

When his mouth found hers again, it was better the second time—hungrier, all of the anticipation, none of the uncertainty. They were actually going through with this. He couldn't believe the lusty spontaneity. And even if, right now, the smoke alarm started blaring and they were forced to stop, scoop up the twins, and run out of the house, he would have to give this almost-shag the following review: two thumbs up, mate!

Tatiana's clothes were slung somewhere outside the tub, and right now she was working fast on getting his pants off. Jack really wished she would at least undo the snap and pull the zipper before she . . .

"Damn!" he cried out.

Tatiana had put forth one terribly impatient, strength of Xena, Warrior Princess yank, getting the pants over and just past his cock. But *painfully*. His trousers were now lodged onto his lower hips, tight as a vise, making all movement impossible. But she didn't care. Now that the vital part of him was free, she mounted him like a mechanical bull, the impact of penetration as complete and necessary as an electrical plug into a wall.

"Oh, damn!" Jack cried out, only this time things were better, all hurt forgotten.

Tatiana clung to him, a soft mewl of desire escaping her.

The lower half of his body (well, most of it, anyway) felt paralyzed. He struggled with his pants, breaking the snap, working the zipper, pushing them down, getting just to his knees. But he could move now. He began to thrust, meeting her passion head-on, increasing his amperage with carefully calibrated movements. "You know what?" he asked, almost panting, really into it. "I've never done it in a dry bathtub before."

"I have," Tatiana answered, her breathing labored, too. "College. Freshman year. Kappa house. Thursday before spring break." She bent forward, chest against chest, face to face. "Worst sex of my life."

Jack's abdominals were sleeked with sweat. Suddenly,

his head fell back, reveling in the pleasure, feeling sensual pulses peck and sting as the feelings shot from brain to erogenous zone and back again. "And this?"

Gently Tatiana bit down on his lower lip. "A vast improvement."

"That's all?" His competitive fire was lit and blazing. "Because." He lifted her hips. "I always"—he thrusted with a galvanic burst of energy—"strive"—his pelvic bone glanced a blow against hers—"to be"—He rocked the boat. Faster, harder, faster—"the very best."

Suddenly, in perfect unison, they both tensed, arched their backs, and gasped in astonishment at the synchronized climax, rippling and straining to squeeze out every blissful moment of hard-won ecstasy. They careened all the way to heaven, hearts pounding, pulses racing, cheeks flushing.

"Yes . . . yes . . . yes!" Tatiana screamed. Loud. Too loud. Enough to wake the twins. And any light sleepers in nearby Malibu.

Jack collapsed. His lungs burned; his body tingled. He just lay there in a heap, listening for the sound of Ethan and Everson. But the house was silent. With a sigh of total contentment, he pushed a wayward tendril of hair from Tatiana's eyes. "That was so . . ."

"Insanely stupid!"

"Not my *first* thought."

"You don't understand," she began apologetically, smoothing a hand down his cheek. "First, let me say that I've never come like that before. It was amazing. I mean, the earth moved. I know that sounds so Carole King, but it did. I could live on that orgasm for months. Hell, I've lived on less for *years*."

"So what's insanely stupid? The fact that we didn't do this sooner?"

"No, silly. We didn't use protection!"

Jack's eyes widened. He mouthed the word, "Oops."

"*Oops* is right."

"I'm usually on top of those things."

"Not this time." She grinned. "I was on top."

"Indeed you were."

"Luckily, I'm on the pill. But that's not foolproof. I've got a sponge in the other bathroom, so I better go use it. You know, just to be safe."

"I feel very much like the cad in one of those after-school specials. Normally, I have a great deal of self-control and can at least settle down a moment to fetch a condom. Of course, you did practically attack me."

"I didn't hear you screaming for help."

An awkward silence settled in, boomeranging between them. How much of what just happened had been heat-of-the-moment passion? How much had been real affection?

"Well . . ." Tatiana said finally, leaning forward to kiss Jack's cheek. "Thanks." She looked around uneasily.

"*Thanks?* You make it sound like I just changed a flat tire for you."

She retrieved her pajama top and bottoms and dressed quickly, holding the buttonless shirt closed with her hands. "What do you want me to say?"

"That this wasn't a mistake."

"Can we please have this conversation tomorrow? I still feel a little tingle. It's too soon for the postgame wrap-up."

"Good use of sports metaphor." Jack managed a grin, but he could see where this was going, and disappointment came raining down on him.

"Anyway, if it makes you feel any better, nothing that great could ever be a mistake." The words made it past Tatiana's lips, but in her eyes, where it counted, there was the rest of the story. And it smacked of instant regret. She gave him a little baby wave and flitted out of the room as fast as she could.

Jack just lay there for a long time, wondering how big a mess they had made of things. It was an irony of the ages: how the greatest sex could lead to the worst consequences.

Chapter Thirteen

"I just slept with Jack."

"Nicholson? How was he?"

"Not him! Jack Thorpe."

"Never heard of him."

This is what Tatiana deserved for waking up September Moore at three o'clock in the morning. "Jack Thorpe is my nanny and personal trainer. You've met him. Remember?"

"I think I slept with him, too."

"No, that was Enrique, my personal assistant."

September yawned into the phone. "How do you expect me to keep up with all the people you're sleeping with? I can't keep up with all the people *I'm* sleeping with."

"Before I even attempt to bring clarity to this situation, tell me what you're on."

"I'm not *on* anything. I just took a Vicodin before I went to bed."

"What did you wash it down with?"

"A few glasses of wine."

Tatiana groaned, shutting her eyes for a moment.

"It's not my fault. I watched that Mariah Carey movie, *Glitter*, on DVD. It really should come with a warning label. As soon as it ended, I headed straight for the pain pills."

"Go back to sleep. I'll talk to you tomorrow."

"No, I'm fine."

"I'm in a crisis. I need you with a clear head." Tatiana stopped to think. This *was* September Moore. "Well, reasonably clear. On a single substance, at least."

"Relax, I've had one pill, a little wine. Stop acting like I'm Judy Garland. We can talk about this."

"Okay," Tatiana said, though still unsure.

"So you've slept with Jack. Big deal. You're not the first married woman to cheat."

"September, Kerr and I got divorced. It felt so good to sign the papers."

"No! When did this happen?"

"Go to sleep, September." She hung up, considered digging out Dr. G's emergency number, but then simply turned off the light and closed her eyes. Slowly, she drifted off.

"It's eight o'clock!" Someone was shaking her awake. "You had a seven o'clock call!" Enrique yelled.

Disoriented, she propped herself up on her elbows and tried to focus. The reality of the situation hit her. "Shit! Call the set! Tell them I had a car accident!"

"Once you get there, they'll see that you didn't," Enrique reasoned.

"Then go wreck the car before I leave!"

He tossed a look to her bedside table. "You have no business reading that Anne Heche book. Talk about the blind leading the blind."

"We have to think of something. Yesterday I was complaining. They'll think I'm pulling a Shannen Doherty."

"Go take a shower. I'll make the call." Enrique pulled back the comforter to force her out of bed.

One breast was exposed. Tatiana quickly pulled her top together.

He gave her a curious look. "Sorry. Forget how to button?"

She swung out of bed and started for the bathroom, head down, arms clutching the pajamas closed. "I need coffee."

"Jack just made a fresh pot. I'll fix you a cup."

Tatiana stopped. "Jack's up?"

"You're surprised? The twins usually start crying at five in the morning."

"Oh ... yeah ... of ... course ... um ... Call the production office. Let them know that I'm on my way."

Enrique waved her inside the bathroom, annoyed. "Go. Take a shower. And run the cold water for a few minutes while you're at it."

Tatiana quietly shut the door. "You idiot." It was all she could think of to say once she faced the mirror. Her eyes were puffy, marred by dark circles. She looked a wreck. That's what a horrible day on the set, a bathtub liaison, and a few hours of fitful sleep could do to you. She went through the motions under the steam jets, then rifled under the sink for a men's moisturizer by Nickel that she kept on hand for emergencies. One of the active ingredients was caffeine, and the product performed miracle work to mask a hard night.

She tumbled into a free T-shirt from a CD release party for Ben Estes, squeezed into some low-riding, hip-hugging gray sweatpants, and kept her hair at bay with a rhinestone-encrusted bandana by China Moon Rags.

Ethan and Everson rushed her the moment she stepped into the living room, demanding hugs and kisses, wanting to show her the Fisher Price people clutched in their tiny hands, then dashed away to finish watching the Teletubbies.

"Good morning," Jack said.

He was standing in the kitchen, wearing a white sleeveless undershirt and faded jeans. There was stubble on his face, a dirty diaper in his hand, and a spit-up stain on his shoulder. But Tatiana's heart still picked up speed because, even like this, the son of a bitch looked better than Richard Gere dolled up in that starched white uniform to come fetch Debra Winger from the factory in *An Officer and a Gentleman*.

"Good morning," Tatiana replied. It came out stiff, awkward, almost blind-date uncomfortable.

Enrique snatched her *Lady Cop Undercover* promotional mug from the microwave and handed it to her. "I'll take you to the studio. I drive faster and know more shortcuts."

Normally, she hated riding with Enrique. He fancied himself to be Vin Diesel from *The Fast and the Furious*, which scared her into an extra Xanax every time. But today her mind was in a million places. If she got behind the wheel, there was no telling where she might end up. Maybe Iowa. So she relented with a groggy nod, accepted the hot drink, and asked, "What did the production office say?"

"To get there right away. They're waiting for you."

Tatiana glanced at Jack, but no words came to mind. She had no idea what to say.

He gave her a half smile and retreated to the living room to stop Ethan from climbing on the coffee table.

She watched him, secretly envying the time he spent with the twins, all the little moments he got to witness, the way they sought him out for every need, big or small.

Enrique slapped her on the butt. "Let's hit the road, movie star."

Tatiana followed him out, feeling more in the world now after a few sips of coffee. She savored it like a precious nectar. Jack's was better than Starbucks. What a great wife he would make. *Freeze*. Okay, thank God that was an internal thought. She was officially insane. That's exactly what Kerr had been. Not a *great* wife, of course. Merely so-so. With a headache every night.

"You had sex with Jack." Enrique said this with the kind of casual certainty one might employ to announce, "You have pepper in your teeth."

She tumbled into his Jeep without a word.

Enrique hopped inside, turned the ignition over, and peeled away like a stunt driver.

"Jesus Christ! Slow down!" Tatiana's stomach did a somersault, and coffee splashed onto her sweatpants. Damn! "Who taught you how to drive—Halle Berry?"

Enrique had this smirk on his face that was irritating the hell out of her.

She gave in after holding tough for all of thirty seconds. "How did you know?"

"Listen, I might not be the most educated guy around. For instance, I have no idea what a stem cell is, and don't ask me to name our vice president."

"Dick Cheney," Tatiana grumbled, still pissed about the spilled coffee.

"Really? I can't picture that guy working side by side with Bill Clinton."

"I'll never lose you to a career in politics; that's for sure."

"Ha, ha. Funny. My point is this: I don't know a lot of stuff, but when two people are doing it . . ." Enrique gestured to himself with his thumb. "The kid knows."

"So you're the Rain Man of sex. Congratulations. Tell me, did Britney and Justin do the deed, or is she still a virgin?"

Enrique's eyes fell upon a comely runner while the Jeep took on a dangerous curve.

"Hey!" Tatiana screamed. "Watch the road!"

"Take it easy." He glanced at her mug, only about a quarter of the way full, the rest stained on her lap. "Do you want me to stop for a latte? I can't handle you without the right amount of coffee in your system. You're like Jack Nicholson in the last twenty minutes of *The Shining*."

"Just drive. I want to get there before Greg smokes too many cigarettes. Yesterday I felt like I was simulating sex with the Marlboro Man. You know, I should suck on a clove of garlic just to get him back."

Enrique sped onward, gunning through yellow lights blinking onto red. "Okay, out with it. What happened with you and Jack? I know what *didn't* happen with Jack and Kara."

"Who's Kara?"

"Mandy's roommate. She woke us up at six o'clock to gush over how sweet Jack was, how he wasn't after the one thing she thought all guys wanted. I was polite and listened for a few minutes. Then I could've sworn she gave me the eye, so I suggested a three-way. Suddenly, they got all Victorian era on me and chucked my ass out. That's how I made it to your house so early this morning."

"Lucky me."

"Lucky you is right." He winked. "Twice, I guess. Once last night, once this morning. So . . . on a scale from one to ten . . ."

Tatiana stared straight ahead. "I'm not talking to you about this. Your job is to get me in with Dr. G as soon as possible."

They drove in silence for a few minutes, listening to Jennifer Lopez and Usher attack the airwaves with their latest hits.

Finally, out of the blue, Tatiana said, "Nine point five." She turned to Enrique and smiled.

He high-fived her and zoomed through another red light.

This time Tatiana didn't mind. Maybe she should try stealing a page from Enrique's notebook, stop obsessing over every event, quit thinking things through from A to Z, just start living a little. She breathed in the California morning air, relished the whipping wind. Suddenly, she began to relax. So what if she banged the nanny in the bathtub? They were both adults. Neither party was married or involved. How complicated could it become?

Tatiana was heading straight for makeup when a production assistant stopped her.

"David and Kip want to see you in Greg's trailer right away."

She searched his face for the rest of the story. P.A.s were always full of gossip. "What's going on?"

He shrugged, offering nothing. But he knew something. She could tell. Prick. No wrap-party gift for him.

Her purse began to ring, startling her. She fished out the cellular and recognized Kitty Bishop's number on the screen. Today Tatiana could give a shit about public image, and burning up the line was the publicist who always spoke from the depths of her media-seeking heart. She tried to sound upbeat. "Hi, Kitty."

"You are a fucking Lana Turner for the fucking new millennium!"

Tatiana stopped in her tracks. This made no sense. Did she have five marriages under her belt? Had a gangster boyfriend been stabbed to death in her bedroom? Where was the L. T. connection?

"I'm looking at the new *In Style*," Kitty went on. "Everyone who sees this is going to want to live in your house!"

"Well, maybe they can. That's not my house, remember? And I believe it's still on the market." Tatiana thought back to how ridiculous she'd felt on that photo shoot, posing in a foyer, lounging on furniture, relaxing in a kitchen, and dipping in a pool—none of which were hers. The only authentic things in that spread were her children and her breasts. It was the *House Beautiful* version of Milli Vanilli. But Kitty had insisted, and when Kitty insisted . . .

"I'm already getting calls. People *love* a new sex symbol. When I got in this morning, there was a message from Howard Stern's people."

Tatiana clutched her stomach, feeling a stab of nausea. "He's a pig. All he wants women to do is take off their clothes and talk about sex."

"Exactly!" Kitty responded exuberantly. "Is Thursday good for you?"

Tatiana had her finger on the END button and was ready to fire.

"I want to start building heat now so that by the time *Sin by Sin* opens, you'll already have a name out there. I've got a call in to Greg Tapper's publicist, too. We should coordinate a sighting to start the columnists panting. I'm thinking a casual dinner at Spago. That worked wonders for Tom and Penelope."

Tatiana tried to pinpoint the origin of her sudden distaste for the big celebrity machine. A few months ago she would've done anything for some PR coverage, even gone on *Fear Factor* to eat worms or be immersed into a giant bucket of human placenta. Now the former just struck her as ridiculous and the latter as, well, completely repulsive and not even worth a *Vanity Fair* cover.

"I'm also thinking about another *Playboy* pictorial," Kitty continued. Obviously, she'd had her Wheaties Energy Crunch this morning. "Sharon Stone did the same when *Total Recall* opened. It was a good profile booster, something to talk about. Otherwise she would've been trampled in the stampede for anything Arnold, and all but forgotten. We run the risk of being overshadowed by Greg if we don't have that extra something to push. I told the Playboy people that it's a cover deal or no deal. How does a million sound?"

Tatiana, navigating her way toward Greg's trailer, almost lost her balance. *"One million dollars?"*

"That's where I'm starting. The bastard didn't laugh in my face, so I know it's gettable."

Tatiana's head swam in the possibilities. She could pay off the house, secure Ethan and Everson's education fund, buy a minivan. Oh, God! What was happening? She was thinking like a frugal housewife! That personal finance guru Dave Ramsey had obviously brainwashed her. There must be subliminal messages in his weekday radio broadcast. A seven-figure payday? It was beyond her wildest dreams. Still, the prospect of taking it off again for a skin mag, even a classy one like *Playboy*, filled her with trepidation. "I'll have to think about this."

"Think about what?" Kitty asked.

"Posing. For *Playboy*."

"What's to think about? You did it for a hundred grand. Why wouldn't you do it for a million?"

"Things have changed, Kitty," Tatiana said tersely. "I've tried to have this conversation with you before. I'm a mother now. I can't be rolling around in the desert naked or discussing blow jobs with Howard Stern. There's a certain dignity I want to uphold."

Kitty fumed silently for one long second before she launched her tirade. "*Dignity?* You want to talk to me about dignity? Joan Collins was in her forties and showed up in soft-porn shit like *The Stud* and *The Bitch* just to pay the bills. Mamie Van Doren sells her own nipple prints on the Web. You're in your *thirties*, sweetheart. This is your chance at the big time, and you got to the party late. The last round is being served. Be smart, take everything you can get, and run to the bank. There are twenty thousand actresses in this town—all of them younger, lots of them prettier—and not one would think twice about getting naked for a passport photo. If you don't take this shot, somebody else will. Now I'm going to start lining up these opportunities, so get your fucking act together." *Click.*

Tatiana looked up, stunned to find herself standing in front of Greg's trailer. The walk over was just a blur. *A million dollars.* It could solve a lot of problems. It could create a lot of new ones. There was so much to sort out. She punched in Enrique's number.

"I hope you've had your coffee," he said right away.

"Have you called Dr. G?"

"Not yet."

"I need to see her. Today. Tell her it's an emergency."

"Worse than your mother coming for a visit?"

Tatiana thought about it. "A close second."

"Shit. This is serious. I'm all over it." He signed off.

Tatiana took a deep breath and raised her knuckles to the trailer door.

It flung open before she made contact. David Walsh stood on the other side. He didn't smile at her. "Glad you could join us."

As she stepped inside, her stomach immediately began to knot. The vibe was ominous. It just hung in the air, thick and humid. Something big was going down. Greg Tapper and Kip Quick were seated on couches. So was Cleo Mars. Tatiana looked twice, shocked to find her new agent here, slumped against an enormous pillow, more pregnant than ever.

David and Cleo shared a secret look.

"Is this some kind of intervention?" Tatiana asked lightly. "Because the prescriptions are all legitimate, and I only have wine at night."

Everybody laughed a little. Her joke brought some levity to the scene, but the tension remained.

Tatiana zeroed in on Cleo. "What's going on here?"

David spoke up. "We have a situation, Tatiana." He gestured to the seat next to Cleo. "Please, sit."

She sank down with a sick feeling. They were replacing her. Someone more bankable became available. Thandie Newton. Jennifer Connelly. Elizabeth Hurley.

"The studio needs a rush on this picture," David went on. "A big budget science fiction film set for Christmas release tested poorly with preview audiences. They're going back for reshoots to get it right."

Tatiana stared back at him. What did Kevin Costner's latest disaster have to do with their movie?

David cleared his throat. "That leaves a hole in Univision's holiday schedule. They've asked us to put a rush on *Sin by Sin* to fill the gap. Greg always delivers huge box office numbers, and Univision needs a hit to close out the year."

Tatiana tried to do the math. Always a difficult thing. She gave up fast. All this was very interesting. *Entertainment Weekly* would give it the Watergate treatment. But what the hell did it have to do with her? Why had she been summoned here?

Greg spoke up next. "The shooting schedule's going to

be intense. Kip will be working around the clock to edit as we go along. If you're not up to it, we need to know now.''

Tatiana had no idea what to think. The B-movie world of the Dobsons was anything but ambiguous. A firing went something like, ''Get the hell off this set and never come back, you lousy piece of shit.'' Basically, an up-front approach. This was all double-talk and furtive glances. Finally, she turned to Cleo and simply asked, ''Are they asking me to quit?''

David provided the answer. ''We're asking if you want to stay.''

Tatiana swallowed hard.

Kip finally spoke up. ''Yesterday you made no secret about your problems with the love scene. Half the footage will have to be scrapped. There's no passion. It looks like you're having a root canal.''

Tatiana remained impassive. The truth was, compared to what she'd gone through with Greg Tapper in that bed while eighty-plus people watched, a root canal didn't sound so bad.

''We have another actress on standby,'' Greg said. ''You can bow out now, if you wish. No hard feelings. We'll issue an innocuous statement about creative differences.''

''Translation: I'm a bitch who's difficult to work with,'' Tatiana said hotly.

Smugly Greg leaned back in his seat. ''If the shoe fits . . .''

Tatiana thought of Sean Young, the talented actress who scored with Kevin in the back of the limousine in *No Way Out*. Word had spread about her. Now she was lucky to land a USA Network movie every few years. There were plenty of examples to learn from. This could ruin her career. The *Playboy* deal would disappear. Not that she was sure she wanted it, but still, a nice offer to have on the table. And it

wasn't as if another *Lady Cop Undercover* movie was waiting in the wings as a back-up plan.

David shook his head. "No one is suggesting that you . . ."

Tatiana tuned him out. There were four other people in
this room—a seasoned producer, a major movie star, a hot
young director, a powerful agent (*her* agent!)—and not one
of them was on her side. She felt alienated, picked on, alone,
and scared. She wanted Jack's coffee! She wanted his strong
arms wrapped around her! She wanted kisses from Ethan
and Everson!

Cleo was talking now. Something about money. Tatiana
decided that she better listen up.

"I've negotiated with David to pay you twenty-five percent of the contract. That more than compensates you for
your preparation and one day of shooting."

Tears welled up in Tatiana's eyes. It was a forgone conclu-
sion. Everyone expected her—hell, they were practically
pushing her—to walk away. The talk of money sobered her
up a bit. Face it, she needed the dough, and one quarter of
the contract didn't cut it. There was a mortgage to consider,
Jack's salary, the twins' seemingly endless expenses, and
Enrique—an indulgence, yes, but one she couldn't live without. "I don't understand. One bad day, and all of you want
me to get lost. So I offered a few suggestions. I just—"

"Tatiana," David interrupted, "I saw yesterday's dailies.
We can salvage some of the footage, but most of it's crap. No
sexual energy. No chemistry. You were somewhere else."

*Yeah, a place called Tobacco Road. You try kissing Greg
after one of his cigarette breaks.* She wanted to say it, but
instead she just listened.

"This morning you held up shooting for hours and had
your assistant call with some bullshit story about you having
an epileptic attack."

"What?" Firing Enrique would be letting him off easy. She would just have to murder him. Slowly.

"To our knowledge, you don't have epilepsy," David said severely. "At least, you didn't disclose it in your medical history to the insurance company."

"Forgive my assistant," Tatiana stated emphatically. "He's an idiot. I overslept today. That's why I missed my call. It's that simple."

"Allow me to make it simple for you, too," David said, obviously the designated bad cop here, although there didn't appear to be a good cop among them. "As of this moment, production of *Sin by Sin* is in the fast lane. It can't afford a bad shooting day or a late call because the leading lady didn't hear her alarm clock. Our window is tight. But it's manageable. And everyone needs to be on the same page to pull it off." He leaned forward and smiled, giving off a little bit of that sweet-David magic she'd fallen for in Cannes. "Don't take this confrontation the wrong way. We all want Tatiana Fox in this picture. But it's do or die. Where's that tigress who ate me alive in the bar at Hotel du Cap? Where's that great actress who marched into a reading and became Nikki Alexander?"

Oh, God, how she wanted to tell them all to go to hell. But it wasn't just about her anymore. There were people at home to consider, and for now, she would just have to play ball. Tatiana stood up. "She's on her way to makeup."

David rose to embrace her. "That's my girl!"

Tatiana spun to face Greg. "The intimate scenes would go much easier on me if you would introduce yourself to something called an Altoid after smoking those cancer sticks."

Greg smirked. "I'll see what I can do."

"Thanks. I'd appreciate that very much." Tatiana started

for the door, then turned around to face all of them. "Okay, gang, let's wrap this fucker." And she was gone.

Cleo waddled outside to catch up with her. "Tatiana! Wait!"

She halted, pivoting angrily. "Just who do you represent, Cleo? Me? Or them?"

Cleo's breathing was labored. She brought both hands around to support the small of her back.

Tatiana had no intention of falling for the poor-pregnant-woman routine. Cleo Mars was nobody's charity case. With child or without, she was sneaky, manipulative, and out for number one. "I can't believe you gave me that shit about girls needing to stick together!"

"Tatiana, it's more complicated than that. I do a lot of business with David, and Greg is an A-list star. You're an unproven commodity. If this movie falls apart because of your frailties, it would compromise my position with them. And you're simply not worth that risk. Not yet, anyway."

Tatiana calmed down a little. At the end of the day, all anyone cared about was the bottom line, and Cleo's argument did make sense. "You could've at least warned me!"

"David specifically asked me not to. He and Greg wanted to hear your gut reaction, and frankly, I did too. The stakes are high. Everybody wants to make a great picture."

Tatiana's head nodded to the beat of Cleo's pep talk, but her heart didn't buy into the propaganda. Like a fool, she'd thought *Sin by Sin* would take her out of the *Lady Cop Undercover* ghetto and into some fancy neighborhood. Not much had changed, though. Sure, the budget was bigger, the people more respectable, the catering at least edible. But it was the same dirty business, and she was the same leading lady, the kind that could be replaced as fast as you can blink.

Cleo stood there looking at her, *really* looking at her, as if trying to see into her soul. "I thought you were hungry for this."

"I thought so, too, Cleo. Only I'm not so sure anymore."

"Then why go through with it?"

Tatiana blinked back a tear. "I may not be hungry, but I still have to eat."

Chapter Fourteen

"Constance Ann, did you know that Chris has a tooth-ache?"

"Yes, Hallie, and I think I know why," Constance Ann replied, tilting her head to one side in a pantomime of deep thought. "Could it be that he didn't listen to Pappy the Panda's advice about eating healthy snacks?"

"My tooth really hurts," Chris whined, rubbing his right cheek.

"Goddamn it!" Constance Ann screamed.

"Cut!" Will Hayes shouted.

The technical crew ceased taping.

Constance Ann stood up and pointed an accusing finger at Chris. "At the top of this scene he was holding his left jowl. Now it's his right one. Hey, I've got an idea. Figure out where the rotten tooth is and stick with it!" She threw up her hands in disgust. "Is this a television show or a first-grade play?"

Chris started to cry and ran off the set.

Will threw down his headphones. "That's just great, Constance Ann. The kid's already on antianxiety medication. What's next—shock treatment?"

"If it turns the little shit into an actor, I'm all for it." She ripped off her microphone and started for her dressing room.

Will Hayes fell into step behind her. "Maybe it's you who needs to be on medication."

Constance Ann spun fast, her eyes blazing with fury.

Will displayed no signs of backing down. "And I mean medication from the pharmacy, not the liquor store."

Constance Ann loved a good fight, the bloodier the better. Most people were pussies who went down after just a few blows. She smiled venomously. "All this time I thought that was a vagina between your legs, Will. Maybe you do have balls."

"Just one, if you must know. Testicular cancer in nineteen ninety-nine."

"Is that so? Well, too bad. Because one won't get the job done. At least not with me."

Will held his own. "This has to stop. The way you abuse these poor kids is sick. If one of these parents went to the press, it'd be over, Constance Ann. *Over*. Pee Wee Herman jacking off in that porno house would seem like an overdue library book."

She jabbed a finger into his bony chest. "Don't try to paint me as some wicked stepmother, you son of a bitch. I'm tough on these kids because I care. That's right. *I care.* I push them to be better, because if I don't, they'll leave this show only to end up like Corey Feldman and Adam Rich and Todd Bridges and every other bad child actor turned drug addict. And it won't take long, Mr. One-nut.

Treat 'em like babies, and they'll go from hit show to loser alley in the time it takes to smoke a bong. Besides, a little tough love never hurt a kid. It builds character.''

Will shook his head. "Their parents might not see things your way.''

She laughed in his face and walked toward her dressing room.

Will followed close behind.

"You want to talk to me about their parents?'' Constance Ann posed incredulously, as she floated inside her sanctuary and began flipping through a stack of mail. "The parents of these little brats aren't raising children. They're raising meal tickets. Believe me, they'd put them through slow torture if it could guarantee the next Mary-Kate-and-Ashley empire. Wake up, Will! Child actors don't have parents. They have pimps. If Michael Jackson writes enough zeros on the check, it's off to the ranch with the llamas and that goddamn monkey. What does he call it? Buckles?''

"Bubbles," Will corrected. "And he's a chimpanzee.''

Constance Ann kicked back on the sofa. "Oh, excuse me.'' She turned her attention back to the mail. Any hand-addressed envelope in childlike scrawl was a fan letter. Those got tossed. Next came an unusually thick issue of *In Style*. Julia Roberts graced the cover—again. That toothy bitch wouldn't go away. A small headline caught her eye.

A TWENTY-FIRST CENTURY FOX AND HER TWINS

Almost instantly, Constance Ann developed a bad feeling in the pit of her stomach. She whipped through ad after ad after ad until she reached the table of contents. Speed-reading down the page, her grossest fear became shattered reality.

BABY, BABY

Tatiana Fox is juggling twins, a dream home in Malibu, and a steamy role opposite Greg Tapper in the upcoming Sin by Sin.

The rage temporarily blinded her. All she could see was red. Once it passed, she pressed on, adrenalized by fury. It took a long time to find the offensive article. She lost it more than once, tearing pages, hissing the most vile expletives she could think of.

Will stood there, taking in the sideshow. "What is wrong with you?"

She stopped searching and glared at him. "I suggest you get out of here before you lose your other ball." Her voice was low and toneless.

Will Hayes retreated without a word.

Constance Ann slammed the door behind him. *Smart move, asshole. You didn't go to Yale for nothing.* By the time she found the loathsome piece, the magazine was in tatters. Ugh! The showcase was worse than she ever imagined:

Tatiana posing in the entryway like some Hollywood wife with a Candy Spelling complex.

Tatiana gracefully perched on the couch reading *Secrets of the Baby Whisperer for Toddlers.*

Tatiana blowing bubbles to the camera while bathing in her sunken copper tub.

Tatiana dipping two giggling blond twins into her turquoise dream infinity pool.

So sweet. So perfect. Such bullshit.

Constance Ann chased down a stiff drink to prepare herself for the text. She scanned it fast, contempt rising with each passing syllable, outrage building upon outrage as she approached the end and took stock not of what was covered, but, more important, what *wasn't*.

Not a single reference to those exploitative *Lady Cop Undercover* movies that litter Cinemax late at night. No mention of the fag husband who dumped her and the kids for another man. According to *In Style*, Tatiana's life was filled with champagne, caviar, and engraved baby rattles from Tiffany's.

Suddenly, Constance Ann found herself smiling at the glossy layout. Yes, the snow job disgusted her. But it was precisely the sort of family-values pap she needed to set the wheels of Tatiana's destruction into motion. For weeks, the concept had roamed around in Constance Ann's mind like a wolf in the woods. First had come the germ of an idea, then the loose strategy, now the intricately layered plan of attack. And it all hinged upon one person.

Mrs. Herman McKenzie ate dinner every night at a small cafeteria near her Pacific Palisades home. She arrived at the same time (five o'clock), sat in the same booth (third one on the right), and selected the same items (four vegetables, cornbread, sweet tea, and a slice of lemon icebox pie).

"Routine is good," Mrs. Herman McKenzie was telling Constance Ann. "If the youth of today had more routine in their lives, we wouldn't have all these unwed teenage mothers to worry about."

Constance Ann listened patiently. She wanted to point out that teenagers *do* have a routine. They *routinely* have sex. But she merely smiled and nodded in placid agreement.

"Now I really must commend you for the work that you do, Constance Ann. You have a fine program. A very fine program. I know the songs are intended for children, but I enjoy singing along, too." Mrs. Herman McKenzie covered

her mouth with her napkin to hide a giggle. "And I just
adore Pappy the Panda." She regained her composure and
lengthened her spine, then cleared her throat. "That's
enough silliness for one day. My apologies. Now, what can
I do for you?"

Constance Ann pushed her barely touched plate out of
the way. How could this militant tight-ass eat this slop every
night? Men in the pokey got better food. "Before I get into
it, Mrs. McKenzie—"

"Please. Call me Eunice."

"Okay . . . Eunice it is." She put on her best Constance
Ann smile. "First, I just have to say how much it means to
me that you find my work worthy." The words were tough
to push past her lips, but the proper foundation had to be
laid. "I have no children of my own, you see. And I believe
the reason for that is this: The children of the world are my
children." Constance Ann put hand over heart. "I couldn't
just love my own. I have to love them all."

Eunice reached out to pat Constance Ann's hand. "You're
one of God's special angels. You have a gift."

*Yeah, a gift to actually say this crap without going into
insulin shock.* "Please, Eunice, you're embarrassing me. I'm
not special. I just have an extraordinary capacity to love.
And why not focus all of it on the children, the precious,
precious children? As I'm sure you well know, they are the
future."

Eunice shut her eyes and bobbed her head passionately,
as if Constance Ann had just spoken the words of a faith
healer. "Thank you for being a heavenly blessing to our
children."

Constance Ann reached out to squeeze Eunice's hand.
"You're welcome. I just wish our culture would think of
the children and realize that some people are not appropriate
role models."

214 _Kylie Adams_

The eyes of Eunice became slits of steel, and she gave a severe nod. "I couldn't agree more, Constance Ann. Take this Britney Spears. Why, she prances around like a lady of the evening! It's because of my determination—and a lot of hard work from my faithful listeners—that the toy stores in this area no longer carry her dolls and accessories."

"I know," Constance Ann said. "Your campaigns against cultural pollution have always been so effective."

Eunice beamed. "I'm proud to say that we just shut down another Victoria's Secret."

"Amazing," Constance Ann gushed. "And so necessary. I mean, what's next after these lingerie shops—legal brothels in our shopping centers?"

Eunice became visibly excited. "This is unbelievably refreshing. You get it, Constance Ann. So few people do." She glanced around and leaned in to whisper conspiratorially. "And just between us, I'm not finished with that Britney Spears. Do you realize what that blond devil is up to now? She's singing a song called 'I'm A Slave 4 U.' "

Constance Ann feigned what she felt was appropriate outrage. "No!"

"Yes!" Eunice hissed, still stealing glances to make sure none of the surrounding diners could hear them. "Think of all the God-fearing, church-going African Americans out there whose ancestors were manacled in ships and dumped ashore without consultation. They have to listen to this hateful music. It's disgraceful!"

Constance Ann saw her opening and decided to go for it. "Not half as disgraceful as this." She plopped the _In Style_ onto the table, folded open to reveal the first two pages of Tatiana's Malibu mommy spread.

Eunice squinted her eyes and peered closer. "Who is that?"

Constance Ann threw up her hands in exaggerated disgust.

"Tatiana Fox. Apparently, the new role model for mother-hood!"

Eunice, intrigued now, inched the magazine toward her and flipped the page. She gasped. "Those children are in the pool without life jackets!"

"And that's not the half of it." Constance Ann tapped an angry index finger on Tatiana's face. "She takes off her clothes in dirty movies." From underneath the table, Constance Ann produced a brown bag containing the first four *Lady Cop Undercover* videos. "Watch these, if you can stomach the filth." She jabbed a finger at Tatiana again. "Her ex-husband is one of those homosexuals."

Eunice leaned back in horror, bolt upright. "You mean he dresses up in women's clothes?"

Constance stifled a laugh. "No, he's into other men. He lives with a TV executive."

"That's appalling!" Eunice exclaimed. "A TV execu-tive? That's almost respectable. I thought they were all Broadway chorus boys."

Constance Ann nodded her own disapproval. "And get this: Tatiana's next movie is called *Sin by Sin*. Sounds like a great title for her biography, doesn't it?"

Eunice sat silently for a moment, allowing all the fine points to sink in. Finally, she spoke. "This Tatiana woman must be stopped."

The rat had taken the cheese. Constance Ann sighed grate-fully. "Which is precisely why I asked to join you for dinner. With your radio show and legions of worker bees dedicated to your cause, you can take a stand against this so-called actress and morally bankrupt parent. She's not a role model. She's a symbol of cultural erosion and a slap in the face to positive family values." Constance Ann shifted a glance to the full-page photo of Tatiana. "Look at her, smiling to America with such pride when she should be feeling nothing but shame.'' Constance Ann closed the magazine. ''I can't stand to see such depravity, especially where children are involved.''

Eunice raised her sweet tea in a toast. ''You and I were cut from the same cloth, Constance Ann.''

I'm not made of polyester, bitch. It was so close to her lips, but she called on willpower and simply smiled her appreciation.

Eunice scooted the videos and magazine to her side of the table. ''This is a very serious matter. I'm glad you brought it to my attention.''

Constance Ann pretended to wipe away a tear. ''I'm sorry. I shouldn't be so emotional. It's just . . . I think about the children . . . I want to protect all of them.''

Eunice pushed her untouched dessert in Constance Ann's direction. ''Have some lemon icebox pie.''

''No, thank you.''

''I insist. You hardly ate anything at all, and you must keep up your strength. Do it for the children.''

Reluctantly, Constance Ann took a bite.

''When I begin a campaign demanding our right to decency, it's important that I have as much information as possible at my disposal.'' Eunice gestured to the videos. ''Being familiar with this woman's previous work is a good start. But I also find it useful to be privy to future projects. Alerting my followers to forthcoming garbage helps energize them. It gives them a purpose, makes them feel like they can play a role in stopping the immorality before it reaches the marketplace.''

Constance Ann raised an eyebrow. ''Now I understand why you're such a formidable adversary.''

Eunice deferred the praise. ''It's all God's work.''

''And He trusts *you* with the task.''

Eunice nodded demurely. "I'm sure the details will be disturbing, but tell me more about this *Sin by Sin* film."

"I wish that I could," Constance Ann began. "But it stars Greg Tapper. He's a huge star, and his movies are always cloaked in secrecy. Scripts are even printed on special paper that can't be photocopied."

Eunice pursed her lips. "There's no telling what kind of trash will be ushered into our local theaters."

Suddenly, a thought struck Constance Ann. No doubt Tatiana kept a script at home. Shooting the film on the studio sound stage meant sleeping in her own bed every night. Of course, it being there and actually getting it were two different things.

That's where Jack Thorpe came in. She added it all up: pretty-boy looks, former professional athlete, so strapped for cash he turned to babysitting. None of it factored out to reveal brain surgeon smarts. He'd be easy to fool.

"On second thought, Eunice, give me a few days to look into some possibilities. I might be able to get exactly what you need."

Mrs. Herman McKenzie raised her glass once more. "To the moral cleansing of America."

Constance Ann smiled triumphant, saluting as well. "I can definitely drink to that."

Kristin Bonner stepped off the plane and into the American Airlines terminal at LAX carrying a Kate Spade purse and two duffel bags that contained everything she owned.

Good-bye, psycho mom and porno-addict dad. Hello, Los Angeles! A brand-new city. A whole new life. Maybe she'd take up acting, just like her half-sister, Tatiana.

It was hard to strut and lug all these bags at the same time. She had the body for strutting, too. In her skimpy white tank over a black bra and skintight Lycra denim jeans that hung dangerously low on her hips, Kristin was getting checked out in a big way.

She followed the signs to ground transportation. Near the top of the escalator, a hot young limousine driver was holding up a sign that read, "MR. WILCOX."

Ooh, la la. The guy was in his early twenties, she guessed, and really had a Shane West thing going on: tall, lanky muscular frame; a brooding, yeah-I'm-cool attitude. Serious eye candy. Major babe.

Kristin marched right up to him and dropped her bags at his feet.

He just stared at her, eyes eclipsed by Ray-Ban aviator sunglasses. "You don't look like a Mr. Wilcox." He sounded so very Southern California dude.

"Your little sign there is wrong. It's *Ms*. Wilcox. Not *Mr.*"

His lips curved into a sexy grin. "Is that so?"

"Yeah." She glanced down at the luggage, then back up at him. "Any day now, Jeeves."

"Just so there's no misunderstanding, I'm supposed to pick up the new assistant coach for the Lakers. Would that be you?"

Kristin held open her arms. "In the flesh."

He gave her a seductive once-over. "How old are you?"

"I'm not jailbait, if that's what you're wondering."

"Show me your ID, then."

"Why should I? You're buying the beer."

He raised his hands up in the air, slowly waving the MR. WILCOX sign back and forth.

Kristin grew impatient. "Are you gonna give me a ride or not?"

"I could get fired for that."

She inched closer and hooked a finger through one of his

belt loops. "But you'll have a good time. Come on, don't make me take a smelly cab. By the way, I'm Kristin."

He cracked the sign over his knee and tossed it into the nearest garbage bin. "I'm Chad, and I'm crazy for doing this." Then he hoisted her bags over his shoulders and led her down the escalator. "So what brings you to L.A.?" He smirked. "Besides coaching basketball, of course."

"My mom kicked me out of the house, so I moved here to live with my half-sister. She's an actress."

Chad looked at Kristin with heightened interest now. "Really? I'm an actor, too." He gestured to the black-and-white driver's uniform. "Not successful. *Yet*. But I will be. Who's your sis?"

"Tatiana Fox."

"The *Lady Cop Undercover* chick?"

Kristin nodded.

"She's hot." He gave her a ray-gun gaze. "I can see the family resemblance." Then he darted through double glass doors and threw her duffel bags into the trunk of an impressive spit-polished black stretch limousine. With a flourish, he opened the back door and ushered her inside the expansive cabin.

Kristin sank into the rich leather. Totally first class. There was a tiny television! She opened a wood-grain cabinet. And liquor!

Chad ran around to hop into the driver's seat. He started the engine. Soon the glass separating them zipped down. "Where to?"

Stretching her body across the seat, Kristin took a swig of 3 Vodka straight from the bottle. "The craziest party you can find."

Chad gave her a cool smile. "Isn't your sister expecting you?"

Kristin passed him the booze.

He took a quick drink and passed it back.

"She doesn't know I'm coming. I suppose I could get there today. . . ."

Chad shook his head from side to side, as if not quite believing his luck. "But there's always tomorrow." He gave her a long stare. "Are you chem-friendly? I've got some friends that really know how to get wasted."

"Any friend of yours . . ."

Chad nodded his delight, shifted into drive, and eased the limo into motion.

Kristin took another hit of alcohol. Living on the edge. It was a blast.

Chapter Fifteen

Tatiana stared at Dr. G.

Dr. G stared back at Tatiana.

"I don't know where to start."

Dr. G smiled. "Then we can just sit until you're ready."

This drove Tatiana nuts because every minute was costing her three dollars. That meant a half-caffeine, double-short, nonfat, no-whip mocha down the drain! So she just came out with it. "I had sex with Jack."

Dr. G remained statue still.

Tatiana wanted to at least see the pen moving. "You might want to jot that down. First real sex in a couple years. Big stuff. Worth a scribble on the pad. Definitely qualifies for a *notation.*"

Dr. G didn't take the hint. "How did it make you feel?"

"Can you recall the most intense orgasm of your life?"

Dr. G could never be rattled. "Yes."

"It felt like that." She paused. "Of course, after it was

over, I could barely look at him, and the next morning things were awkward as hell.''

"That doesn't surprise me," Dr. G said with her trademark nonchalant directness. ''Your relationship with Jack was complicated even before sex entered the equation.''

Tatiana brushed a tumble of hair back with her hands. God, she was exhausted. Dr. G had kindly agreed to see her after hours, but right now all she wanted to do was sleep. The shooting day had taken its toll. They went after the love scene like independent guerrilla filmmakers financing a movie on credit cards. Sure, they got it in the can, but all the groping, rolling, kissing, and gyrating had left her sore and in dire need of a hot bath, two Ambiens, a lavender-scented candle, and the soft jazzy sounds of Diana Krall. Wearily she looked at Dr. G. It just wasn't in her to deconstruct life tonight.

''Is it accurate to say that your encounter with Jack satisfied your physical needs but left you wanting emotionally?''

Way too probing. Downright rude. Even for a therapist. Tatiana shut her eyes. ''Sometimes I hate you.''

Dr. G didn't pause so much as a beat. ''Let's talk about that.''

Tatiana sighed heavily. No choice left but to surrender. ''Yes. What you said a second ago. You're dead-on.''

''That's not necessarily a bad thing. Sometimes people expect too much from sexual intimacy. It can't always be satisfying on all levels. The key—''

''There's no point in understanding this particular episode,'' Tatiana cut in. ''Because Jack's not sticking around.''

''You're firing him?''

''Are you crazy?'' Tatiana halted, realizing the ludicrousness of that rhetorical question. After all, *she* was on the couch. Clearly, the crazy stain was on her. ''I would never fire him. He's the best thing that's ever happened to . . . the twins." Her heart went bang. She'd come so close to saying "me," only managing to stop herself at the last moment. "I asked Jack to promise that he'd stay with us until Ethan and Everson turned eighteen." She shrugged diffidently. "And he said no."

"Did you ask for this promise in relation to his current capacity as your nanny?"

"*Manny*," Tatiana corrected. "And what do you mean by 'current capacity'? Like it matters. Jack's not in this for the long haul. There's no commitment on his part. The man is twenty-six and free to do anything he wants. For all I know, he could quit next week."

"That's true," Dr. G said quietly. "He could."

Tatiana felt a flush of alarm. "Do you think he's going to?"

Dr. G shook her head. "I can't speculate on that."

"Maybe I should find a psychic. I could take in a piece of Jack's clothing and have an energy reading done."

Dr. G tilted her head briefly to one side. "That's one approach."

"Do you have a better idea?"

"Maybe you should try being honest with yourself."

Tatiana braced for impact. This happened at almost every session. Everything would be going along just fine and then Dr. G would hit her over the head with a psychological sledgehammer. "I admitted that the sex was good. It's a start. I could've easily convinced myself he was lousy in bed."

"How can you ask Jack to make a job commitment eighteen years into the future? That's not fair. And I don't believe his commitment to the twins is your only issue. I think you're equally concerned about his commitment to *you*."

Tatiana just sat there, frustrated. "You won't let me get away with anything."

Dr. G laughed. "These sessions aren't about that, Tatiana. Sometimes I think my job is to help patients expose the frauds in their lives. We all have them. But more often than not, the most hurtful fraud of all is the one you see in the mirror. Don't con yourself into believing that Jack's refusal to commit to a job is also a refusal to commit to a loving relationship."

Tatiana resisted the analysis. Going through life with her usual bag of tricks was so much easier. "Are you suggesting that I ask him to marry me?" She laughed a little.

Dr. G remained stone-faced. "I didn't say anything about marriage."

Tatiana's purse began to ring. She moved to answer. Could be Jack about the twins. The name on the caller ID screen triggered an involuntary groan.

NED BONNER. Justine reaching out from Florida.

Oh, God, was it possible to be less prepared? Hardly any sleep, only one Xanax in her system, no bridge to jump off of. Face it, she was in no shape to talk to her mother. Then she remembered that Dr. G was right there. A flood of relief. "It's my mother. The only reason I'm taking it is because you're here to help me when I hang up. Don't move." She clicked the button. "Hi, Mom."

"I was going to wait to hear from you, but you obviously have no intention of calling."

"Yes, I do. On Christmas. It's only a few months away. Glad that's cleared up. Bye, now."

"How is she settling in? I'm sure she doesn't want to talk to me. And that's fine. Just tell her that I'm putting her green cashmere sweater in the mail. It was at the cleaners."

Tatiana hadn't been this confused since that Saturday matinee of *Memento*. "Are you sniffing whipped cream with the yard boy again?"

"I'm not interested in hearing your stand-up act, Tatiana.

We'll see who's laughing after *you* experience life with Kristin.''

Tatiana clenched her stomach and gripped the cell phone tighter, as if a stronger hold might bring more clarity. ''I have no idea what you're talking about.''

''I put Kristin on a plane to Los Angeles this morning.''

Tatiana couldn't believe it. ''Why didn't you call me?''

''To hear what? That you're too busy?''

Anger and fear played Ping-Pong in Tatiana's mind. She rummaged through her purse for a scrap of paper and something to write with. ''Give me the flight number and arrival time.''

''Hold on. It's on the refrigerator.''

Tatiana sat there, a bundle of nerves and twitches. Finally, her mother came back on the line. She scribbled down the information and experienced a mounting panic. ''Kristin landed *hours* ago! Are you insane? I would've been there to pick her up! She's only seventeen!''

''Don't worry. Your sister's street-smart. You'll learn.''

''Ugh!'' Tatiana hung up. She couldn't listen to another word.

Dr. G sat there expectantly.

''My mother is crazy! She put my seventeen-year-old sister on a plane here to L.A. without a word of warning! It's been hours! She could be anywhere in this city!''

Dr. G put down her pen and formed a pyramid with her fingers. ''How does that make you feel?''

With his arms ramrod straight, Jaron Green lifted the five-pound weights to shoulder height and back down again. ''Look at me! I'm a bodybuilder!''

Jack laughed. ''Let's try three sets of twelve.''

"Hey, go easy on me. I'm not Conan the Barbarian," Jaron cracked.

"You're right about that, mate."

"Like my outfit?" Jaron asked. He was wearing a Cartoon Planet sweatshirt cut jagged around the neckline, black tights, red leg warmers, and Reebok cross-trainers.

"What do you call a look like that?"

Jaron cackled. "I don't know, but Kerr accused me of raiding the closets of Jennifer Beals and Jane Fonda back in the eighties."

"Keep going," Jack instructed, counting as Jaron blathered on. "You're doing great."

Jaron finished up lift number twelve with a pained grunt. "All done. Time for a break. Who wants pizza?"

"No break. And no pizza. I'll treat you to a piece of fruit after we're done." Jack demonstrated proper form again, sans weights. "Two more sets. You can do it."

Jaron started pumping again. "When all is said and done, will I ever look like you, gorgeous?"

Jack smiled, embarrassed but flattered, too. "This took years of hard work, mate. Plus, I come from a good gene pool. You should see my mum. Still a real head-turner."

Jack had just finished giving the twins a bath and putting them down for the night when Kerr and Jaron rushed the scene unannounced.

"This is an emergency!" Jaron had exclaimed. "I saw myself naked in one of those plasma mirrors—you know, the kind that shows every possible angle. Unfortunately for me, there wasn't a single good one. Now, I can either dye my hair and change my name to Camryn Manheim, or I can get in shape and return to my once slim, fabulous self." Flamboyantly—and that was putting it mildly—Jaron had sucked in his cheeks and his gut. "What do you think?"

"He probably thinks I left one neurotic woman for

another,'' Kerr had said, settling in at the kitchen table with his pink Mary Kay notebook.

Jaron had ignored Kerr and began pleading with Jack. ''I know it's rude of us to just storm in like this, but I need a fitness program. *Tonight.* Otherwise, I might just say, 'Fuck it', and wait for the 'Hot Now' sign to blink at Krispy Kreme. This time tomorrow I could be knocking on Carnie Wilson's door, saying, 'Cookie, how'd you do it?' ''

By that point, Jack had warmed to the intrusion. ''Well, I couldn't bloody well stand by and watch you go to those extremes.''

Jaron had turned to Kerr. ''This one's a doll! Love him, love the ex-wife, love the kids. We should all pose for the cover of *Blended Family* magazine.''

While Jack put Jaron through the paces, Kerr worked the telephone, booking clients for a new Mary Kay party, this one at Jaron's house. It struck Jack as odd that Kerr hadn't inquired about the twins. Not even a quick tiptoe back to their room to check on them as they slept.

As soon as Jaron finished his workout, he begged permission to take a shower—something about being allergic to perspiration. Jack got him set up, then headed back to the kitchen. ''Want something to drink, mate?''

Kerr glanced up from studying a Mary Kay order form. ''Whatever you're having.''

Jack grabbed two bottles of Smart Water from the fridge and joined Kerr at the table.

''Thanks,'' Kerr said, twisting off the cap and drinking deeply. ''Got anything to eat? Jaron refused to have anything but celery today. I'm starving.''

''There's some leftover Chinese.''

Kerr nodded excitedly. ''Don't bother warming it up. I like it cold.''

Jack gave him a strange look. This bloke used to live

here. Couldn't he see about his own food? But Jack didn't want to make a case out of it, so he waited on Kerr like any good host would. "Chopsticks or fork?"

"Fork," Kerr said absently, head buried in Mary Kay matters.

Jack set down the cartons and utensils with a little extra force.

Kerr failed to notice and dug in like a teenage boy after a hard game.

"Don't tell Tatiana about this," Jack said.

"About what?" Kerr asked, his mouth full of kung pao chicken. Really gross.

"I won't let her touch the stuff, but I order it on the sly. I figure, since my ass isn't heading for a big screen near you, I can indulge."

Kerr didn't acknowledge the joke. He just rummaged through all four cartons before asking, "No eggrolls?"

"Sorry. All gone."

Kerr shrugged and started in on the sweet-and-sour shrimp.

Jack decided to test him and search for common ground at the same time. "The twins are doing great."

Kerr nodded with vague interest. "That's good."

"Do you miss it?"

Kerr stabbed his fork into the beef-and-broccoli stir-fry. "Being married? Hell no! Nothing against Tat, but we—"

"I meant do you miss being here with the kids," Jack cut in impatiently. He knew the reason why this slacker couldn't stay hitched. In fact, it was taking a shower right now.

"Oh," Kerr said, mulling it over. "I don't know. I haven't really thought about it much. Melina did most of the work. I just played with them once in a while." He toyed with the lemon chicken but didn't take a bite. "Hey, guess what? I think Jaron and I are going to get a puppy."

"That sounds like fun," Jack muttered through clenched teeth. What did Tatiana ever see in this guy? "Can I ask you something, mate? It's personal."

Kerr looked at him curiously. "What?"

"Tatiana's a relatively young woman. Very beautiful. She's bound to—"

Kerr grinned as he interrupted with, "You want to know how I could leave her for a guy like Jaron."

"No," Jack said, shaking his head. "That's not what I'm getting at. It's only a matter of time before Tatiana meets someone. She's likely to marry again. I'm just wondering how you'd feel about another man moving in to assume a fatherly role with the twins."

Kerr narrowed his gaze. "Isn't that what you've already done?"

"Easy, mate," Jack countered, holding up both hands. "I'm just the help."

Kerr gave him a cool nod. "If that's the case, I think I'm done with this." He pushed the takeout cartons over to Jack's side of the table.

Jack stood up, ready to belt the smug bastard. But he maintained his cool. "Understand this, mate. I work *here*. I don't work for *you*. Clear your own shit off the table." He started out, then doubled back. "When do you plan on growing up? At forty?"

"I don't know, Mom."

There was no stopping Jack now. "You're unbelievable. Ethan and Everson aren't some project to get bored with." His eyes blazed contempt. "Do you stick with anything? One minute you're a bad poet and the next you're a Mary Kay girl."

Kerr's face flushed scarlet with anger. "Watch it, nanny

boy! I'm running my own business here! You're looking at an entrepreneur!'' He raised the pink notebook as evidence.

Mockingly Jack widened his eyes. ''Donald Fucking Trump, I presume.''

''Since when is an ex-jockstrap a literary critic? Did you even finish high school?''

Jack returned a hot nod. ''Graduated early. I wrote better sonnets on the bathroom walls of Chingford High, too!''

''Oh, yeah?'' Kerr screamed.

''Yeah!''

Jack felt ridiculous now. He decided to stop before things got completely third-grade with ''mum'' insults or some such crap. ''Since we're running out of clever jabs here, why don't you answer my original question.''

Kerr calmed down a little. ''What was it? I forgot.'' Long pause. ''Oh, about Tat finding a new husband?'' Kerr laughed at him. ''I hope you haven't rented a tux. She'd never marry a man like you. Tat's tired of supporting the men in her life. Trust me, I've heard the tirades. She wants a guy to take care of *her* for a change. Maybe someone like Greg Tapper.''

This hit a nerve, but Jack betrayed nothing. His temples pulsed. ''For sake of argument, let's say that it is Greg. Personally, I wouldn't want to see the name Tatiana Tapper engraved on stationery, but that's just me.'' Pointing to the back of the house, he said, ''What about those innocent kids? They need a father around. Not in between Mary Kay parties and puppy obedience school. All the time.''

Kerr gave him a crazy look. ''Who do you think you are? Head of Social Services? Get a life.''

''Just answer the goddamn question!''

''What *is* the question?''

Jack stepped forward menacingly. He was smack-dab in Kerr's face. ''If a man were willing to step in and be a real

father to those twins, would you transfer your parental rights?
Yes or no?''

The telephone jangled.

At first, Jack let it ring, hoping Kerr might answer, but
the dumb-ass was just staring lasers. He snatched the receiver
and barked, ''Hello?''

A girl was sobbing, loud music blasting in the background.
''Is . . . Tatiana there?''

Jack sensed serious trouble. ''She's not home right now,''
he said gently. ''Who's calling?''

More sobbing. The girl could barely get a word out.

''It's okay, sweetheart. Take a deep breath for me.'' He
waited to hear the intake of air. ''That's good. Tell me your
name.''

''Kristin.'' She lost composure again but settled down
long enough to murmur, ''I'm Tatiana's . . . sister.''

Jack was stunned. He covered the mouthpiece with his
palm and turned to Kerr. ''I didn't know Tatiana had a
sister.''

Kerr looked fuzzy. ''Yeah, I think her name's Carrie. I
can't remember where she lives, though.''

Why did he think this flake would be any help? Jack
focused on the hysterical girl. ''My name's Jack. Jack
Thorpe. I work for Tatiana.'' He kept his voice firm but
soothing. ''You can trust me. Everything's going to be just
fine.''

Kristin's sobs began to subside.

''Are you hurt?''

She sniffled. ''Not really.''

''Where are you?''

A moment of hesitation. ''I'm not sure. A gas station
somewhere. I can't see the street signs. One of the guys said
something about West Hollywood.'' Kristin's voice trailed
off in a slur.

Jack's mind raced, a million worst-case scenarios flashing. "Are you on a pay phone?" He talked louder this time.

"Uh-huh."

"Go inside and ask the clerk for an address."

There was a clang, then nothing but white noise. He waited for long seconds, feeling helpless, putting the face of his own sister in this tableau, anxiousness building.

Suddenly, Kristin came back on the line to mumble out her whereabouts.

"Don't move. I'm on my way." Jack grabbed Kerr's pen and scratched the information onto the first thing he could find—a Mary Kay catalog.

"Hey!" Kerr protested. "That's got the new line of—"

Jack ripped off the cover. "Kristin's in trouble. I need you and Jaron to stay here—"

"But we have plans to—"

Jack picked up his keys. "Those plans are canceled."

Jaron shuffled into the kitchen wearing Tatiana's pink terry cloth robe. "Do you mind giving me a massage, Jack?" He rubbed his shoulder. "All that exercising made me really sore."

The telephone jangled again.

Jack recovered it on the first ring. "Hello?"

"Is my sister there?" Tatiana, sounding just a smidge better than Kristin. "Please tell me she is, and if so, why the hell didn't anyone call me?"

"Calm down, Tatiana."

"Don't tell me to calm down! This isn't *The Poseidon Adventure!* I'm not Shelley Winters!"

Jack sighed. "Kristin just called. I'm heading out the door to pick her up."

"What about—"

"Kerr and Jaron are here to watch the twins."

"But—"

"Come home and wait for us here." Jack's tone was absolute, father to petulant daughter, headmaster to out-of-line pupil. "And drive carefully. The last thing we need is you in hospital as a result of a foolish accident." He hung up and started out, stopping fast to address Jaron. "Tatiana's on her way. I wouldn't be in that robe when she gets in. Remember, you're the home-wrecker."

Jaron covered his face in shame.

Kerr glared at the messenger.

Jack tumbled into his new SUV and burned rubber down the drive, praying he would find Kristin in better shape than she sounded.

Chapter Sixteen

Some man in a black Lexus was staring at her.

Kristin tried to avoid his gaze.

Slowly he coasted over to the pay phone, window down, no doubt running a quick assessment. Lone teenage girl. Two duffel bags. Total Runaway Hotline case. "Need a ride?"

Up close, he didn't look so bad. Still, there was that perverted-older-businessman vibe going strong. It creeped her out. "No, thanks."

"A girl like you shouldn't be out here all by herself. It's dangerous."

Kristin gave him a polar look. "I know. Strangers like you might want me to hop in their cars."

His smile was plastic, like any jerk with a certificate from a Dale Carnegie seminar. "I'm not a stranger. You can call me Bill."

Kristin scowled in response. "Bill? Are you sure about that? You look more like an asshole to me."

No more slimy-sales-guy sheen. Just another angry loser. She thought fast. "My uncle will be here any minute. So get lost."

"Little bitch." And then *Bill* screeched away, disappearing into the traffic of the night.

Kristin felt enormous relief but stood tough, ready for anything. The next man who approached her better be a dude named Jack with a killer Australian accent.

Running off with Chad, the out-of-work actor, had been a stupid move. He'd taken her to some raggedy apartment where he shacked up with two other guys—another wannabe thespian (really a waiter, probably a bad one) and a muscle rat with biceps for brains who worked at a gym called Crunch.

The roomies had attempted to pull together a last-minute funk ball. Kristin had been to one before back home in Florida. It was like a grown-up version of musical chairs. Guys set themselves up in a circle formation. Girls dance to wild songs inside the testosterone ring and plop down on boys' laps when the music stops. Whoever a girl lands on is the boy she hooks up with for the night. Major fun if lots of cool people are making the scene. But the scarce crowd Chad and his posse had gathered up was lame.

Even the Foxy hadn't been able to get Kristin in the party mood. Foxy was the latest club drug, better than Ecstasy according to lots of friends who'd tried it. They said the trip was like riding a long, sensual wave. Obviously, Chad had completely underdosed her, because all she felt was a dull buzz and occasional dizziness.

Still, she was ultimately thankful for the botched hit. After all, Kristin had just wanted to canoodle with the cute limousine driver, only one of Chad's ugly friends (a morning

DJ with a face for radio) had other ideas, forcing her onto his lap when the music stopped and expecting her to let him have his way. Yeah, right. Not even with a *full* dose of Foxy running through her.

Of course, the DJ had acted all pissed off, and Chad had taken his buddy's side, calling her a pain in the ass, shoving her out of the apartment, and dumping her bags onto the sidewalk. The whole scene had frightened the hell out of her. There she'd been, pitched out on the street like garbage, and nobody had a clue about where she was. So far, L.A. boys were no improvement over the Florida variety.

A silver Nissan Xterra peeled into the lot and headed straight for the pay phone, braking fast in front of her. The driver hopped out, his expression full of hope. "Kristin?"

She recognized the voice immediately. "Jack?"

He moved closer, breathing a sigh of relief as he took in the questionable surroundings. "Let's get out of here."

Kristin rushed to embrace him. She didn't know why, exactly. It just seemed like a normal way to respond to a rescuer, especially one this hot.

Jack was stiff at first, but then relaxed, giving her a tight squeeze.

Kristin imagined that a big brother's hug might feel this way.

"I'm not going to interrogate you," Jack said, leaning down to fetch her duffel bags and toss them into the back of the SUV. "Your sister's at home waiting to do that." He gave her a look. "I suggest that you get your story straight."

The implication that she was some kid about to be grounded for staying out too late infuriated her. Jumping up and buckling herself in, Kristin rolled her eyes. "I don't have a *story*."

"Sure, you do," Jack argued easily. "Fifty bucks says it

involves a guy. And judging from your eyes right now and speech pattern on the phone earlier, probably a drug or two.''

Kristin wasn't accustomed to anyone getting the better of her. ''Who *are* you?''

He nodded, more to himself than to her. ''Definitely drugs. Memory loss already. I'm Jack, remember?''

''I know *that*. I meant what do you do for my sister?''

''I'm responsible for the children.'' He made a smooth lane-change and glanced at her. ''That happens to include you tonight.''

Kristin twisted in her seat. ''I'm *not* a child.''

Jack took his eyes off the road long enough to level another pointed look. ''You may have a point. A child would have better sense than you displayed tonight.''

''You don't know anything about me!''

''You'd be surprised. How old are you? Fifteen?''

''Seventeen!''

''I've got eight years on you, sweetheart, and I've forgotten more tricks than you've actually pulled.''

Kristin stared straight ahead. ''Whatever.''

He gestured to the luggage in the backseat. ''I take it this is more than a weekend trip. How long are you staying?''

She shrugged.

Jack pulled over and stopped the car.

Kristin's psychic gifts predicted boring lecture ahead.

''Do you have any drugs?''

Kristin hadn't expected this. ''Why? Do you want some?''

He stared back without a trace of humor. ''Answer me.''

She shook her head.

''I don't believe you. Show me your purse.''

''I swear. I don't have anything. I took a small hit of Foxy. That's all.''

''Powder or pill?''

His knowledge of the trade surprised her. This dude would be tough to fool. "Powder. They mixed it into a drink."

He shook his head. "Do you have any idea how dangerous that is?"

"Do you always talk in public service announcements?"

"You know, for a smart-ass, you're not so bright. Foxy, Ecstasy, Mystic—these drugs can kill in one hit, and you're trusting the lab work to some dope fiend who didn't pass high school chemistry."

His point was sobering, but she played it cool. "Oh, please. People do it all the time."

"And some of them die. A friend of mine did. She was only nineteen."

Kristin said nothing. There was a look in his eyes, a palpable sadness, a buried memory that still haunted.

"Here's the deal, Kristin. Your sister's raising twins, and she's under a lot of pressure on the set of her new movie. Having you show up to play Jane Dean, teen rebel, could push her over the edge. So these are the rules: No drugs. No bullshit. You'll go to school, you'll help out around the house, and you'll show respect at all times. Got it?"

Kristin just stared at him. It sounded like a military academy. "What?" she scoffed. "I can't have any friends?"

"Just one. Maybe two. But they'll have to be honor roll students, and I'll want to meet their parents first."

Tatiana sat slumped in the pool chaise, staring mindlessly at the water. The California night was cool, but she braved the elements, bundled up with a fleece throw. It seemed impossible that everything had happened in one day.

Almost being booted off the set of *Sin by Sin.*

Showdowns with Kitty Bishop and Cleo Mars.

A miserable day in the sack with Greg Tapper.

Dr. G's psychological truth game.

Telecommunications warfare with her mother.

And the cherry on the sundae: Kristin. First lost. Then found. Now an indefinite house guest.

Tatiana clutched the blanket, wrapping it more snugly around her. She longed for chemical assistance. Prozac to ward off depression, Klonopin to fight the anxiety, an Ambien or two to insure sleep. But she was too lazy, too immobilized by fatigue, even to consider going to the medicine cabinet. And asking Jack to do so on her behalf would probably mean a one-way ticket to Promises, the celebrity rehab center.

She didn't hear Jack approach. Suddenly, he was offering her a glass of red wine. "It's not the morphine you were probably hoping for, but . . ."

Delighted, Tatiana rose up slightly to accept. "Anything will do." Instead of sipping, she guzzled, like a gunslinger in a hot saloon.

Jack smiled and produced the bottle from behind his back, refilling her glass instantly.

"I promise to make this one last . . . a little more . . . right there . . . Thank you."

He sat down beside her and chugged straight from the bottle with great comedic flair.

Tatiana laughed at him. "Want to talk about it?"

"Don't you have enough problems?"

"Actually, I do. I was just trying to be polite."

Part of her—well, okay, every cell in her body, to be perfectly accurate—burned with the ardent need to curl up on Jack's lap, rest her head on his chest, complain about all her woes, and listen to him murmur something generically supportive along the lines of, "Everything's going to be just fine, baby," as he stroked her hair and occasionally kissed the top of her head.

Instead, she just gazed at him, wondering what they were to each other.

Abruptly, he stood up. "I'm going for a swim."

"Are you crazy? The water must be freezing!"

Jack's shirt was off. Next came the jeans. He ran to the edge of the pool in his boxers, turning around to beckon her. "Come on. It'll be invigorating."

Feeling a surge of energy, Tatiana pushed the blanket away. Her body tingled. "You first."

He spun around to drop the boxers, mooning her before diving in headfirst, emerging in the middle of the pool. "Whooh! This feels fantastic!"

Tatiana dashed over, infinitely intrigued. "Is it cold?"

"Jump in and find out."

She tested the water with her big toe. It felt like ice water. "I can't!"

Jack swam toward her, his muscular buttocks bobbing up and down. "Trust me. This will do more for your spirits than the wine."

Tatiana inched away, just beyond his grasp, quickly stripping down to her delicates. She glanced back at the house.

"Don't worry," Jack assured her. "Kristin is fast asleep in your bed, and the baby monitor is right over there."

Suddenly, Tatiana's aversion to cold water was superseded by her desire to be with Jack. Her fingers started to work on the clasp of her bra. "Close your eyes."

Jack obeyed, smiling, shaking his head. "It's not like I haven't seen you naked before—*Playboy*, the *Lady Cop* movies, that time I walked in on you getting dressed."

"I don't care. No peeking." She slipped off her panties.

"And, of course, there was last night."

Tatiana halted.

Jack stole a glance.

A disapproving finger was waved in his face. "Bad boy!"

And then she sucked in a deep breath and negotiated a graceful dive, bracing herself for the freezing blast. It was Antarctica, but the body shock felt amazing. She glided through the water, like a mermaid, almost making it to the other side but coming up for air a few feet short. Wiping the chlorine from her eyes, she searched for Jack but couldn't find him anywhere.

"Looking for me?"

Tatiana's heart lurched. She whipped around.

Jack stood directly behind her, a playful grin on his face.

"You're such a little boy."

He glanced down at his crotch in faux horror. "It's the cold water. One must allow for shrinkage."

Tatiana giggled, wrapping her arms around her shoulders for any bit of warmth she could produce. "I don't know how long I can stay in. My teeth are chattering."

Jack's hands dipped down to her waist. "Come here. I'll be your underwater blanket." He pulled her close.

Instinctively, she locked her legs around his hips and clung tight, feeling a rush of body heat as he squeezed her, rubbing his hands up and down her back with such delicious speed that she actually felt toasty.

"Better?" His breath was in her ear.

"A little," she whispered, not about to let go.

"How about this?" Jack posed. His mouth found hers for a kiss full of passionate hunger. It went on forever, lips crushing, tongues probing, desire flaming. Finally, he pulled back, but only to let them breathe.

"Definitely better," Tatiana gasped, feeling weak. She clung to him as they floated, like two lovers lost at sea, until they beached themselves onto the cascading steps in the shallow end of the pool. It took a moment to get right, but soon their body knot of tangled limbs became blissful comfort.

"Who needs wine?" Jack asked softly, his chin cupping her shoulder as she lay on top of him, her back to his chest, her body locked under his arms.

Tatiana's mind was at war. This felt so good. She wanted simply to enjoy it. But a stronger part of her needed things defined. When she spoke, her tone was unusually pensive. "What are we doing, Jack?"

"I don't know."

Tatiana tensed. She felt the urge to flee but fought against it.

Jack seemed to pick up on her discomfort. He relaxed his hold. "This is getting complicated."

Slowly she flipped over, facing him now. "What if we mess things up? I don't want you to leave because of me. That's not fair to Ethan and Everson. You're too important to them."

Jack smiled wryly and tapped a finger to his temple. "If memory serves, I tried to have this conversation last night."

"Yes, you did," Tatiana agreed, silently shaming herself. "And I behaved like an animal."

"A very inconsiderate animal. You didn't send flowers. You didn't call."

She laughed and clamped a hand over his mouth. "Stop being silly."

"I'll be serious. If you're sure that's what you want."

Tatiana hesitated at first. "Yes, it is."

"Here's what I'm certain of: You fascinate me. Sometimes I think I've got you pegged, and then you go and surprise me. It makes me curious. About *you*. I've never felt that way about a woman. You hold my interest in all sorts of wild and wonderful ways."

His words were blowing her away. She could only watch his lips move.

"And last night's bout in the loo wasn't so bad," Jack

went on. "Until you ran off like you were catching a bus."
He pursed his mouth into a pout. "I like to cuddle."

She grinned at him. "First of all, I'm a minor celebrity.
You won't find me running after a bus. A cab, maybe, but
never a bus."

"Preferred method of travel noted." He traced the outline
of her lips with his finger. "Your turn. Say something
serious."

"Okay . . . Something serious . . . I've never been a home-
body. Everything that mattered to me was outside—acting,
shopping, being seen at the latest hot spot. Now I can't wait
to come home. I miss it when I'm gone, and nothing seems
as important anymore. Look what you've done to me, Jack.
You just appeared out of nowhere and helped me get a life."

He smoothed back her hair with his hands. "Right back
at you."

"So where does that leave us?"

"In your bedroom, I hope. Kristin can take the sleeper
sofa. It's murder on my back."

She tugged at his hair playfully. "It's not that simple,
and you know it."

"It could be."

"Nothing ever is."

"Does it bother you that I'm not rich?"

"What?"

"Kerr tells me that you're tired of making all the money,
that you want the next man in your life to take care of you."

"That's ridiculous. And leave it to Kerr to miss the point
entirely. Yes, I want a provider. An *emotional* provider.
What do I need a man's money for? I've been supporting
myself since I left high school. Besides, wealthy men are
too distant. In my experience, all they did was worry about
the stock market and think up different ways to control me.
Until they got bored, of course, and traded me in for a

younger version of myself. Trust me, I've been there. Rich guys suck.''

"But rich men have power," Jack countered. "I thought women loved power.''

"Have you been reading my *Cosmopolitan* again? Yes, power pushes buttons in some women. I mean, why else would pudgy Bill Clinton be swooned over like Mel Gibson? But at the end of the day, what can a rich man really do? Can he move back call times, so I can get an extra two hours of sleep? Force Regis Philbin out of show business? Make a pair of Manolo Blahnik strappy heels that don't kill my feet? The answers are no; oh, how I wish; and hell no, respectively. But who cares? I can buy my own diamonds.''

Jack snapped his fingers and teased her with, "Yes, you can, Beyoncé.''

Tatiana laughed and began singing the Destiny's Child hit. "All the honeys making money, throw your hands up at me. . . .''

He ravished her neck with tiny nibbles and quick kisses. "How do you know I'm not just after you for your money?''

"Have you seen my debt-to-income ratio? Everson's got more liquidity with just a few savings bonds in her name.''

He stopped abruptly. "You mean there's no yacht?''

"Not unless you count Ethan's plastic one in the bathtub.''

Jack shrugged. "That'll have to do.'' And he started on her neck again, this time with more fervor.

Tatiana pulled away to study him: that perfectly symmetrical face, those sensual lips, the hungry eyes reflecting her own desire. Pressing her body into him, she could feel his growing excitement. Boldly, she reached down to touch his hard promise of ultimate fulfillment. It made her shiver.

She loved his body. He had the build of a natural athlete in peak form. Wide shoulders, utterly flat abdominals, a high, drum-tight ass, muscled arms, and large, masculine hands.

A thought flashed into her mind, and Tatiana started to laugh. For the past two days, she'd spent no fewer than eighteen hours in bed with Greg Tapper, Hollywood's twenty-million-dollar stud. Up against Jack, though, cinema's dream god wasn't worth the loose change you could dig out of a couch. Greg was short, deeply committed to Rogaine, in merely decent shape, and even fully erect, had no business hiding his manhood inside a long tube sock when the simple ankle-high variety would suffice. Oh, and he couldn't kiss worth a damn.

"What's so funny?" Jack asked.

Tatiana debated whether or not to tell him. "Nothing."

"Normally, I wouldn't be so inquisitive, but you just touched my penis and laughed. As foreplay goes, I've had better."

"It's not you. I promise." She stroked his cheek. "I've been doing this love scene with Greg Tapper for two days, and not once has the experience conjured up any feeling other than nausea, which is funny to me because women actually faint in his presence. And there I am, just waiting for the director to yell 'Cut,' so I can get the hell out of Dodge."

Jack smiled. "You better be a damn good actress."

"Honey, Meryl Streep's not that good. Multiple camera angles and sophisticated editing have never been so necessary." She wrapped her arms around his neck and pressed against him. "I think you'd be a natural for love scenes. No movie magic needed. Just raw talent."

Jack's hands wandered down her body, following the curves of her breasts, her hips, the cheeks of her ass. "I'm new at this. I might need a lot of rehearsals." His tongue traced a line toward the hollow of her throat.

"You know what they say," Tatiana whispered. "Practice makes perfect."

Jack met her gaze, the desire in his eyes so intense that it felt like penetration.

For a heartbeat she stood there, immobile, crazy with anticipation.

"Hold on to me."

She tightened her grip around his neck as Jack ventured backward, toward the center of the pool, taking her to the deepest area. Their toes could barely touch. "Take a breath."

Tatiana's soul was aflame. She just stared back, momentarily uncertain, then followed his order to the letter, filling her lungs with oxygen.

Jack took her down.

She opened her eyes. The chlorine burned for a few seconds, but her vision adjusted quickly.

Jack swam between her legs, head first, burying his mouth into the most vital part of her, his lips and tongue playing at the gate, teasing her, refusing to enter at first, then plunging inside.

Tatiana's lungs were straining. She arched her hips toward him, every thrust of his tongue, every probe of his fingers a throbbing, glistening, unbearable joy. Suddenly, a tingling heat engulfed her, ameliorating the cold, releasing a pressure valve of sensual spasms that stretched on and on until she cried out underwater.

Jack pushed her to the top, as if in tune with her desperation for air. He gave her just enough time to take in a heaving breath before covering her mouth with his own. They glided through the water until her back hit the pool wall. His kiss was bruising, unrelenting, deliciously dominant.

Tatiana turned away from his lips and panted for more air. Guiding his head down to her breasts, she pulled at his waist, silently begging him to feed the aching hunger within.

His tongue had tantalized. She needed more to satisfy. And anything but Jack inside her would be completely unbearable.

His mouth concentrated on one nipple at a time, bathing each with hot breath and a warm, velvet tongue. Pleasurable, yes, but the exhilarating expectation of what was coming next robbed all of her attention. She could actually feel the heat of him, lingering at her very core—hard, huge, ready to please yet refusing to submit.

"Please, Jack." It escaped her as a moan.

He kissed her again. "Please what?"

She knew what he wanted to hear, but she'd never begged a man before. The longing became so excruciating that her breath was coming in little gasps. Finally, she relented. After all, they were only words. And the reward would be so sweet. "Please put it inside me."

Instantly, he inserted himself, impaling her.

Tatiana's body was engulfed by a searing near-pain that quickly transformed itself into a marvelous feeling of completeness. Three thrusts later she climaxed, riding the dizzying crest to the end of the erotic rainbow. When it was over, she fell against him, struck down by all the intensity.

Jack withdrew from her, equally spent, chest heaving "That . . . was . . . incredible."

"Amazing."

"My legs feel like cooked spaghetti."

She laughed. "I saw a strange white light."

"My feet are still vibrating."

Tatiana knew how to put an end to this contest. "Bet you can't top this: I love you."

Jack punched at the water, the competitive part of him obviously hating to lose, no matter what the game. But after a single glance at the moon, his face broke into a wide, satisfied smile. "I love you more."

"Prove it."

He floated onto his back, proudly displaying the evidence.

Greedily, Tatiana swam toward him. "Did you spike that bottle of wine with Viagra?"

Chapter Seventeen

Tatiana had to stop waking up like this.

Enrique, armed with Starbucks, stood over her, his eyes bright with amusement.

She stretched, still sleepy, but it was a deliriously wonderful sleepy. "That better be my regular." Sitting up to accept, she quickly pulled the sheet over a zonked-out Jack to cover his bare ass.

Enrique laughed. "Since you crawled into bed with him, do you mind if I get cozy with the hot chick in your room?"

Tatiana practically lurched in protest. "That's my sister, and she's only seventeen."

"I can respect that." One beat. "When's her birthday?"

"Enrique!"

"I'm kidding. You know, a woman who just got laid two nights in a row shouldn't be so uptight." He parked on the edge of the sleeper sofa. "The twins are up and in their playpen." A pointed glance to Jack. "Do I have to do everything around here?"

Tatiana drank deep on the coffee. "Why are you here so early? Don't get me wrong. I'm not complaining." She smiled. "It's just that I'm used to you not being around when I need something."

Enrique smirked. "Dr. G really needs to help you with this passive-aggressive side. It's not attractive."

"Oh, speaking of Dr. G, get me in pronto."

"Maybe you should think about adding on to the house and just giving her a room."

Tatiana grinned sweetly. "Nothing you say is going to spoil my mood this morning."

"Your sister sleeps in a thong."

Tatiana closed her eyes. "Enrique, I'm warning you. Kristin is off limits."

"Don't worry. Anyway, I've actually given up sex. I'm trying to improve myself. I started drawing again."

She didn't buy it. "*You've* given up sex?"

"Well, only in the morning. Those are the hours I dedicate to my art. I do have a year of animation school under my belt, and Jaron's got big pull at Cartoon Planet. Who knows? Maybe I'll come up with the next Powerpuff Girls phenomenon."

Tatiana was pleasantly surprised. She'd never known Enrique to think in terms of career goals or the future. Usually, his only concern was the remote possibility of a condom breaking.

Jack stirred and, with a start, bolted upright, his hair a sexy pillow-static mess. "What time is it?"

Enrique checked his watch. "Almost seven."

"I can't believe I slept this late." Jack began to tumble out, realized he was naked, and covered himself back up.

Tatiana laughed. "Relax. The twins are fine."

Enrique nodded, pleased with himself. "I put them in the playpen."

Jack rubbed his eyes. "Their diapers need to be changed."

"Already done," Enrique said. "I was lucky. No poop. They're saving that for you, I guess."

Jack was clearly threatened by the fact that the first part of the morning had gone so well without him.

Tatiana thought this *very* cute. She loved him more already.

"Ethan's crib sheet usually turns up damp by morning. It needs to be—"

"Washed, I know," Enrique cut in. "It's in the hamper."

"Did you—"

"Yes, I spot-treated it. What do you think I am? A pig?"

Tatiana watched the rapid-fire exchange like a tennis match. It was better than McEnroe and Borg's legendary battles at Wimbledon.

Jack surrendered. "I give, mate."

Enrique grinned triumphant and turned to Tatiana. "Need a ride to the studio?"

"Not until noon. They're shooting one of Greg's fight scenes this morning."

Enrique shrugged. "What can I do?" He gestured to Jack. "Besides his job, of course. He's obviously taken on other duties."

Jack good-naturedly tossed a pillow at Enrique's head.

Tatiana took a deep breath. "There's so much that needs to be done. We have to get Kristin into a good high school, secure my appointment with Dr. G, call-block my mother—"

"That reminds me," Enrique interrupted. "Your mother called. In fact, she's holding right now."

Tatiana gave him an incredulous look. "No."

Enrique shook his head yes. "Kitchen phone. Don't worry

about staying on too long. I can do some sketching until you're done.''

"Ugh!" Tatiana jumped out of bed and yanked the top sheet for cover, leaving Jack to fend for himself.

Enrique gave Jack a knowing nod. "Serious mother-daughter issues."

"So I've gathered," Jack replied, casually placing a pillow over his unmentionable.

Tatiana stomped into the kitchen, the sheet haphazardly wrapped around her like some toga from Mars. She saw the receiver dangling off the hook and rushed to pick it up. "Mom?"

"Do you have any idea how long I've been waiting? How rude! This call is going to cost me a fortune."

Tatiana sighed wearily. "We're on the same long-distance plan. A nickel per minute. You're probably out fifty cents."

"It's still a waste of money!"

"I could call some celebrity friends, maybe get a telethon started."

Justine Bonner huffed. "What's going on there? A strange man answered the phone."

"That's just Enrique, my personal assistant. He'd only be considered strange in, say, the Midwest or certain parts of the South. He's a California native."

"A *personal* assistant. Must be nice to have one of those. I wouldn't know. I'm not a big *star*."

"Not yet. But I could see you making a strong impression on one of those reality shows. Would you consider *Real World Afghanistan*?"

Justine seethed in a long second of silence. "I didn't call to be ridiculed. How's Kristin?"

"Still sleeping." Tatiana considered sharing the details of Kristin's L.A. adventure—the limo driver, the funk ball, the club drug experimentation—but in the end decided against it. Her mother knew exactly what kind of trouble she'd put on that plane.

Justine clucked. "I expected a call last night. Never got one."

This infuriated Tatiana. "You ship Kristin to California like a package from Fingerhut, no word of warning to me, no cell phone for emergencies, and now you want updates on the hour? Mom, you don't have to live like this. There's medication for bipolar disorder."

"I was testing her!" Justine hissed defensively. "And she failed. Kristin's old enough to know that you're the first person she should've called. Might as well give me the sordid details. Where did she go?" Her mother pressed on before Tatiana could answer. "Probably ran off with some guy to a crazy party where everybody gets high on that drug they call Agony."

"Ecstasy."

"What?"

"The drug is called Ecstasy. Agony is this conversation."

Jack stepped into the kitchen, the pillow still over his crotch. "I need to get dressed and see about the twins' breakfast. Make me some coffee?"

Tatiana nodded yes, pointed to the phone, and used the same hand to form a pretend gun that she aimed at her own head.

Jack laughed and sauntered off.

Tatiana watched his beautiful ass until he disappeared from sight. It belonged to her now. Sorry, Constance Ann. She made a mental note to have Enrique call-block her, too.

"Who was that?" Justine demanded.

"Jack. He's the twins' nanny. Actually, I call him a manny—"

"You have a personal assistant *and* a nanny? Are you

sure it's okay to talk to me, Tatiana? Maybe you should hire someone to do that, too.''

''Believe me, if I could afford the salary that job would demand . . .''

''What was I thinking to send Kristin to live with someone like you?'' Justine asked hotly. ''She'll become worse than ever. You and your personal assistants and nannies and dirty movies—that's not real life!''

A scream was itching at Tatiana's throat. She could feel her blood firing up. This time Justine had gone too far. ''Let's not forget the central issue here—you kicked Kristin out of the house,'' she began, striving to keep her voice computer cool. ''Any guilt about the way you handled the matter is something for *you* to wrestle with. So don't go off point and start judging me. It's all I can do to make sure that Kristin has everything she needs and feels welcome in my home. Sorry, Mom. You're going to have to dump this on someone else. Or better yet, deal with it yourself. Because I don't have the time.''

Justine's silence was deafening. It went on for over a minute.

Tatiana beamed. She was so proud of herself. If only she had that on tape! She could play it back for Dr. G, then sit and listen as the good therapist praised her emotional growth. What a breakthrough. A typical argument with her mother used to end with Tatiana making up a story to get off the phone. Example: she had to chase down Winona Ryder, who'd stolen her purse. But this time Tatiana dropped the games and glib comments for the simple truth in her heart. It felt glorious!

And she decided to quit while she was ahead. ''Listen, I have to go. Jack wants coffee, and I'm not even dressed yet. There's a lot to do.''

"You make coffee for the nanny?" Justine inquired haughtily.

"He's not just the nanny, Mom. He's also my lover." *Click.* That seemed as good a time as any to hang up.

"Constance Ann, why is Pappy the Panda sad?" Hallie asked.

Because he's stuck on this piece-of-shit show with pint-sized hacks like you. It was her fantasy script. But she plastered on the Constance Ann smile and delivered the real line. "Pappy misses his grandparents. They live very far away, and he doesn't get a chance to visit them often."

Chris piped in next. "What can we do to make Pappy feel better?"

Constance Ann widened her eyes and clapped her hands. "I have a great idea! Let's help Pappy the Panda write a letter to his grandparents! He can tell them about all the fun things he's been up to lately!"

The children cheered their approval and jumped up and down. Then, as up-tempo electronic pop music filled the studio, the young tykes segued into a simple dance routine.

Hallie, ever the pro, hit her mark like gold to sing the first lead.

>   *If somebody you love lives far away*
>   *It doesn't have to be a sad day*

Chris grooved next to Hallie to belt out his part.

>   *There's a great way to start feeling better*
>   *It's called writing a special letter. . . .*

"Jesus Christ!" Constance Ann screamed. "Is the fat one tone deaf?"

"Cut!" Will Hayes bellowed, burying his face in his hands.

"The girl is homely, but at least the little rodent can carry a tune!"

As if on cue, Chris and Hallie started to cry.

Constance Ann shook her head. If only the whiny cretins could dance in perfect synchronization, too. Then maybe a show could get wrapped before the tech goons clocked in on overtime, which blew the budget and cut in on her gross points.

Chris and Hallie were really pouring on the tears now.

"Listen to them!" Constance Ann yelled. "Wailing like I took away their pacifier. Maybe I should fix 'em a sugar tit and put 'em to bed with a baby bottle."

Chris usually scampered away like a rat, but today, even with his eyes dripping like a leaky faucet, he stood his ground. "I sang just like my voice coach taught me to!"

Constance Ann got right up in his chubby face. "Is that so?"

Defiantly, Chris nodded.

"Who is this shit-for-brains coach?"

"Mr. Bessell!"

"Well, you can give *Mr. Bessell* this message from me: He wouldn't know the right key if it came up and clamped itself to his hairy balls!"

The kid's cheeks turned red. "You're mean!"

She gave him her most evil smile. "I know. And I'm going to prove just how mean I can be right now. You're fired. So get your rotten-singing, line-flubbing, Little Debbie Cake-eating ass out of here." She lunged at him. Just for kicks.

Chris ran like hell.

Constance Ann cackled. "Let that be a lesson, kiddies. Nobody messes with the star of the show!" She blazed her angry eyes at all the shocked little faces. "Anybody else want to take me on?"

"We're breaking for lunch!" Will shouted. He rushed Constance Ann, taking her firmly by the arm and into the corridor that led to her dressing room.

She twisted her elbow free. "Don't manhandle me, you son of a bitch! Save those moves for your S-and-M hookers."

His expression was pleading. "I appreciate your eye for detail and commitment to excellence, Constance Ann. It's why this show—"

"*My* show."

Will conceded. "It's why *your* show is so successful. But we have to find a way to identify these missteps without terrorizing the other actors. It disrupts the whole shooting day."

Constance Ann smiled the smile of the wicked. "Is this a new approach that you practiced in the mirror, Will? So sorry. Patronization doesn't work with me." She turned to leave.

"I've mentioned that Chris is Sam Taylor's nephew, haven't I?" His tone carried a hint of a threat.

Constance Ann stopped dead in her tracks. "Yes. On more than one occasion. Each time it gets less interesting."

"Sam is nobody to tangle with. He *owns* Tycoon Productions. He owns *you*."

She laughed in his pallid face. "Nobody owns me. Sam owns the show, and the show brings in megabucks." She put on the trademark Constance Ann grin, all sweetness and light and Pepsodent bright. "This mug paid for his new home in Aspen last year. Do you really think he gives a damn if I get a little cranky with the bit players?"

Will just stared at her. He looked tired and run-down.

Constance Ann thought about firing him, too. But she discarded the idea. Making this Ivy League sap miserable was too much fun. "How do you do it, Will?"

"How do I do what?"

Constance Ann patted his clammy cheek. "How do you manage to get around with your head so far up your ass?" And then she walked down the corridor, through the side exit, and into her brand-new customized convertible, just off the boat from Germany.

She checked her voice mail on the road, hoping to have heard from Jack Thorpe. There were three messages: two hang-ups and a thank-you call from Mrs. Herman McKenzie. Shit. The four dollars and eighty-nine cents it had cost to feed the bitter cow a vegetable plate at that prison mess hall she called a restaurant hardly warranted the gesture. Even worse, Eunice's babble revealed nothing about future plans. Just a bunch of mindless chatter and religious pabulum. Constance Ann exercised her favorite option—delete.

On a lark, she decided to drop in. If Jack didn't come to her, then she would go to Jack. Besides, she had to get her hands on that *Sin by Sin* script. No point in delaying morality's top cop and her faithful God squad's public annihilation of Tatiana.

Constance Ann knew better than to seek out the Malibu estate. That house featured in *In Style* belonged to Tatiana about as much as that sprawling ski lodge in Vail from the *In Style* a few months back had belonged to Constance Ann—for the length of the photo shoot and not a nanosecond longer. Hell, she couldn't blame the cheap starlet. It was all part of the celebrity machine, and, face it: dreamy-eyed yacks struggling month to month in dingy digs needed something to daydream about. That's who forked out good money for those rags.

Snaking through the Hollywood Hills, BMW roof down,

sun shining, Chris Isaak crooning, she came upon Tatiana's home and almost laughed out loud. Constance Ann's pool shack was bigger than this. She was dying to know how much Tatiana had paid for this stucco outhouse. Granted, the view was great. But who could survive in such cramped quarters on a daily basis?

Constance Ann tried the front door. It was open. She let herself in.

Jack Thorpe stood in the kitchen, exquisitely shirtless, the rest of him vacuum-packed into faded and tattered Levi's. The sight reminded her of that classic Diet Coke commercial with Lucky Vanous. Only better. Because Lucky had never spoken, and Jack had an accent that could turn her body to butter.

He was hovering over those blond brats, patiently feeding them yogurt by the spoonful, every bite cause for some minicelebration of coos and effusive praise. "That's right, Ethan. Eat it up. Big-boy style. What a man! And Everson's hungry, too. Say, 'I'm the most beautiful girl in the whole wide world, and I love my lunchie wunchie. Yes, I do. Oh, yes I do.' "

Constance Ann questioned Jack's sanity. He could do so much more than play nursemaid to Tatiana's tots. Sure, the knee might be shot to hell, ruling out pro sports altogether, but the rest of him remained intact. There was modeling, acting, broadcasting—anything but this mindless slavery to children. Jesus, he was like her alter ego, only worse— *sincere* about it. A kid sucking down a blot of yogurt actually brought him real happiness.

Suddenly, the girl spotted Constance Ann, a fearful expression clouding her face. She pointed a finger and grunted like a cave dweller, in an all-out bid for Jack's attention.

He responded instantly, concentrating hard, eager to

understand her. His gaze followed the little hand, leading him straight to . . .

"Surprise!" Constance Ann sang.

Jack was genuinely stunned.

"The door was open," she explained. "I didn't want to ring the bell in case they were napping."

"We're having lunch," Jack said. There was great pride in his voice, as if it were an accomplishment along the lines of "I saved a life today; my album went double platinum, I built a new house." *We're having lunch.* Did the media know about this? Maybe she should call a press conference.

"I see that!" Constance Ann gave it her all, really turning on the charm. She moved closer, ratcheting up the sweetness. "Is the lunch for their tummies or their faces?"

Jack wiped a messy chin. "A little of both, I'm afraid." He looked at her curiously.

"We kept missing each other on the phone, and I was in the neighborhood, so . . ."

He glanced away, continuing to fuss over the kids, all but ignoring her.

Constance Ann cleared her throat. "I stopped by to discuss my fitness needs."

Jack smiled kindly, but his eyes seemed to carry an apology. "Can I get you anything to drink? Juice, water . . ."

Did she look two years old? "Bourbon."

"Ah, the hard stuff." He thought for a second, and then his brow furrowed. "Tatiana's teenage sister is staying with us, and the liquor cabinet was locked up last night. I'm not sure where the key is. I can scare up some wine, perhaps."

Constance Ann was still hung up on his choice of pronoun. Us. She felt her stomach churn a bit. The first sip didn't help. What he offered tasted like the cheap stuff she gave out as Christmas gifts every year. She put it down, never to be touched again.

She noticed a splash of yogurt just above Jack's nipple and experienced a sudden longing to lick him clean. Running her tongue across her upper lip, she fixated on his hairless chest. "Now, about my needs . . ."

The boy—at least she thought it was the boy—chose this moment to break into a high-pitched wail, kicking his feet and flapping his hands.

Jack extricated him from the high chair.

The boy stopped crying but clung to Jack like a baby koala, fearfully turning away from Constance Ann.

"He's shy," Jack explained. "And tired. Refuses to nap today for some reason."

She hated parents who gave a running telegraph of every burp, bump, doo-doo, and spit-up. Jack reminded her of the typical child addict strolling the aisles of Baby Gap, looking for a fix.

Now the girl was pitching a fit, stirring up enough commotion to make you think she was acting out a scene from *The Towering Inferno.*

Indulgently Jack scooped her out of the seat with his free arm. Peace restored. "This is a tricky part of the day."

Constance Ann just stared at him. Her oh-the-kids-are-so-cute routine was used up. What now?

Jack shifted uncomfortably. "I should tell you that my situation has changed. Making time for fitness training has been a challenge. Now with Tatiana's sister living here and shooting schedules being extended for the film, it's only going to get worse."

Constance Ann couldn't believe it. Jack Thorpe, master of the Jack Attack, once as big in the U.K. as Michael Jordan was right here in America, sounded like a frazzled suburban housewife. "What about your work with the Junior League?"

He smirked. "Going very well. Thank you for asking."

She was almost ready to forgive him. "It's still there."

"My sense of humor? It better be. I'd bloody well go mad without it."

"Surely Tatiana gives you a night off. You know what they say. All work and no play makes Jack a—"

"Very involved boy." He smiled. "Another new development since I left that message on your machine."

Constance Ann's calm expression belied the inner disgust. "You and Tatiana?"

Jack nodded. "For two nights, now. I think we might have a future together. We've only broken up once."

"Impressive. But don't order monogrammed towels yet. By the time a Greg Tapper movie wraps, you can always count on a few ex-husbands and ex-boyfriends to start a support group."

This hit a nerve. She noticed a sudden tightening along Jack's jawline.

"Maybe you'll be the exception. Stranger things have happened." She started for the door. "Please tell Tatiana that I wish her all the happiness she deserves."

"And in your shrewd estimation, Constance Ann, how much would that be?"

"Who am I to say?"

"Just how long are the two of you going to carry this grudge? It's been *years*. Move on. Life's too short."

Constance Ann didn't know what to make of him. There were moments of keen intelligence and sharp humor, but then he could ruin everything with sugary clichés like this, rendering him nothing more than an unoriginal hard-body. Any second now he could be quoting Rodney King. *Can't we all just get along? Please.* It also pissed her off that this male Hazel from Down Under presumed to know what her grudge was. Because he had no idea.

She hated dredging up the memory. The animosity it triggered made her body feel hot, almost radioactive. The Beasley Acting Workshop's showcase production of *A Streetcar Named Desire* should have been her moment. By that point Greg Tapper had dropped out of the class, on to bigger and better things, leaving the smoldering role of Stanley Kowalski to some beefy hack who was probably delivering pizzas today. It hadn't mattered, though. She would have wowed them as Stella, maybe hooked an agent, even become a real actress instead of some Shari Lewis clone.

Remembrance of the botched scheme smoked inside her mind. Constance Ann had poisoned food intended for the actress she understudied. Not enough to kill, just enough to take the bitch out of commission for a few days. But in a sadistic twist of fate, the actress Tatiana was shadowing had consumed it. The switcheroo still burned her to this day. That redheaded tramp had got the chance to shine. And Constance Ann had practically presented her the opportunity on a silver salver.

"You're both successful now," Jack was saying. "Who cares about what happened years ago in some stupid acting class?"

I do. She shrugged easily. "Maybe I should bury the hatchet." *In her back.*

"My football mates and I used to have legendary rows— shoving, throwing punches, name-calling of the vulgar sort. But it was never anything a few bottles of ale couldn't repair."

Constance Ann nodded with vague appreciation. His soccer-field friendship lessons didn't interest her. She wanted that fucking script. "I really should be going. Do you mind if I visit the bathroom first? It's a long drive back to the studio."

Jack started to show her the way.

"Don't be silly," Constance Ann said. "You've got your hands full with those little ones. I'll find it myself."

And she did. On the bedside table. Mission accomplished.

Chapter Eighteen

"Have you ever undergone hypnosis?" September asked.

"No," Tatiana answered.

"I'd like to try it. You don't know what happened that night, but we might be able to find out by tapping into your subconscious."

Tatiana gave September a savage look. "My mind is like a bad neighborhood, doctor. It's no place for you to visit. Trust me on that."

"Are you afraid of what I might find?"

"No, I'm not," Tatiana said coolly, pausing a beat. "But you should be."

September registered a moment's pure fear.

"Cut!" Kip Quick yelled. He left his director's chair to join them on the cramped but impeccably designed set, this one the dark-paneled office of Dr. Beverly Hoffman, the psychiatrist played by September Moore in *Sin by Sin*.

"Great scene." Kip flopped a nasty wad of gum back

and forth to push out his words. "Let's try another take." He put his arm around September. "This time, show more fear after Tatiana's last line."

September nodded her understanding and did exactly what she was told, emoting with all the subtlety of a jackhammer. By comparison, Faye Dunaway's wire hanger scene in *Mommie Dearest* was low-key.

But Kip loved it, ordered the take to print, and called for the next setup.

The crew rocketed into action.

September tossed an annoyed look in Kip's direction. "Can you believe that *boy* questioned my instincts? I probably won my Oscar the same year he had his birthday party at Chuck E. Cheese. Does he not realize that I have an Academy Award for Best Supporting Actress?"

"He should. You posted signs at the catering table."

"Thank God I thought of that. It's important that everyone know they're working with an Oscar winner. Helps build morale." She laughed ruefully. "And this picture could use some."

"What do you mean?"

September reared back in astonishment. "Have you read the script?"

Tatiana just looked at her, puzzled. She held up a battered copy of the screenplay, scribbled with notes. "This is my main copy. I keep a second one on my bedside table. Ask me anyone's line from any page. I mean it." She shut her eyes to prove her mettle, working straight from random memory. "Page sixty-one. Nurse number two. 'You're going to have to wait out there. The surgeon will be with you as soon as we know something.'"

September seemed amused by her commitment. "Honey, sometimes you need a little distance to see things objectively. This script is bad. Like, *Silk Stockings* in its final season

267

bad." She took her voice down to a faint whisper. "They would probably fire me for saying this." A furtive circular glance. "But I think it's worse than *Body of Evidence*. You know, that terrible Madonna movie where she burns Willem Dafoe with candle wax."

Tatiana remembered the film well. An unintentional comedy.

"It's worse than *Color of Night*, too," September went on. "Bruce Willis was in that one. Freeze-frame the director's cut, and you get a good look at his willy." She giggled. "It's no wonder Demi divorced him."

Tatiana managed a wan smile. She couldn't believe September was trashing the *Sin by Sin* script. It was great. Everybody said so. David Walsh had worked like hell to get this Greg Tapper vehicle into production.

"Honey, what's wrong? You're looking just like I did after I found out Joan Van Ark got my spot on *Hollywood Squares*."

Tatiana went on the offensive. "If you think this script is so horrible, why did you accept the role?"

"It's a big movie, and I needed the money. Come on, there's only a handful of great projects in a given year, and Julia Roberts, Gwyneth Paltrow, and Nicole Kidman lay claim to those. The rest are shit. That's why I do so much television. And it's not much better. All I did in *Just A Few Bites, Jenny!* was scream at Katie Holmes until she ate a bagel."

Tatiana stared blankly ahead as they walked in the direction of September's trailer, her friend's words fading to white noise. She tried to imagine the script through less enamored eyes. If you took away the fact that Greg Tapper was the star, that a powerful studio like Univision was behind it, and that industry legend David Walsh was ushering it to the big screen . . . then you had . . . Oh, God!

The realization began to take shape. Subtract all those things and what you had was just another B movie, only this time without those awful producers, Don and Glee Dobson, which, technically, bumped it up to a B-plus, possibly A-minus, if you took into account catering and wardrobe improvements.

September stepped inside her enormous trailer. Greg Tapper's beat it in terms of size, but only by a few hundred square feet. She'd purchased it herself before the career slump, knowing that down the road she would need some star trappings to nourish her inner diva.

Tatiana halted dead in her tracks.

Kristin was going at it hot and heavy with a half-naked man in September's bed. The guy—ripped muscles, bleached hair, tanning-bed pallor—gave off strong Chippendale vibes.

"Kristin!" Tatiana shrieked.

"Rob!" September screamed.

As if not a peep had been uttered, their game of tonsil hockey played on.

September slipped off one of her low-heeled pumps and threw it at Rob, hitting his right shoulder.

Finally, their tongues separated.

"You were supposed to stay in here and watch television!" Tatiana roared.

"I was," Kristin explained, shrugging a little. "But then Rob came in. Anyway, I was sick of *Judge Judy*."

Tatiana regarded Rob as if he were toxic waste. "She's only seventeen, and you look like you've had six years of high school."

Rob jumped off the bed before the last syllable dropped. He pointed an accusing finger at Kristin. "She swore that she was eighteen!"

Everyone boomeranged glares to Kristin now.

Except September, who turned to Tatiana. "Seventeen? I thought she was twelve. What's the big deal?"

At first, Tatiana thought this might be a sick joke. But then she realized that September Moore was talking. "Does she look twelve?"

The loopy actress gave Kristin a critical once-over. "Now that you mention it, I guess not. I wasn't paying attention when I first met her. You know how I feel about children. They should all be cordoned off somewhere until they're of voting age."

Tatiana went back to the subject at hand. She scowled at Rob. "Who are you?"

September looked puzzled. "I thought that was your sister, Kathy."

"*Kristin,*" Tatiana hissed. "Who's he?"

September glowered at the chiseled Adonis. "He was *formerly* known as my masseur."

Tatiana rolled her eyes. "Well, this rubdown is over."

September nodded severely. "You're damn right it is!"

Rob thought fast. "It's not my fault. She was all over me." In the weak-excuses-from-creepy-guys category, this ranked right up there with "The dog ate my homework."

Now Kristin turned on him. "All over *you?* I guess it's true what they say about steroids and memory loss. Because you were totally into *me.*"

Rob's face flushed red.

Kristin thundered on. "Normally, I don't even go for the muscle-bound-shaved-body-Clairol-blond-kit-ready-for-my-close-up-in-a-gay-porno look. But I was bored, you didn't completely repulse me, and your breath tasted like spearmint. So, I thought, whatever."

Tatiana tried to fight back a smile. She lost the battle.

September nodded the way politicians do when the president says something patriotic in his State of the Union

address. "I like this girl! She reminds me of myself. Oh, to
be thirteen again."

Tatiana elbowed her friend and costar. "She's *seventeen*."

"I know. She's like I was at thirteen, though. Only more
innocent."

Rob slipped on his white Calvin Klein tank in a hurry.
"I'm out of here."

"And don't you dare come back!" September yelled.
Watching him go, she chewed on her lower lip. "Until
tomorrow at ten o'clock!"

Tatiana lit into Kristin. "First the limousine driver at the
airport. Now September's masseur. You meet a guy and five
minutes later you're on his lap. It's girls like you who make
people believe those letters to *Penthouse*."

"As if *you* can lecture me!" Kristin fired back.

"I can, and I will!"

Kristin plugged her ears. "I can't hear you!"

There was nothing more annoying than this tactic. Naturally, Tatiana wanted to strangle her. Instead, she mouthed
the words, "You're on the next plane to Florida."

Kristin dropped her hands. "What?"

Tatiana spoke with cucumber cool. "You read my lips
correctly."

September rejoined them. "I didn't. What'd you say?"

"I said that if Kristin doesn't listen to me, she'll be on
the next plane back to Florida."

September gave Kristin a horrified look. "Listen to your
sister. Once I was desperate for work and had to do dinner
theater in Florida. The worst two nights of my life."

Tatiana gave her a strange look. "Two nights?"

"The veal was bad, and the health department shut the
place down." September perched herself on the edge of the
bed next to Kristin. "I just can't get over how much you

remind me of myself at your age.'' She patted the girl's hand. "I was always seeking out older boys—college guys, fathers of the really cute college guys, in some cases the grandfathers if they were exceptionally virile like Sean Connery. I didn't think boys my age could do anything but make fart noises under their arms.''

Kristin laughed, turning to Tatiana. "Is this woman for real?''

Tatiana opened her mouth to answer.

September beat her to the punch. "Of course, I'm for real. I won the Academy Award for Best Supporting Actress in *Postcard from Paris*. Don't they teach you anything in school?''

Kristin smirked. "I guess not. They waste our time with those other subjects—math and science.''

September reached out to grab one of the signs that she'd posted around the set. "Here, take a flier.'' She shook her head in disbelief. "And they wonder why Japanese kids are so far ahead.''

"Is there a point on the way?'' Tatiana pressed.

"Yes!'' September clapped her hands. "What Kathy needs is—''

"Kristin," Tatiana corrected.

September turned to the girl. "Do you mind if I call you Kathy?''

Kristin offered a diffident shrug.

"What Kathy needs is a whirlwind high school romance. I remember mine. Mark Cameron. He was kicked off the football team for bad grades but excelled in shop class. A real go-getter.'' September winked. "And good with his hands, too.'' She sighed wistfully. "All these little trysts with older guys are ultimately fake and kind of sad. You need a sweet high school love to set things right. Every girl deserves an Archie. Who do you relate to more—Betty or Veronica?''

"Veronica," Kristin said quickly.

September beamed with pride. "Me, too. You know, Betty was such a tomboy. Personally, I think she was a lesbian."

Tatiana chimed in with this pragmatic announcement: "Before she finds her Archie, we need to find a good school."

Kristen made a face.

"Beverly Hills High!" September exclaimed. "It's the most famous high school in the world. And my alma mater, I'm proud to say. I graduated the same year as Nicolas Cage."

Kristin's eyes sparkled. "Really? He's hot."

September waved a dismissive hand. "All I remember is that he hardly ever washed his hair. Oh, Kathy, you can join the ranks of internationally recognized alumni! First, there's me, an Academy Award winner, class of . . . not that long ago. There's also Jamie Lee Curtis, Angelina Jolie, Antonio Sabato Jr., even the *Menendez* brothers."

Kristin gasped. "Those guys that killed their parents?"

"Yes! Horrible people. But very famous. They were precursors to O. J. He wouldn't have received half the attention if it hadn't been for those boys. I think he owes them a great deal."

Frustrated, Tatiana broke in. "September, please. We're not even zoned for that school."

"I am," September said. "Use my address."

"Does that mean I can live with you?" Kristin asked hopefully.

September put hand over heart. "Oh, Kathy, how sweet. But the answer's no. You see, children bore me."

Kristin was offended. "I'm not a child. I'm seventeen."

"Not a selling point. Teenagers like you can be so self-centered. I tried the Big Sisters program once. You know, because I like to give back. But the orphan girl they assigned me to was just out for herself. It was awful. Not once did she plan or do something special for me. Luckily, I quit in time to put a stop-payment on my donation check.'' She breathed a sigh of relief.

There were three fast knocks on the door.

September gasped. "Rob's back already? You two might have to get lost.''

It was Enrique.

Kristin took note of her posture and jutted out her breasts.

Enrique glanced around appreciatively. "Nice digs.'' He turned to Tatiana. "I thought *you* were the star.''

She gave him a look. "September *owns* this.''

"Yeah, but I got stuck with the towing bill to get it onto the lot,'' September spat. "Cheap bastards. Meanwhile Greg Tapper gets a girl to hold an umbrella for him just so he doesn't get any sun from the trailer to the studio door.''

Enrique reviewed a list on his small steno pad, the kind reporters use. "Your mother is call-blocked, Dr. G can see you at seven, and all the bills are paid. Regarding schools for Kristin, I need to know if you're thinking public, private, religious, military, or boarding.''

Kristin appealed to Tatiana, her expression pleading.

Tatiana gave in. "I'm thinking Beverly Hills High. We'll use September's address to get around the zoning issue.''

"Ah,'' Enrique said, breaking into a big smile. "I remember those days well.''

"You went to that school?'' Tatiana asked.

"Not exactly. My high school was in East L.A. But I dated a hot Jewish girl at Beverly who gave the best—''

Tatiana held up a stop-sign hand. "Don't you dare!''

"*Parties*. What did you think I was going to say?'' He winked.

Kristin giggled.

"I've got an idea. Why don't I take Kristin by there right now to get the enrollment process started. I can pretend to be September's assistant."

Tatiana couldn't resist the opening. "Please do a better job of pretending to be her assistant than you do pretending to be mine. We want this plan to work."

"And since you're pretending," September said, "Pick up some dim sum for me. There's a Chin Chin on Beverly Drive near the school."

"Come on, Kristin," Enrique said. "I'll show you how to forge lunch passes. The in crowd goes off campus to this pizza joint called Mulberry Street."

"Cool!" Kristin jumped up and headed out, so excited that she offered only a vague good-bye.

The matter of the lousy *Sin by Sin* script came back to haunt Tatiana. She turned to September with an imploring look. "Tell me the truth. Do you really think this movie is going to be bad?"

"Honey, you know what they say. If it ain't on the page, it ain't on the stage."

Jack stood inside the tiny pool cabana, concentrating hard. Ideas were jumping inside his head faster than he could process them. But with a little imagination, he knew this could work.

"I say we just do it, kiddos."

"Daddy . . . do it," Everson murmured, having graduated from the fractured *Da Da* in the last few days.

Ethan giggled and kicked his feet. "Do it!"

"OK, team, make me a big promise. No sleeping in the car. If I'm going to get this done, I'll need you to take a long nap in your cribs when we get back."

"Po?" Everson asked.

"Yes, Po will take a nap with you."

"Elmo?" she inquired.

"Yes, Elmo will take a nap with you, too."

She went through the entire list of bed buddies that had to be present and accounted for before she would submit to sleep: Po, from the Teletubbies, Elmo from *Sesame Street*, Barney, BJ, and Baby Bop, Buttercup Hippo, and a plush monkey of unknown origin that Enrique had brought home from that overly service-oriented sales associate at Saks Fifth Avenue.

"Let's go bye-bye, gang. We've got a lot to get done before Mommy comes home."

Jack secured the twins in their car seats and pressed "Play" on the video machine that had cost him an extra five hundred bucks. But soon the Wiggles were singing, Ethan and Everson were rocking strong, and it felt like the smartest money he'd ever spent. He didn't miss the BMW Z8 anymore. His new sports utility vehicle was much more practical—more storage space, no bending over when buckling kids in and out, and lots of head and leg room.

Together they made the rounds: Home Depot, Target, a funky furnishings store called Zipper, and a warehouse that dealt only in European beds. Ethan and Everson never fussed once. They were too fascinated with the slapdash pace of it all, breathing in frenzied excitement at each new stop. When strangers peered over the double stroller to covet the blond wonders, they merely smiled as if to say, "Yes, we're adorable. Still a slow news day."

It was their charm that had been Jack's secret weapon to insure immediate delivery and on-site assembly of two items: a multiuse futon that went from cozy love seat to sofa to bed in just a few lifts and pulls, and a funky wardrobe cabinet with crystal hardware. With Ethan and Everson grinning in matching red gingham-print overalls, the clerk couldn't talk of jammed schedules and driver shortages. These kids were Kryptonite to the word *no*.

After shopping, they shared two Happy Meals at McDonald's and watched a gaggle of screaming toddlers wear themselves out in the Play Land's ball jumper. A new Barney video (something about the purple dinosaur going to the zoo) held their interest during the ride home. By the time Jack reached the driveway, Everson was yawning. It had worked out perfectly. He put them to bed and didn't hear a peep for three and a half hours. That had been just enough time to paint, navigate the delivery men, and put all the extra touches in place.

Later, Jack was preparing dinner when Enrique and Kristin arrived, joshing each other like close cousins and sipping drinks from Coffee Bean and Tea Leaf.

"I want to play lead in the spring production of *Hello, Dolly!*" Kristin said.

"But you can't sing. That's usually a prerequisite for musicals," Enrique teased.

"I can sing!"

"I heard you massacre the new Shakira song in the car. You're so bad you should lip-synch in the shower."

Kristin pushed him, giggling, clearly loving the abuse. She glanced at Jack, then traded a secret look with Enrique. More giggles.

"Uh, Jack," Enrique began, hardly able to keep a straight face, "Kristin and I were just wondering . . ."

"Yes?"

"Well, you seem to have your hands full with the twins." Enrique tried to continue but cracked up. "The last thing you need . . . is another baby in this house, so I sure hope that you and Tatiana are . . . practicing safe sex!"

Kristin lost her composure. Ditto Enrique. They were doubled over, clutching stomachs, gasping for relief.

Jack shook his head in mock disapproval but found himself laughing, too. "Very funny, Cheech and Chong. Now make yourselves useful and go check on the twins. *Bear in the Big Blue House* is almost over."

L.A.'s newest comedy team headed into the living room, still breaking themselves up, just as Tatiana came in through the kitchen door.

Jack opened his mouth to speak.

Tatiana hushed him with a finger, a sexy smile curled onto her lips. She cased out the situation and dashed into his arms for a deep, passionate kiss.

He drew back a little, tracing the length of her lower lip with his tongue. "I wasn't expecting you until much later. But I'm not complaining."

Tatiana sighed the sigh of the exhausted. "I only have a few minutes. I've got an appointment with Dr. G at seven, and two scenes to shoot after that. It's going to be a late night."

Jack's hands skated down her body and hooked onto her waist. "I don't care. I'll wait up."

She hugged him tightly and moaned out her fatigue. "I'd rather just crawl into bed and find you sleeping there and cuddle up beside you."

"I think that can be arranged." He kissed the top of her head.

"I drove all the way home to kiss my babies. One down, two to go. How are they?"

"Operating at the genius level, of course. Everson can operate the VCR and count to ten."

"Hmm, that's one more thing than Enrique can do."

Tatiana caught sight of something on his forearm and inspected it more closely. "Is that paint?"

Jack's grin revealed nothing. *Almost busted.* "Come out to the pool. I want to show you something." He pulled her by the hand, leading her out to the deck, playfully covering her eyes as they approached the cabana.

Tatiana loved all the mystery. She couldn't stop laughing, her hands pulling at his wrists. "What's going on?"

Jack set her free.

Tatiana opened her eyes. "Oh, my God!" She glanced around, trying to get her bearings. "This is the cabana?"

Jack nodded proudly and watched her take in the transformation.

The old white interior was awash in wild pink—a great color called Hot Lips from Benjamin Moore. The queen-sized futon ruled the small space, but there was just enough room for a bedside table, the wardrobe cabinet, and a desk. The tiny haven was ready for occupancy, complete with a thirteen-inch color television and a portable stereo.

Tatiana turned to him, confused. "What's this for?"

"It's for Kristin."

"Oh, Jack!" Her eyes welled up with tears.

He wrapped an arm around her waist and pulled her closer. "Kristin's seventeen, and for this arrangement to work, she's going to need her own space. Nothing was in here but storage, so I rearranged things in the garage and put it there."

Tatiana's eyes were wide with amazement. "How did you do all this in one day?"

"It's called multitasking. The twins helped me. Everson picked out the paint color."

Tatiana laughed and wiped a tear from her cheek. "Has she seen it?"

He shook his head no.

"She's going to love it."

"Rule number one: no boys in the cabana."

Tatiana laughed. "I couldn't agree more. We'll probably spend all our time enforcing that one."

Jack nodded. "I'll keep a baby monitor in here. Just in case."

Outside on the deck, he heard Kristin and Enrique and called them into the cabana. They sauntered inside, each carrying one of the twins.

Tatiana rushed to take Ethan and Everson, who were delighted to go to her.

"This is awesome," Kristin remarked. "I didn't even know this was here."

"It's yours," Tatiana said.

Jack smiled. "We thought you needed a little privacy."

Kristin dove onto the bed and jumped up and down like a little girl. "Are you serious?"

Enrique turned to Tatiana. "I've been with you for two years, and I don't even have a file cabinet."

Jack laughed. "I'll make an Office Depot run tomorrow, mate."

"It's big enough to have a small party," Kristin said.

Tatiana was brushing a tendril of hair away from Everson's eyes, barely paying attention. But suddenly Kristin's announcement registered. "No parties!"

Jack heard the faint sound of the telephone and left the group to dash into the kitchen and pick up. "Hello?"

"Jack! Is that you?" It was Hugh Haliwell.

Jack remained silent. This was the last bloke in the world he wanted to talk to. A few of his mates had told him to sue the pants off the bastard, but that was all the bastard had left—his pants. Besides, Jack didn't have a thirty-six-inch waist.

"I begged your mum for this number."

Jack stiffened. "I don't know why. We've got nothing to talk about."

Hugh's voice boomed when he said, "Oh, I think you're wrong about that! How soon can you get home?"

"You're unbelievable, Hugh. Christ, you should be bloody thankful that I didn't kill you! So listen very carefully when I say that I'm not interested in anything you have to say."

"The new coanchor for that BBC sports magazine show just got pink-slipped. Research ran some attitude surveys, and you tested highest with males *and* females. They want you, Jack."

Chapter Nineteen

"I'd like to thank Mrs. Fred Lampert for being our special guest today and playing such beautiful organ music," Mrs. Herman McKenzie was saying.

Constance Ann swilled back her second martini of the morning.

"It was my pleasure to be here," Mrs. Fred Lampert said. She paused awkwardly. "I have to go to the doctor now. He changed my medicine. I used to take a blue pill in the morning for my low blood pressure, but for the last week or so I've been taking a white pill."

Ensconced in her dressing room with a DISTURB AND YOU DIE sign tacked to the door, Constance Ann snarled in the direction of the radio.

Mrs. Herman McKenzie cut in with a meek attempt to resuscitate an already dead program. "Stay in touch and let us know how that works out. Right now we're going to take a break and hear from our sponsors. I'll be back after that with today's 'Shame on You' segment.''

A male announcer's voice boomed. ''That's next on the *Mrs. Herman McKenzie Show*, with your host, Mrs. Herman McKenzie, positive talk radio for listeners who believe in true family values. Exclusively on all-talk FM Ninety-eight Los Angeles.''

Constance Ann suffered through commercials for a new Vitamin C compound, Hooked on Phonics, a mutual funds provider, and life insurance. Balls! She'd been listening to this goody-goody torture for ninety minutes. And not a single word about Tatiana. If Mrs. Herman McKenzie didn't deliver soon, then Constance Ann planned to shove this radio straight up her big ass!

''Good morning! Wasn't that a nice break? I got the chance to freshen up and make myself a hot cup of coffee. Hope you did, too.'' The sigh that came next was heavy. ''Something is troubling me today, listeners. It's the culture around us. So dirty, so indecent. All of you know how I feel about this Britney Spears and the way she's brainwashing our young girls. It's disgraceful. Now I feel that it's my duty as a God-fearing woman of substance to tell you about another she-devil in our midst.''

Constance Ann shook up another martini—this time, to celebrate. Ha!

''Tatiana Fox is her name. You should see her parading around in the latest issue of *In Style*, talking about the sanctity of motherhood while she poses seductively. I have it on good authority that this woman's ex-husband is one of those homosapiens. And I know firsthand that she makes her living off smut. Last night I had the misfortune of sitting through a few of her movies. Some trash called *Lady Firefighter*. Beware, listeners. These are not heroic films for the family. They are filled with sex, violence, and nudity. Just like what you see on the Lifetime channel. Don't even get me started on the trickery involved in marketing this garbage. With a title like *Lady Firefighter*, you would expect to see something honorable, like the rescue of an elderly citizen from a burning building. But there's not a single fire in the movie or its three sequels. For that matter, no one even lights a match!''

Constance Ann just sat there, fuming. Right now the three martinis were feeling like one glass of Tang. What the fuck was this bitch talking about?

"Listeners, my primary concern is this Tatiana Fox person's next movie. We must put a stop to it. That's right. We must band together to prevent this filth from stinking up our neighborhood cinemas. I have perused the script, and I know it was written with Satan's pen. It's called *Sin by Sin*. Clever, aren't they? Trying to fool us into believing it might be a well-meaning film with a biblical message, when in fact it's outright sludge from the gutter. Does society need a movie about a woman who kills her husbands? First and foremost, murder is wrong. Why glorify it? And secondly, showing multiple marriages on film does nothing but undermine the institution itself. Tatiana Fox has opened fire on family values. Let's strike back!''

Constance Ann relaxed a little. This last diatribe sounded better, and with enough momentum, it just might work.

Tatiana was on her knees in front of Greg Tapper, freezing water cascading down from the shower jets. She was cold and miserable, but all the camera saw was lusty hunger. They didn't call it acting for nothing.

"Give me more head-bobbing," Kip shouted. "I won't get it past the MPAA, but I can use it for the director's cut."

She obliged, thinking about what September had said

about the script. Maybe it was bad. Granted, they were shooting out of sequence, but so far, she couldn't imagine this nonsense being spliced together to create a cohesive story.

"Cut!"

Greg smiled at her. "Having fun down there?"

"It's cold," Tatiana said. She gestured to his limp tube sock. "Obviously."

Greg's assistant rushed to offer him a warm terry cloth robe.

He slipped it on and took off, leaving her there, shivering and wet.

She looked around for hers, but someone had swiped it. Figured. With zero clout and an early reputation for being difficult, she was hardly getting the star treatment. At least the crew on the *Lady Cop* movies had been like family. Granted, family you wished would relocate to Bosnia, but family nonetheless.

Finally, a burly boom operator tossed her a bath towel.

She smiled her thanks and was starting for September's trailer when she heard a ruckus near one of the entrance doors.

"Show me *your* credentials. Any asshole with fifty bucks can rent a security guard costume and fake badge from a costume shop." It was Kitty Bishop. Who else?

The poor guard; he didn't stand a chance.

"It's okay!" Tatiana called out. "She's my publicist."

Kitty bulldozed past, muttering something about his being the product of a brother-sister union. She looked at the skimpy towel. "Don't they give you robes around here?"

Tatiana rolled her eyes. "Somebody lifted mine. Anything to see me naked for ten extra seconds."

"We need to talk."

"Let's go to September's trailer. She's off today, but I've

got full access." Tatiana led the way. "I hope you didn't come here to pressure me about the new *Playboy* deal. I still haven't decided."

"It's not that," Kitty said. "You're the center of a protest."

Tatiana gave her a strange look. "A protest? I don't wear fur."

"Not that kind. A moral protest. Some bible bitch has it in for you. She thinks you're corrupting the culture."

"What? That's insane. The only jobs I can get are in racy movies and men's magazines. If anything, I'm a *victim* of the corrupted culture. Who is this woman?"

Kitty gave her a quick rundown on Mrs. Herman McKenzie and paraphrased this morning's rant on the airwaves.

"I'm shocked that she even knows who I am. Please. Someone pass her Pamela Anderson's number."

Kitty shook her head. "For some reason she's fixated on you and this movie."

Tatiana shrugged it off. "Speaking of this movie, have you read the script?"

"Not exactly. I skimmed a summary report that Cleo's assistant drafted. Why?"

They stepped into September's trailer, and Tatiana slipped into one of her friend's robes. "Because it's finally dawning on me that this could be a real turkey. When I first read it, I thought, 'Wow, this is amazing.' But I think that's because I *knew* it was a Greg Tapper project. I *knew* that Gwyneth and Nicole and all the other A-list girls were being considered. I just had stars in my eyes, I guess."

"Honey, nobody's going to confuse this picture with *A Beautiful Mind*. Show me a man who pays eight bucks and sees blood, tits, and a great car chase, and I'll show you a happy moviegoer. Trust me. The box office will be there.

You could make a movie about Greg Tapper on the crapper
and still open at number one on the first weekend.''

Tatiana sank down onto the sofa. As if it mattered. All
she wanted was for this shoot to end. And forget signing
for the sequel. Even with an offer of ten million or more!
Well, she'd at least think about that. Okay, she'd do it.
Hmm. Maybe this is how *Speed 2* got made. ''Did you just
come here to tell me about Anita Bryant?''

''Yeah, I thought you might be upset.''

''Why? I've never heard of . . . What's her name?''

''Mrs. Herman McKenzie.''

''I bet more people saw me give the finger to that man
in a black Jetta on the freeway this morning than listen to
her dumb show.''

Kitty considered the situation. ''Maybe. But she was successful in getting the Britney dolls off the shelves in several
stores. Don't think we're going to take this like a couple of
chumps. If the thing gets bad enough, I've got connections.
Forget a horse's head. This wacko will wake up with a giant
dildo in her bed.''

Tatiana pulled a blanket over her. She was still cold from
the shower scene. ''Don't waste your time. What could
possibly come of it?

SHAME ON YOU, TATIANA
SHE-DEVIL GO HOME
NO MORE FILTH
SAVE THE WHALES

As demonstrations go, it was pretty lame. Only four protesters. And the last sign holder was obviously confused,
though well intentioned. They were assembled outside the
studio gates. No one among the quartet appeared particularly

passionate. Without the homemade picket signs, she would have just assumed they were waiting for a bus.

The most ridiculous part of all: These dopes had no idea who they were protesting against. They'd actually offered her a friendly wave as she drove out of the gate. Honestly. Her movies weren't worth a shit; at least her protests could be good.

Suddenly it occurred to Tatiana that she hadn't heard from Enrique all day. Miffed, she buzzed his cellular.

"Don't feel slighted," he said off the bat. "I've been dealing with Kristin and the Beverly High saga. But everything's set. She's enrolled and starts tomorrow. That's not good news for the American Express bill, though. She needed new school clothes, so I took her to Fred Segal."

"How much? Never mind. Don't tell me."

"The weirdest thing happened today. We were just getting home and a protester shows up at the house with a picket sign that says, 'SHAME ON YOU.' She insisted that you were the target. Anyway, I convinced her that it was September she was marching against and sent her over there."

Tatiana laughed. "Why did you do that?"

"Because she still thinks I'm her *pretend* assistant. She badgered me to go pick out a birthday present for Rob. Then she sent me back out to get a refund because she ended up giving him a video of her Oscar-acceptance speech."

"That's what I got for Christmas."

"Hey, did you and Jack have a fight?"

Tatiana's brow crinkled. "No." Last night she'd fallen asleep right away. This morning she'd only seen him for a few minutes. There'd been no time to argue. "Why?"

"He's been unusually quiet today and spending a lot time on the phone with the door closed. Kristin thought she overheard him making travel plans. Maybe she's wrong."

Tatiana experienced an overwhelming feeling of dread. It

seemed to shake her central nervous system. "He's probably planning a quick visit home," she managed to say.

She signed off and floored it home, her fear bringing clarity, putting everything into perspective. The wrath of Mrs. Herman McKenzie. The hellish shoot of *Sin by Sin*. The lingering issues with her mother. None of these things registered in importance against the possibility of Jack's leaving.

By the time Tatiana got home, she was a nervous wreck. It felt as if the foundation of her life were cracking. To her surprise, the twins were down for the night. Normally, they weren't in bed for at least another hour.

She discovered him out by the pool with a bottle of wine and what appeared to be an awful lot of guilt.

Tentatively she ventured onto the deck. "Hi," she said softly. "The house is so quiet."

Jack barely looked at her. "Ethan and Everson didn't nap today. And Enrique treated Kristin to a movie." Wordlessly he poured a glass of wine and offered it to her.

"No thanks," Tatiana said. "If you have something to tell me, I think I'll take it like a man."

There was a long stretch of silence before he started to talk. "I got a call from Hugh, my former manager."

"The man who stole all your money."

"He didn't *steal* my money. He lost it."

Tatiana didn't see the difference. "What did he want?"

"I'm up for a coanchor job on a BBC sports magazine show."

Tatiana swallowed hard. She wanted the wine now. She wanted whatever was in the medicine cabinet, too. Not enough to harm herself. Just enough to deal. Her whole world went dark. "When do you leave?" It seemed a fair question. After all, that's what men do. They leave. Her father, Kerr, and now Jack.

"In a few days. But I won't be gone long."

"What if you get the job?"

"It's just a short trip."

Tatiana stood up. Tears were close, but she fought them back. "I knew this would happen. Deep down, I knew."

He started to say something.

"Come on, Jack. You knew, too. The original plan was just to get me through the shoot of this film." She threw up her hands. "And you're not even sticking to that."

"Is that what you're concerned about? The stupid movie?"

Instinctively, her defensive mechanisms kicked in. "*Sin by Sin* is a major motion picture, thank you very much."

"Bollocks! I read your script on the pot one morning, and it's bloody awful. None of it makes any sense."

A small part of her wanted to pause the real argument and get his thoughts on the screenplay. But now wasn't the time.

"I don't want to fight," he said, softly now. "This is just for a few days—"

"Jack, please." Tatiana had to stop him. "If they offer you this job, you're going to say yes. You won't even have to think about it."

"You're sure of this? Because *I'm* not."

"Don't act torn for me, Jack. You're twenty-six years old. London's where you grew up. Sports are your life." She shrugged. "Game over."

He shook his head. "You don't understand."

"I understand enough. Let's face it. We never quite got this right. I had to twist your arm to take the job. Before we jumped into bed, we must've second-guessed ourselves a hundred times. The latest joke is that we've been playing house and fooling ourselves into believing that we have something solid. How could it be, when one phone call from out of the blue changes everything?''

"You make it sound so black and white. It's not. This is tough. A big part of me doesn't even want to go, but I'd be crazy not to. I owe it to myself to at least hear what they have to offer.''

Tatiana hated the ambiguity. She wanted to hear him say, "I'm taking whatever's on the table. No more diapers and burp cloths for me, baby. Adios. And don't expect a post-card." It'd be so much easier if he were a cold bastard. But she could see the conflict in Jack's eyes. This was incredible news for him, yet he looked as if he'd just lost a dear friend.

"I called a nanny agency. They're sending over some candidates tomorrow. There's even a guy in the lot." He smiled. "Imagine that. I'll pick out the best and go through the twins' routine for a day or two. I want everything to be seamless while I'm gone. You've got enough on your plate.''

She wanted to scream. Even in the act of dumping her and the kids he could be so goddamn charming. Well, she just couldn't take it. Already her heart was breaking. The smartest thing she could do for herself was make it a clean snap. None of this leaving for a few days, coming back, announcing a departure, taking the twins to the park for the last time, making love to her as a final good-bye. Why prolong the painful reality? It wasn't fair.

"That's not your place," she said, her tone cold and detached.

He didn't understand.

"To just assume the role of hiring another nanny."

"I thought—''

"You're not their father, Jack, even if you get a cheap thrill out of Everson calling you Daddy." Her own capacity for cruelty surprised her. But this was the only way.

There was a long silence. He stared into the deep end of

the pool, and then he looked at her with tears in his eyes. "You bitch." It was almost a whisper.

Tatiana hated herself, realizing that she'd gone too far and hurt him in a way she never intended. But she still didn't go to him.

Jack sat there, teetering on the emotional edge.

All she had to do was give him one more push. "It's better that you just leave. The twins need stability. You going and coming back and going again will only confuse them. I'll hire the new nanny. I'm their mother. It's my responsibility."

"I haven't quit," Jack whispered. The pain in his voice almost melted her.

"Then I guess you're fired." Tatiana left him to lock herself in her room. Desperate to talk, she tried to phone September, but voice mail clicked on. For the longest time she just curled up in bed and attempted to cry it out. The two pills didn't do anything for sleep. She started to take a third but decided against it at the last minute. Too *Valley of the Dolls.*

The next morning she looked terrible. Her makeup artists would really have to work some magic. Today's courtroom scene called for her character to be supermodel perfect. But when Kip yelled, "Action!" hours later, that's exactly what she was. And people said Tatiana Fox couldn't act.

They were rapidly approaching the end of the film. It was a blessing when the shooting schedule became more demanding than ever. Tatiana wasn't even home when Jack left for the airport, which made things easier.

She didn't have to say good-bye.

The new nanny reminded her of Melina. The similarities were there. Sarita Rosa had a quiet demeanor, spoke in a thick accent, and bonded instantly with Ethan and Everson. Tatiana hated her.

Jack had been the epicenter of so much positive energy in the house, and his departure left a huge emptiness that sent Tatiana into a serious depression. Dr. G and Prozac could only do so much. But while she sank to new depths, Kristin managed to soar, embarking upon an exciting life at Beverly Hills High.

Her sister had declared an interest in acting and joined the school's Theater Arts Workshop. Much to Enrique's dismay, she snared the lead role in the spring production of *Hello, Dolly!* September had taken an immediate interest in this development, hiring the same vocal coach who'd trained Madonna for *Evita* to get Kristin's pipes into shape.

Her sister's impressive blossoming helped lift Tatiana's spirits. So did the fact that Kristin's relatively smooth assimilation into Los Angeles life was driving Justine mad. Still, it bothered Tatiana that her mother didn't want to hear about the improved Kristin, the one who now loved school, pursued artistic interests, and had kissed off older guys for her first real Archie, a Jewish cutie named Emmanuel Abramson.

He was Beverly High's resident Matt Lauer, a staple on the school's own television station, KBEV. The local NBC affiliate hired him to file teen-oriented news reports, and his hard-hitting exposé on the dangers of club drugs such as Ecstasy, Foxy, and Mystic had a profound impact on Kristin, who vowed never to experiment again. She openly adored the classy and driven Emmanuel, going so far as to modify her personal style to impress him. Much to Tatiana's delight, Kristin had donated her video vamp fashions to charity and studied photographs of the late Carolyn Bessette as inspiration for her new sophisticated look.

What bothered Tatiana about Kristin's relationship with Emmanuel was his nickname. Everybody called him Manny, including Kristin. And she mentioned him at least two hundred times a day. Manny said this, Manny did that, Manny's coming over, etc. Each time Tatiana heard the name, an image of Jack flashed in her mind, immediately followed by a tiny piercing in her heart. Silently she wondered where he was, how he was doing, but she never spoke of him out loud. In fact, she'd forbidden Enrique and Kristin from mentioning Jack at all. It was difficult enough to endure the occasional murmur about him from Ethan and Everson.

But no matter what steps she took to forget him, no matter how many weeks passed, Jack's absence only seemed to amplify. Sarita, though perfectly competent as a nanny, attended to things differently. She didn't go to great lengths to prepare Ethan and Everson's meals, her affection for them was only perfunctory, and she inadvertently got them hooked on *The Constance Ann Show*. It drove Tatiana crazy that she might eventually have to give in and buy Everson a stuffed toy of Pappy the Panda.

And the Jack-of-all-voids didn't end there. Whereas he'd brought a certain lovely, madcap atmosphere into the home, Sarita was all business. The Mexico City native tended to the twins, went about chores, and talked very little. Kristin interacted with her as little as possible, preferring to cocoon herself in the cabana that Jack built. The same could be said for Enrique. He spent less time at the house than ever, partly because of the dour Sarita, but maybe equally, if not more so, because of Tatiana.

She'd been nobody's party girl the past few weeks. In fact, Enrique had asked to reduce his hours in order to accommodate a part-time job at Cartoon Planet that Jaron had offered. Ostensibly, the queen who stole her husband saw promise in an animation project Enrique had been toying around with. Something called *Super Wowie Girl and Goo Goo Bunny*.

Thinking of Jaron, Tatiana actually cracked a smile. Losing Jack as a personal trainer had sent him on a Krispy Kreme bender, which resulted in a five-pound gain. He'd cited fear as the reason for not exercising on his own, claiming Jack's close attention to proper form prevented injury. And he denounced the idea of hiring someone else. So Jaron focused all his energy on planning a big party for Kerr, who'd written a poem about skin exfoliation that made it into the Mary Kay corporate newsletter. It was his first published piece, and for him, the equivalent of a *New York Times* bestseller.

The sudden opening of September's trailer door startled Tatiana. She'd been sitting here alone in the dark, thinking, remembering, regretting, all to the fortune-cookie-analysis sounds of Alanis Morissette on the CD player.

September stormed inside and cut off the music. "How can you listen to that? No wonder you're depressed." She turned on a light. "Enough of this. Get dressed. You're my date for the wrap party at Linq."

The *Sin by Sin* shoot was finally over. Now all Tatiana had to do was get through looping, the press junket, and the premiere. Adding the wrap party to that list would be overkill. "I'm not going."

"It's a wrap party. You're one of the stars. If you don't go, everybody will think you're a bitch."

"They already think that."

September considered this point. "True. And they probably think the same about me." She shrugged. "We could go to Spago for dinner instead."

Tatiana begged her off. "I need to get home to the twins."

"I guess I'll go to the party, then. But don't worry. I'll do our bitch rep justice by screaming at a waiter."

Tatiana attempted a smile.

"You've got to get over this Jack business. I've never seen you like this before."

"I've never felt like this."

"I could loan you Rob for a night. He'll bring you back to the land of the living. Just don't let him talk about skateboarding. Or the time he met Fred Durst of Limp Bizkit. Or how he keeps his body fat at eight percent. Okay, no talking at all. He'll just come over and fu—"

Tatiana stopped her. "Not interested."

"What if I sent Simon Baker? The guy from *The Guardian*." She sang the last selling point: "He's got an Aussie accent."

Tatiana shook her head no.

September sighed. "This is beyond my abilities. I give up. What does your therapist say?"

Tatiana stood up. Weakly. Her energy level was below zero. "Not much. These days we spend most of the sessions just staring at each other."

"I hope you're getting a discount."

Tatiana started to go.

"Hey," September said brightly. "Maybe this will cheer you up: The Save the Whales people outnumber the losers picketing you five to one. I saw the last holdout reading their literature this morning. She's bound to cave any day."

Leaving the trailer, she ran into Greg Tapper, freshly done up in fake blood from his last scene.

"Will I see you at the party tonight?"

She smiled faintly. "I'm afraid not. But please give everyone my best."

"What about the after party at my Malibu house?"

"I don't think I was invited to that one."

He flashed the famous Tapper Chicklet grin. "I'm planning it as we speak. A low-key affair. Very private. No tube sock. I promise."

The worst offer she'd had all day. So why was she actually considering it? Tatiana's brain fired up, and she heard the voices of David and Greg and Cleo and Kitty and September talking inside her head:

Be good to the picture, and the picture will be good to you.

My fans want to believe that the love they see on-screen is real.

You could do worse than be known as the Greg Tapper girl.

I promised his publicist that you'd never wear heels in public with him.

How do you think it feels to endorse a twenty-million-dollar check?

The voice of Jack was gone. Long gone. He'd returned home to his world, and she'd remained here in hers.

Maybe September was right. She had to start the process of getting over Jack. Why not start right now? After all, there was a movie to promote, other jobs to line up. The Hollywood game beckoned. She took the bait. What the hell.

Tatiana Fox smiled at Greg Tapper, one player to another. "Have your publicist call my publicist."

Chapter Twenty

The weeks leading up to the debut of *Sin by Sin* were murder on Constance Ann. Greg Tapper and Tatiana Fox being branded the hot couple of the moment was driving her mad.

Restaurants, charity events, award galas, film premieres. They showed up everywhere. How did she know? Because she couldn't turn on the damn water faucet without a picture of them spitting out of it.

"It should've been me!" Constance Ann shouted, tossing the new *Us Weekly* across the dressing room. Photos of Greg and Tatiana littered the "Hot Stuff" *and* "Faces and Places" sections. Consider her subscription canceled. Up yours, Jann Wenner. He was the publisher of that fish-paper rag.

Today marked the last taping of *The Constance Ann Show* for a few months. Perfect timing, too. Her nerves were shot to hell. She needed a break from all the snaggle-toothed brats in the cast.

But the real issue gnawing at her insides was Mrs. Herman McKenzie. She claimed to be a moral crusader with a legion of militant soldiers dedicated to her cause. What a joke. Constance Ann's plumber had more pimples on his ass than this Tammy Faye wannabe had followers.

Every morning Constance Ann had cruised by the studio gates to see if the number of protesters had grown. And they had. For saving the goddamn whales! Oh, she'd come so close, so very close, to pulling a Lizzie Grubman and plowing right into those morons with her BMW, but in the end she thought, screw it. Why scratch up a beautiful paint job?

All Constance Ann needed was an opportunity to regroup. Get away from the same old surroundings. An exotic place. Maybe Florence, Italy. She loved to visit during this time of year. The summer heat was gone, the tacky tourists were thinning. Yes! An excellent idea. She could stroll the banks of the Arno river and plot out a new scheme to destroy Tatiana. And it had to be foolproof! No more bullshitting around.

Constance Ann heard a sudden commotion in the corridor.

Urgent footsteps. Muffled voices. The noise stopped right outside her dressing room door.

"No! You can't go in there!" It was Will Hayes.

Boom! Boom! Boom! Someone pounded on the door.

"This is trespassing!" Will again.

She didn't know what to do. Gut instincts told her not to open the door, but there was no other way out of here.

"Constance Ann, are you in there?" The rude female voice rang familiar.

For a long second she tried to place it, yet ultimately came up with nothing.

"This is Piper Perry from *In Your Face*. I've got some

questions for you, Constance Ann. My crew and I will wait all day and all night if we have to.''

She knew the voice, the name, and the show. A cold current of fear raced through her bloodstream. Piper Perry's *In Your Face* was the extreme-sports version of exposé television journalism. She was righteous, bloodthirsty, and lethal. The running joke in the industry was this: If Piper Perry's got your number, pray that she finds you on the roof of a tall building. So you can jump.

Boom! Boom! Boom! Harder this time. The cheap door buckled.

Constance Ann's mind took off. Piper always did her homework. That double-barreled bitch was more than a muckraker. She was a scandal anthropologist. The lengths she would go to knew no boundaries. Hidden cameras. Garbage digging. Secret photographs. And when she struck gold, it was damning stuff. Ask the congressman who voted against gay rights but cruised runaway boys after dark. Or the squeaky-clean talk show host whose private cancer foundation was revealed to be a front for fake salaries and first-class vacations.

"I've got a video here, Constance Ann." Piper's voice was taunting. "I think you'll find it interesting. A little friend of mine named Chris wore a camera for us. You remember him, don't you? He used to be on your show."

Constance Ann didn't have to look in the mirror. She already knew that the blood had siphoned from her face. Frantically she searched for her purse, a hat, and some dark sunglasses. If she could just run to her car and drive to her lawyer's office . . . Hank was the king of sleaze. He'd tell her what to do about this barracuda.

She flung open the door and tried to rush past them, but the corridor was too narrow. And Piper Perry was too fast. Even worse, her camera guy was shooting Constance Ann's every ill-fated duck and dodge. Now she was cornered like some wounded animal.

Piper stuck a portable DVD player in her face. The picture quality was grainy but good enough to be unimpeachable. The sound was crystal clear.

"Well, you can give Mr. Bessell this message from me: He wouldn't know the right key if it came up and clamped itself to his hairy balls!" She came off like a monster.

"You're mean!" The fat little shit sounded sympathetic.

"I know. And I'm going to prove just how mean I can be right now. You're fired. So get your rotten-singing, line-flubbing, Little Debbie Cake-eating ass out of here." Had she actually said that?

The camera operator shifted positions to gain a different angle.

Constance Ann saw an opening and went for it. With every bit of her speed and strength, she broke past them, making a dead run for the car.

Piper and company trailed her, nipping at her heels like junkyard dogs. "You're the honorary chair of the National Children's Council, Constance Ann! What do you think the board of directors will say about this? How will your young fans feel? What about their parents?"

Constance Ann made it to the car just steps ahead of them. And then it dawned on her. No keys. Goddamn it! She wasted precious seconds rummaging through her purse. Finally, she found them, turned the engine over, and shifted into drive.

"Why are you running, Constance Ann?" Piper stood directly in front of the BMW. "I just want to talk."

Constance Ann's foot wavered. To keep it on the brake or slam it on the gas? She could actually run Piper down and end this problem. But it would only open up a host of new ones. Swerving around them, she gunned it, peeling out of the studio and onto Sunset Boulevard.

The reality sank in fast. She was over. So over they would need a new word for *over*. Oh, God! That nanny-cam-style video would get played again and again and again. Chris would get his fifteen minutes, too, making the poor-pitiful-me media rounds, from Katie Couric to Larry King to Diane Sawyer, telling the world about the real Constance Ann, exposing the beast behind the fraudulent image.

She drove like a demon. She cried tears that burned. But nothing could have prepared her for what came next. A new billboard had just gone up to promote *Sin by Sin*.

Greg Tapper and Tatiana Fox.

Larger than life.

Locked in passionate embrace.

That hurt more than the specter of a doomed future.

"When you woke up this morning, what were you looking forward to?"

"My Prozac," Tatiana said.

Dr. G raised an eyebrow. "Name something else."

Tatiana sighed and really mulled the question this time. The answer that came to her actually brought a smile to her lips. "Ethan and Everson's hands. They're beautiful and always busy. I love their little thumbs."

Dr. G gave her an encouraging nod. "That's a lovely thing to look forward to. Keep going."

Tatiana took a moment to think. "Every morning Enrique brings me coffee from Starbucks. I drink it out by the pool, and he shows me his sketches for the animation project he's working on. I love that part of the day. He's so talented. I hope something happens for him."

Dr. G smiled. "Not such a bad day, is it? Two healthy

children and coffee with a friend. That's plenty of reason to get out of bed.'' She shifted in her seat and leaned forward. "What if you did this every morning? Made a list of everything you were looking forward to and stuck to it. Think how wonderful the day could be.''

Tatiana liked the idea, even though it made her out to be more fragile than she felt. "I was just kidding about the Prozac. You know that, right?''

"There's an element of truth in all humor, Tatiana. Especially yours. It's how you defend yourself. It's how you cope.''

"I can't laugh about Jack yet. Does that mean I'm not coping?''

Dr. G tossed it right back to her. "Is that what you think?''

Tatiana hated this trick. "I don't know. When he was around, you didn't have me making lists to get out of bed.''

"You're depressed. Jack leaving is part of that, but it's not the whole story.''

"So what's the rest of it? Enlighten me.''

"You mean sit here and tell you what your problems are?'' Dr. G shook her head. "That's not how I work. You know that.''

"Yes, but you owe me for all those sessions when we just stared at each other.''

"Owe you?''

"You charged me a full rate. One hundred fifty dollars an hour for staring? I can get that for free from the produce guy at Ralph's Market.''

"Then maybe you should schedule your next session with him.''

Tatiana laughed a little. "Dr. G! That was bitchy. Good for you. But I'm sticking to my guns. I want some heavy-duty analysis. Or at least a free week of sessions.''

Dr. G stared back, expressionless.

"Come on." Tatiana's voice was almost pleading. "I've seen Dr. Phil on *Oprah*. He yells in people's faces and tells them everything that they're doing wrong. It seems very productive."

Dr. G took a deep breath. "I'll share some observations, Tatiana. But I'm not going to yell in your face."

She shrugged. "Fair enough."

"I think Jack's departure unearthed some feelings from your childhood that you're not fully cognizant of. That's why this depression has been so insidious."

Tatiana rolled her eyes. "I know, I know. My daddy left me when I was a little girl, blah, blah—"

Dr. G stopped her. "It's not about being left, Tatiana. Because Jack didn't leave as much as you pushed him away. He didn't get the chance to choose between staying here and returning home. You made that decision for him."

Tatiana sat there, uncertain whether she wanted Dr. G to go on or not.

"Anyway, I don't think the root of your pain is about Jack leaving you. I think it's about Jack loving you. One of the most precious gifts of all is to find someone who *learns* us. What we like. What we don't like. To cater to our needs and take joy in contributing to our happiness. That's what Jack did for you, and it touched you so deeply because that's what your mother didn't do. Typically, our first experience with that kind of love is from a mother. Don't get me wrong. I'm not saying that Justine doesn't love you. She does. It just isn't that learned, nurturing kind of love that wraps you up like a warm blanket. When I was a little girl and I got sick, my mother knew exactly what to do to make me feel better. She'd bring me 7-Up and Lipton's Cup of Soup with the tiny oyster crackers, scratch my back in circles, and tell me how everything was going to be okay. That's what I do for my family. And that's what Jack did for you. He *learned* you. He *learned* the twins.''

Tatiana felt a tear cascading down her cheek. "We were learning him, too." She sniffled.

"I know," Dr. G said, reaching out to pass her a Kleenex. "I know."

Tatiana wiped her eyes and felt more depressed than ever. She remembered something Dr. G had mentioned earlier. "You said Jack was only part of the story."

"There's the matter of your career."

Tatiana feigned devastation. "Too much for one session. You'll have to put me on suicide watch."

Dr. G looked at her with something close to admiration. "You seem to be figuring out the career stuff all by yourself. Think of the resolve it took to turn down a million-dollar offer from *Playboy*. You didn't have that a year ago."

"A year ago I would've done it for a new car."

Dr. G chuckled. "You see? That's growth."

Tatiana allowed the point to sink in. "I turned down a million dollars!"

Dr. G beamed proudly. "Yes, you did."

Tatiana spoke emphatically when she said, "I could use a million dollars."

Dr. G laughed again. "I could, too."

Tatiana felt an amazing calm. And a sudden need to vent. "I guess the reason I was able to say no is because I'm not her anymore. The sex bomb, I mean. I think she's dead. I *hope* she's dead. Of course, if this movie's a hit, she'll probably come back to life, and I'll have to figure out what to do with her. God, it's like Cher, isn't it?" She giggled to herself. "Maybe I'll do one of those calendars. You know, roll around on the beach in a tiny bathing suit. But no more nudity! It's not that I'm ashamed of what I've done. Everything was tasteful—R-rated movies, *Playboy*. I only

showed my boobs and my butt. I could count the number
of men who've seen my vagina with both hands and one
foot and still have some toes left. I was the hot girl for a
few years. That's not such a bad thing. No one got hurt. I
probably helped some marriages along the way. Lots of
couples are too shy to go to the back room of a video store,
so they pick up *Lady Cop Undercover* instead. Anyway, the
decisions I make now aren't just about me. I have to think
about Ethan and Everson, too."

Dr. G nodded. "Being a mother changes everything."

Tatiana curled her legs onto the couch. "I know. It's like,
I want to do something in my work that they can enjoy,
too." She laughed. "I'll have to keep *Sin by Sin* under lock
and key until they're seventeen. That's no fun. And some
of this has to do with Kristin, too. She wants to be an actress.
Can you believe that? It scares the hell out of me. I had a
dream the other night where she came home and announced
that she'd accepted the lead role in a movie called *Lady
Park Ranger*. The dream ended with me chasing the Dobsons—those are the loser producers I used to deal with—
around a room with an eggbeater in my hand. Any thoughts?"

Dr. G smiled. "I think the dream speaks for itself."

An image of Jack popped into Tatiana's mind. Only this
time it wasn't followed by a pang of sadness. Today's session
seemed to be moving her beyond something. She felt free,
eager to share. "Do you want to know what the best thing
about Jack was?"

"Yes, I do."

"He made me never want to answer the phone after six
o'clock."

"What do you mean?"

"That's the ultimate test. If you want to answer the phone
after six o'clock in the evening, then honey, you've got
problems in your relationship. Don't you get it? I was at

home with Jack. He had a bottle of my favorite wine. The twins were there. We had a pint of Haagen-Dazs chocolate chocolate chip in the freezer. Why would I want to answer the phone?''

Dr. G gave her a knowing nod. "Indeed."

"I miss that most of all. I say that because I've been going out with Greg Tapper to help promote the movie. Nothing's happening. It's just a publicity romance. But I know that if I ended up with a guy like him, I'd jump for the phone if it rang after six o'clock. Hell, I'd talk to anyone. A telemarketer. Even my own mother. Am I rambling? God, I haven't talked this much in weeks. It feels great. Let me know if I change subjects too often. I'm bad about that. September and I are going shopping for premiere dresses together. That'll be fun. I'll add it to my things-to-look-forward-to list. Oh, have you been keeping up with the Constance Ann scandal? Her show was canceled, and it doesn't look good for her on the legal front. I heard that bootleg copies of the hidden camera video are being sold all over town and on e-bay. Apparently, it's more popular than the new edition of *Wild Girls of Spring Break*. Kristin turned up in one of those once. She was in Panama City for—"

"Tatiana," Dr. G interrupted, pointing to her watch. "We have to stop."

Epilogue

Ziegfeld Theatre, New York

Tatiana had been relieved when everyone honored her request to stay home from the premiere. With Greg on one arm, Kitty pulling on the other one, and anxiety going strong over seeing herself on the big screen for the first time, it just seemed like a good idea to keep the entourage strictly business.

Still, it hurt to realize that no one had put up a fight. Come on. A little resistance please. At least act as if you care. But Tatiana let it go. They had lives as busy as hers.

Kristin was joining Manny and his family on a trip to San Francisco's wine country. With Jaron's help, Enrique was finishing a presentation short of *Super Wowie Girl and Goo Goo Bunny* for Cartoon Planet executives. And Kerr was hard at work on another poem for the Mary Kay newsletter, this one about perfumed body lotion. The twins, naturally, were safely ensconced at home with Sarita.

So here Tatiana was, playing movie star, holding the hand of a man she didn't even like, pretending to care about whatever Kitty chose to whisper in her ear every five minutes, waiting for the do-or-die reviews. Would the critics approve? Would the audience applaud? How much would the movie gross on opening weekend? All of this was supposed to matter. But none of it did. Not one damn bit.

Tatiana used to think that people who walked away from the spotlight were insane. She just couldn't wrap her head around the notion of anyone saying no to stardom. Like Sissy Spacek. The actress had never let the Hollywood machine grind her up. She lived on a farm, worked only when she felt like it, and showed up to collect awards wearing no makeup and her husband's shirt. A true original. And there was Demi Moore, who gave up everything to dedicate her life to her three daughters. Of course, having millions in the bank helped. But what struck Tatiana most was the sentiment of leaving it all behind, that clarion call to the world saying, "This is what really matters to me." She never understood the concept before. She did now.

The closing credits were moments away. But all Tatiana could think about was the post-premiere party. How long would it last? Would they notice if she slipped out? Factoring the time difference in Los Angeles, she knew that it was possible to get back to the Hudson Hotel and call the twins before Sarita put them down for the night. This would mean a mere cameo at her own party. *Yes, I'm the star. Like the dress? It's Carolina Herrera. What's next? I'm reading scripts, taking meetings. Kiss, kiss. Have to go now. Bye-bye.* But Tatiana didn't care. She had to hear Ethan and Everson's sweet voices tonight. Everything else paled in importance.

A PR flack flitted down the aisle to deliver a fax to Kitty, who promptly fished a tiny flashlight from her handbag and focused the beam on the page. "That son of a bitch!"

Tatiana peered over Kitty's shoulder. The headline screamed out at her.

SIN BY SIN A VIOLATION OF CINEMATIC LAW

She recognized the byline. The writer was a respected syndicated film critic whose reviews turned up in newspapers across the country.

Kitty tried to put a positive spin on it. "Doesn't matter. This picture is critic-proof. We'll be laughing all the way to number one. Just wait."

Tatiana reached out to steady the flashlight in Kitty's hand. She wanted to see this.

The new Greg Tapper vehicle, Sin by Sin, *gets one thing right—it lives up to its title. Everything in this film is sinful. Bad acting, terrible script, amateur direction. Name the transgression; this movie's probably guilty of it. Maybe Univision rushed this junk out because they knew it would contaminate the vault.*

Greg Tapper's all-out bid to steam up his screen image produces laughable results. The love scenes don't resemble sex at all. More like practice sessions for synchronized swimming. He should stick to jumping through windows and disengaging bombs ten seconds before they blow. Speaking of bombs, why couldn't he stop this one?

The newcomer here, an auburn-haired bombshell who calls herself Tatiana Fox (yeah, I'm sure that's on her birth certificate) does what she can in an underwritten, preposterous role. Fox escaped the B-movie

world of Lady Cop Undercover *but might want to get
her uniform dry-cleaned. This movie is sure to put her
back on the beat.*

Tatiana looked away from the page. When Kitty tried to
pass the flashlight and fax over to Greg, she blocked the
move. "Not tonight. He can read that tomorrow if he wants."
Kitty shrugged and stuffed the items into her purse.
Tatiana actually felt bad for Greg. Stardom meant everything to him. Rave reviews, big box office numbers, and
throngs of awe-struck fans were rich food for his soul. The
cruel barbs from that critic would hurt, and it served no
purpose for him to read them minutes before facing his peers
at a party.
She turned to him as the closing credits began to scroll.
A drop of perspiration trickled down the side of his face.
He knew how bad it was. You could see it in his eyes, feel
it in the tension that radiated from his body.
The lights went up.
No cheers. No whistles. The applause was tepid, obliga-
tory.
Tatiana could see the exchange of secret looks, hear deri-
sive giggles, make out casual inquiries about where the party
was.
Greg leaned over to say, "My publicist thinks we should
arrive at the party separately. Do you mind?"
Tatiana smiled at him. "Not at all." And it really didn't
matter to her. This wasn't personal. It was Hollywood. Greg
was already taking measures to distance himself from the
movie, and if that meant ditching his costar as his date, then
so be it.
There were a few friendly comments as she made her
way toward the lobby.
"You looked fantastic."

"I'm so jealous. I would kill for your boobs."

September was holding court on the sidewalk, offering sound bytes to a gaggle of news media, definitely in her element. "What's my favorite movie? I don't really have one. Of course, *Postcards from Paris* has a special place in my heart. You know, I won the Oscar for that one . . ."

Tatiana laughed to herself, then maneuvered around to the other side of Kitty, using her as a shield to escape notice. "I'm going back to the hotel."

"Honey, there's a party. Lots of photo opportunities. Let me put a muzzle on loony tunes over there and stick you in front of the camera."

"I don't care, Kitty. I want to call my kids."

The superpublicist shook her head but conceded. "I'll never understand my mommy clients. Why can't you just get a cat?"

They moved toward the line of black limousines, so long it looked like an oil slick. Two drivers were just pulling out. The opening gave Tatiana a straight line of sight across Fifty-fourth Street. What she saw knocked the breath from her body.

Jack smiled at her from the opposite sidewalk, Ethan and Everson flanking him on either side. They were all dressed up in matching black tuxedos.

Tatiana covered her heart with one hand and clutched Kitty's arm with the other, if only to steady herself. The tears came instantly. Emotion lodged in her throat like a fireball. She could barely breathe.

Kitty followed her gaze. "Isn't that John?"

"It's Jack," Tatiana corrected her. "It's Jack!" And she darted into the street, holding out her hand to stop a limousine, forcing it into a herky-jerky stop.

The driver blared his horn. "Lady, are you crazy?"

"Yes!" Tatiana screamed. "Yes, yes, yes!" Only she

wasn't answering the driver's question. She was answering Jack's.

Down on one knee, holding open a small black box that contained a beautiful square-cut diamond, he shook his head with great humor. "At least let me ask the question!"

Tatiana finally reached them. "Fire away."

Jack stood up, scooping Ethan and Everson into each arm. "Will you marry me?"

"I've answered that question four times already."

And then he kissed her lips. And the twins leaned in to kiss her cheeks. And it was the greatest happiness Tatiana Fox had ever known.

"Quick! Somebody take a picture. That gown is to die for, and they look scrumptious in their tuxedos!" It was Jaron. The sweetest home-wrecker a girl could ask for.

Tatiana drew back. Suddenly, everyone was in view: Enrique, Kristin, Manny, Kerr, and Jaron! Right there on the sidewalk, dressed to the nines, looking fabulous. She hugged them all, still reeling from surprise, touched beyond words. "I can't believe this!" she screamed and kissed Jack again.

"What about the picture?" Jaron whined.

"Cameras are rolling," an unfamiliar voice said.

Suddenly a microphone was pushed in Tatiana's face.

All the crews that minutes ago were under September's spell had crossed over to their side of the street.

"Congratulations on the engagement!" It was Roshumba Williams from *Entertainment Tonight*. "Have you set a date?"

Jack stepped up to the mike. "As soon as possible." He paused a beat. "Who's up for the red-eye to Vegas?"

Everybody laughed.

"This is a big night for you." Jeannette Walls from

MSNBC had shoved her way to the front. "A film premiere, a proposal. This must be a dream come true."

Tatiana looked at Jack. "You have no idea."

Across the street, Kitty Bishop was doing the double thumbs-up sign. "Honey, you're a star!" she shouted. "Whether you like it or not!"

Sin by Sin died a quick death at the box office, and Cleo's phone never jingled with more offers for Tatiana Fox-Thorpe. But that was okay. Tatiana found a new career in animation, lending her voice to the title character in Enrique's Super Wowie Girl and Goo Goo Bunny creation. The show had been an instant smash on Cartoon Planet. Kids went wild for it. So did twenty-year-old college stoners.

Tatiana even modeled the costume—colored spandex unitard, cape, pushed-up boobs, pink mask—to help Enrique with the illustration models of the crime-busting heroine who protected the idyllic town of Wowie Land from evildoers with the help of her trusty sidekick, a magical rabbit who could turn inanimate objects into carrots.

Luckily, she'd posed before her third month.

"I felt a kick," Jack said, slowly moving his hand around her belly. "Did you feel that?"

Tatiana, beached in bed with swollen feet, just looked at him. "Must be a boy. He kicks all the time. It's like a World Cup championship going on in there."

Jack grinned. "Just like his dad." He kissed her forehead and rose up to leave. "Kristin and Manny are watching TV. Just yell if you need anything."

Tatiana looked at him, so handsome in his starched Thomas Pink shirt and tie. "I promise not to fall asleep before your report." And then she yawned.

"You'll be out before the Law and Order case is solved."

"Which reminds me. September guest-stars tonight. She plays a crazy movie star."

Jack laughed. "And how does a crazy movie star prepare to play the role of a crazy movie star?"

Tatiana giggled. "I think all you have to do is show up on time and know your lines."

He kissed her again, this time full on the mouth. "I'm off. Several teams have won games in various sports, and it's my job to inform the city about such matters. Stay off your feet. Love you."

"Love you more."

"Love for infinity."

Jack wiggled her toe on his way out. "Eternal love."

Tatiana released a blissful sigh. She loved reflecting on the comical collusion that had taken place to get Jack back to Los Angeles. Manny, who worked at an NBC news affiliate as a teen-issues reporter, had casually remarked to Kristin that the sports anchor was leaving. Enrique's recent affair with a British tourist had actually ended on a high note, so he had no qualms about asking her to air-mail sample tapes of Jack doing his thing on BBC. And as luck would have it, one of Kerr's Mary Kay clients happened to be the wife of the news director making the hiring decision. Jack had an offer before he even knew there was a job. Of course, it had taken Kitty to close the deal. Jack had printed out her e-mail and saved it.

FROM: KittyB
TO: JackAttack
SUBJECT: The Rest of Your Life
Kitty Bishop here. I'll get to the point because this shit reminds me of seventh grade. Tatiana can barely stomach Greg Tapper. It's just publicity for the movie,

*you idiot. So take the L.A. job. And bring a ring for
Christ's sakes.*

Kitty had been furious at both of them for framing the
message and hanging it next to their wedding portrait. She
didn't want anyone to know about her soft side.

The telephone jangled.

Tatiana reached it by the third ring. Pretty good considering her size and limited agility. "Hello?"

"You'll never believe who I just saw!" It was September.

Tatiana gave up. "Who?"

"*Constance Ann.* She's selling bras at Saks!"

Tatiana didn't believe it. "No!"

"Yes! When all those child actors sued for workplace
harassment and mental cruelty, she lost everything. You'd
think she'd be friendly since she needs the job, but she was
snippy with me about a return. Should I call management
and get her fired?"

"No, I think she's miserable enough."

Ethan and Everson suddenly appeared in the doorway.
They performed a giggle duet, then raced in and jumped
onto the bed, sandwiching in Tatiana.

"I have to go, September."

"Don't forget. I'm on *Law and Order* tonight. I could
get an Emmy for this one!"

Tatiana hung up, tickling the twins until they squealed.
"Why aren't you two in bed?" she asked in the silly voice
she usually reserved for Super Wowie Girl. "Tell me right
now. I want to know."

"I want Daddy . . . TV . . . See Daddy," Everson said.

"Daddy on TV," Ethan echoed.

Tatiana felt another kick. Whoa. A big one. "Sweethearts,
Daddy comes on too late. You'll be sleeping."

"Video!" Everson shouted. She stretched for the remote

control on the bedside table, grunting when she couldn't reach it.

Tatiana allowed her to have the bulky device.

Everson pressed "Play." Last night's segment of Jack delivering sports news filled the screen. The twins settled back peacefully to watch their daddy, and he was their daddy by every definition now since Kerr had signed over parental rights.

Tatiana couldn't take her eyes off their little faces, so serious, hanging on Jack's every word, nodding occasionally as if they understood every play, trade, and coaching blunder being reported.

Finally, her gaze drifted to the screen, to the man she loved, to the amazing force that had turned her life upside in the most wonderful ways: Jack Thorpe. Now, *there* was a movie star.

Darling!

I hope you had a blast with *Baby, Baby*. Raise your hand if you want a househusband like Jack and a personal assistant like Enrique. OK, hands down. They could get stuck that way waiting for such a perfect scenario!

If this is your first Kylie book, then you'll simply have to dash out and get my others to be fully informed. Why? Because my characters don't live in one book. They travel! Tatiana's sassy publicist, Kitty Bishop, showed up in *Fly Me to the Moon* first, and Tatiana herself, not to mention a certain creep named Greg Tapper, were major players in the romance between Candace Rowley and Strider Moore in "Sex and the Single Chocoholic," a novella in the anthology *The Only Thing Better Than Chocolate*. Who will be the next to leapfrog across books? The muse can be a mysterious thing, but I know you can count on seeing Enrique Santiago again soon. After all, he's much too wild to stay cooped up in the pages of *Baby, Baby!*

Up next for me is a novella called "Holiday Stud," part of a Christmas collection entitled *Santa Baby*. That's out in October. I think you'll get a hoot out of Audra, a fashion attorney who takes a gigolo home for Christmas to meet the family. Hey, it's better than showing up with one of those ghastly fruitcakes that gets shoved in the recycled gift closet! And next summer prepare yourself for my craziest, sexiest, coolest book yet—a romp called *Ex-Girlfriends* that's sure to leave skid marks on your bedside table.

Air Kisses,

Kylie

P.S. Darling, don't forget to visit my Web site, www.kylieadams.com and add your e-mail address to my VIP Section. That way you won't miss my regular e-newsletter.

Or write to me the old-fashioned way, or as I like to call it, Jackie Kennedy style . . . c/o Zebra Books, 850 Third Avenue, New York, NY 10022